ERLE STANLEY GARDNER

- Cited by the Guinness Book of World Records as the #1 best-selling writer of all time!

- Author of more than 100 clever, authentic, and sophisticated mystery novels!

- Creator of the amazing Perry Mason, the savvy Della Street, and dynamite detective Paul Drake!

- **THE ONLY AUTHOR WHO OUT-SELLS AGATHA CHRISTIE, HAROLD ROBBINS, BARBARA CARTLAND, AND LOUIS L'AMOUR *COMBINED!***

Why?

Because he writes the best, most fascinating whodunits of all!

You'll want to read every one of them, coming soon from
BALLANTINE BOOKS

SO-AUY-547

By Erle Stanley Gardner
Published by Ballantine Books:

The Case of the
Caretaker's Cat

Erle Stanley Gardner

BALLANTINE BOOKS • NEW YORK

Copyright © 1935 by Erle Stanley Gardner
Copyright renewed © 1963 by Erle Stanley Gardner

All rights reserved under International and Pan-American Copyright Conventions. Published in the United States by Ballantine Books, a division of Random House, Inc., New York, and simultaneously in Canada by Random House of Canada Limited, Toronto.

http://www.randomhouse.com

ISBN 0-345-32156-1

This edition published by arrangement with William Morrow & Company, Inc.

Manufactured in the United States of America

First Ballantine Books Edition: February 1985

10 9 8 7 6 5 4 3 2 1

CAST OF CHARACTERS

1

PERRY MASON, CRIMINAL LAWYER, FROWNED AT CARL Jackson, one of his assistants. At the corner of the desk, knees crossed, pencil poised over an open notebook, Della Street, Perry Mason's secretary, regarded both men with level, contemplative eyes.

Mason held in his hand a typewritten memorandum. "About a cat, eh?" he asked.

"Yes, sir," Jackson said. "He insists upon seeing you personally. He's a crank. I wouldn't waste time on him, sir."

"Shriveled leg and a crutch, I believe you said," Mason observed musingly, consulting the memorandum.

"That's right. He's about sixty-five. He said he was in an automobile accident about two years ago. His employer was driving the car. Ashton—that's the man who wants to see you about the cat—got a broken hip and some of the tendons in his right leg cut. Laxter, his employer, had his right leg broken just above the knee. Laxter wasn't a young man himself. I think he was sixty-two at the time of his death, but his leg healed up okay. Ashton's leg didn't. He's been on crutches ever since.

"I suppose that was one of the reasons why Laxter was so careful to make provision for the caretaker in his will. He didn't leave Ashton a sum of money outright, but stipulated that the beneficiaries under his will should give Ashton a perpetual job as caretaker so long as he was able to work, and furnish a home for him when he was no longer able to work."

Perry Mason said, frowning, "That's an unusual will, Jackson."

1

The young lawyer nodded agreement. "I'll say it's an unusual will. This man, Laxter, was a lawyer. He left three grandchildren. One of them, a girl, was completely cut off by the will. The other two divided the property share and share alike."

"How long's he been dead?"

"About two weeks, I think."

"Laxter . . . Laxter . . . wasn't there something in the paper about him? Didn't I read something about a fire in connection with his death?"

"That's right, sir, Peter Laxter. He was said to be a miser. He certainly was eccentric. He had a mansion here in the city and wouldn't live in it. He left this man Ashton in charge as the caretaker. Laxter lived in a country house at Carmencita. The house caught fire at night, and Laxter was burned to death. The three grandchildren and several servants were in the house at the time. They all escaped. Ashton says the fire started in or near Laxter's bedroom."

"The caretaker there at the time?" Mason asked.

"No. He was in charge of the city house."

"The grandchildren living there now?"

"Two of them are—the two who inherited. Samuel C. Laxter, and Frank Oafley. The granddaughter, who was disinherited, Winifred Laxter, isn't there. No one knows where she is."

"And Ashton is waiting in the outer office?" Mason inquired, his eyes twinkling.

"Yes, sir. He won't see anyone except you."

"Specifically, what's his trouble?"

"Sam Laxter admits he's obligated, under the will, to furnish Ashton with a job as caretaker, but claims he isn't obligated to keep Ashton's cat in the house. Ashton has a big Persian cat. He's very much attached to it. Laxter's served notice that Ashton can either get rid of the cat, or it'll be poisoned. I *could* handle it, only Ashton insists on seeing you or no one. I wouldn't take up your time with it—only you insist upon knowing all about the clients

2

who come to the office and won't let any of us handle their cases."

Mason nodded, and said, "Right. You can't ever tell when something seemingly trivial may develop into something big. I remember the time Fenwick was trying a murder case and a man came to the office and insisted on seeing him about a battery case. Fenwick tried to turn him over to a clerk and the man left the office in a rage. Two months after Fenwick's client had been hanged, Fenwick found out the man wanted to see him about having the prosecuting witness in the murder case arrested for assault and battery growing out of an automobile accident. If Fenwick had talked with that man he'd have found out the prosecuting witness couldn't have been where he said he was at the time the murder was committed."

Jackson had heard the story before. He nodded with courteous attention. In a tone which showed very plainly he thought the troubles of Mr. Ashton had occupied far too much of the time allotted for the morning conference, he inquired, "Shall I tell Mr. Ashton we can't handle it?"

"Has he any money?" Mason inquired.

"I don't think so. Under the will he was left a perpetual job as caretaker. That job pays him fifty dollars a month, and his board and room."

"And he's an old man?" Mason inquired.

"Reasonably so. An old crank, if you ask me."

"But he loves animals," Mason remarked.

"He's very much attached to his cat, if that's what you mean."

Mason nodded slowly, and said, "That's what I mean."

Della Street, more familiar with Mason's moods than the assistant attorney, entered the conversation with the easy familiarity of one who works in an office where there is but little formality.

"You just finished a murder case, Chief. Why not let

the assistants handle things while you take a cruise to the Orient? It'll give you a rest."

Mason regarded her with twinkling eyes. "Who the devil would take care of Ashton's cat, then?"

"Mr. Jackson could."

"He won't see Jackson."

"Then let him find some other attorney. The city is overrun with attorneys. You can't afford to take your time to bother with a cat!"

"An old man," Mason said, almost musingly, "a crank . . . probably friendless. His benefactor is dead. The cat represents the only living thing to which he's attached. Most lawyers would laugh the case out of the office. If some lawyer took the case, he wouldn't know where to begin. God knows there's no precedent to guide him.

"No, Della, this is one of those cases that seems so trivial to the lawyer, but means so much to the client. A lawyer isn't like a shopkeeper who can sell his wares or not as he chooses. He holds his talents in trust for the unfortunate."

Della Street, knowing what was to come, nodded to Jackson and said, "You may ask Mr. Ashton to step in."

Jackson gave a half-hearted smile, gathered up his papers and left the room. As the door clicked shut, Della Street's fingers closed about Perry Mason's left hand.

"You're only taking that case, Chief, because you know he can't afford to pay any other good lawyer to handle it."

Mason, grinning, replied, "Well, you must admit that a man with a shriveled leg, a crabby disposition, a Persian cat, and no money, is entitled to a break once in a while."

The sounds of a crutch and a foot alternated in the long corridor. Jackson held open the door after the manner of one who, having counseled against an unwise act, is very definitely keeping clear of the consequences.

The man who entered the room was wizened with age. He had thin lips, bushy white eyebrows, a bald head, and

4

unsmiling features. "This is the *third* time I've been in to see you," he said irritably.

Mason indicated a chair. "Sit down, Mr. Ashton. I'm sorry. I've been trying a murder case. What's the name of your cat?"

"Clinker," Ashton said, sitting down in the big, over-stuffed, black leather chair, standing his crutch straight in front of him, holding it with both hands.

"Why Clinker?" Mason asked.

The man's lips and eyes remained unsmiling. "A bit of humor."

"Humor?" Mason inquired.

"Yes, I used to have a job firing a boiler. Clinkers get in the way and clutter things up. When I first got the cat, I called him Clinker because he was always in the way—always cluttering things up."

"Attached to him?" Mason inquired, in a voice which was elaborately casual.

"The only friend I've got left in the world," Ashton said rather gruffly.

Mason raised his eyebrows.

"I'm a caretaker. A caretaker doesn't really work. He just keeps an eye on things. The big house has been closed up for years. The master lived in a place at Carmencita. All I did was just putter around the big place, keep up the yard and sweep off the front steps. Three or four times a year the master had the place throughly cleaned; the rest of the time the rooms were all shut, locked, and the shutters drawn."

"No one lived there?"

"No one."

"Why didn't he rent the place?" Mason asked.

"It wasn't his way."

"And he left a will providing for you?"

"That he did. The will keeps me in my job while I'm able to work and takes care of me whenever I can't work."

"The heirs are two grandchildren?"

5

"Three. Only two are mentioned in the will."

"Tell me about your troubles," Mason invited.

"The master was burned to death when the country home caught fire. I didn't know about it until they telephoned me the next morning. After the death, Sam Laxter took charge. He's a nice boy to look at, and he'll fool you if you let him, but he doesn't like animals and I don't like people who can't get along with animals."

"Who was in the house at the time it burned?" Mason asked.

"Winifred—that's Winifred Laxter. She's a granddaughter. Then there was Sam Laxter and Frank Oafley —they're grandsons. Mrs. Pixley was there—she's the housekeeper. And there was a nurse—Edith DeVoe."

"Anyone else?" Mason asked.

"Jim Brandon, the chauffeur. He's a smooth one. He knows which side of the bread his butter's on, all right. You should see the way he toadies to Sam Laxter."

Ashton pounded on the floor with the tip of his crutch to emphasize his disgust.

"Who else?" Mason asked.

Ashton checked off the people he had named on his fingers, then said, "Nora Abbington."

"What's she like?" Mason asked, very evidently enjoying seeing these various characters through Ashton's cynical eyes.

"A big cow," Ashton said. "A docile, trusting, good-natured, big-eyed clod. But she wasn't there when the house burned. She came in and worked by the day."

"After the house burned there was no more work for her?" Mason inquired.

"That's right. She didn't come any more after that."

"Then I presume we can eliminate her from the picture. She really doesn't figure in the case."

"Wouldn't," Ashton said significantly, "if it wasn't that she was in love with Jim Brandon. She thinks Jim's going to marry her when he gets money. Bah! I tried to tell her

6

a thing or two about Jim Brandon, but she wouldn't listen to me."

"How does it happen you know these people so well if you were in the city house and they were out in the country?"

"Oh, I used to drive out once in a while."

"You drive a car?"

"Yes."

"Your car?"

"No, it's one the master kept at the house for me so I could drive out to see him when he wanted to give instructions. He hated to come to the city."

"What sort of a car?" Mason inquired.

"A Chevvy."

"Your bad leg doesn't keep you from driving?"

"No, not that car. It has a special emergency brake on it. When I pull up on that brake lever the car stops."

Mason flashed an amused glance at Della Street, turned back to the wizened, bald-headed man. "Why wasn't Winifred provided for in the will?" he asked.

"No one knows."

"You were in charge of the house here in the city?"

"That's right."

"What's the address?"

"3824 East Washington."

"You're still there?"

"Yes—and so're Laxter, Oafley, and the servants."

"In other words, when the house burned at Carmencita, they came to live in the city house. Is that right?"

"Yes. They'd have moved in anyway as soon as the master died. They're not the sort who like country life. They want city stuff and lots of it."

"And they object to the cat?"

"Sam Laxter does. He's the executor."

"Specifically, what form has his objection taken?"

"He's told me to get rid of the cat or he'll poison it."

"Has he given any reason?"

7

"He doesn't like cats. He doesn't like Clinker especially. I sleep in the basement. I keep the basement window open. Clinker jumps in and jumps out—you know how a cat is—you can't keep him shut up all the time. With my leg the way it is, I don't walk around much. Clinker has to get out some. When it's raining, he gets his feet dirty. Then he jumps in through the window, and gets my bed muddy."

"The window is over your bed?" Mason inquired.

"That's right, and the cat sleeps on my bed. It has for years. It hasn't bothered anyone. Sam Laxter says it runs up the laundry bill, getting the bedspreads all mussed up. . . . Laundry bills! He throws away enough in one night at a night club to pay my laundry bills for ten years!"

"Rather a free spender?" Mason asked good-naturedly.

"He was—he isn't so much now."

"No?" Mason inquired.

"No, he can't get the money."

"What money?"

"The money the master left."

"I thought you said he left it share and share alike to the two grandchildren."

"He did—what they've been able to find."

"They haven't been able to find it all?" Mason asked, interested.

"A bit before the fire," Ashton said, as though the recital gave him great satisfaction, "the master made a complete clean-up. He cashed in something over a million dollars. No one knows what he did with that money. Sam Laxter says he buried it somewhere, but I know the master better than that. I think he put it in a safety deposit box under an assumed name. He didn't trust the banks. He said that when times were good, the banks loaned his money and made a profit on it, and when times were bad, they told him they were sorry they couldn't get it back. He lost some money in a bank a couple of years ago. Once was enough for the master."

"A million dollars in cash?" Mason asked.

"Of course it was in cash," Ashton snapped. "What else would he take it in?"

Perry Mason glanced at Della Street.

"How about Winifred—you say she's disappeared?"

"Yes, she pulled out. I don't blame her. The others treated her shameful."

"How old are the grandchildren?"

"Sam's twenty-eight; Frank Oafley's twenty-six; Winifred's twenty-two—and a beauty! She's worth all the rest put together. Six months ago the master made a will leaving her everything and cutting off the other two grandchildren with ten dollars each. Then two days before he died, he made this new will."

Mason frowned, and said, "That's hard on Winifred."

Ashton grunted, said nothing.

"Just how much money did you plan to spend in enforcing your rights to keep Clinker?" Mason asked speculatively.

Ashton whipped a billfold from his pocket, pulled out a sheaf of bills.

"I'm not a piker," he said. "Good lawyers come high. I don't want anything but the best. How much is it goin' to cost?"

Mason stared at the thick bundle of bills.

"Where did you get all that money?" he asked curiously.

"Saved it. I don't have any expenses, and I've been saving my salary for twenty years. I've put it in gilt-edged stuff—stuff that the master recommended—and when the master cashed in, I cashed in."

"On Mr. Laxter's advice?" Mason asked, eyeing his client curiously.

"If you want to put it that way."

"And you're willing to spend your money to keep your cat?"

"I'm willing to spend a reasonable amount of it; I'm

9

not going to throw it away. But I know it costs money to get a good lawyer, and I know I'm not going to get a poor lawyer."

"Suppose," Mason said, "I should tell you it was going to cost you five hundred dollars by way of retainer?"

"That's too much," Ashton said irritably.

"Suppose I should say two hundred and fifty dollars?"

"That's reasonable. I'll pay it."

Ashton started counting bills.

"Wait a minute," Mason said, laughing. "Perhaps it won't be necessary to spend any large amount of money. I was just trying to determine exactly how attached you were to the cat."

"I'm plenty attached to him. I'd spend any reasonable amount to put Sam Laxter in his place, but I'm not going to be stuck."

"What are Laxter's initials?" Mason asked.

"Samuel C."

"Perhaps," Mason told him, "a letter will be all that's necessary. If that's the case, it isn't going to cost you much."

He turned to Della Street.

"Della," he said, "take a letter to Samuel C. Laxter, 3824 East Washington Street. Dear Sir: Mr. Ashton has consulted me—no, wait a minute, Della, better put his initials in there—I've got them here on the memo—Charles Ashton, that's it—has consulted me with reference to his rights under the will of the late Peter Laxter. Under the provisions of that will, you were obligated to furnish Mr. Ashton with a position as caretaker during the period of his ability to work in that capacity.

"It is only natural that Mr. Ashton should wish to keep his cat with him. A caretaker is entitled to pets. This is particularly true in the present case, because the pet was maintained during the testator's lifetime.

"In the event that you should injure Mr. Ashton's pet,

it will be necessary for me to contend that you have breached a condition of the will and have, therefore, forfeited your inheritance."

Perry Mason grinned at Della Street. "That should throw a scare into him," he remarked. "If he thinks he's fighting over his entire inheritance instead of just a cat, he'll decide not to take any chances."

He turned to Ashton, nodded reassuringly. "Leave ten dollars with the bookkeeper as a retainer. She'll give you a receipt. If anything develops I'll write to you. If you find out anything, ring up this office and ask for Miss Street—she's my secretary. You can leave any message with her. That's all for the present."

Ashton's gnarled hands tightened about the crutch. He pulled himself to his feet, slipped the crutch under his arm. Without a word of thanks or farewell, he hobbledy-banged from the office.

Della Street looked at Perry Mason with surprised eyes.

"Is it possible," she asked, "that this grandson might forfeit his inheritance if he threw out the cat?"

"Stranger things have happened," he answered. "It depends on the wording of the will. If the provision about the caretaker is a condition to the vesting of the inheritance, I might be able to make it stick. But, you understand, all I'm doing now is throwing a scare into Mr. Samuel C. Laxter. I think we'll hear from that gentleman in person. When we do, let me know. . . . That's what I like about the law business, Della—it's so damned diversified. . . . A caretaker's cat!"

He chuckled.

Della Street closed her notebook, started toward her own office, paused at the window to look down at the busy street. "You saved him two hundred and forty dollars," she said, her eyes aimlessly watching the snarl of city traffic, "and he didn't even thank you."

A breath of wind, blowing in through the open window stirred her hair. She bent forward from the waist,

11

leaning out to catch the breeze, filling her lungs with the fresh air.

"Probably he's just peculiar," Mason said. "He certainly is a shriveled-up specimen. . . . Don't lean too far out there, Della. . . . You must remember he likes animals, and he's not a young man any more. Regardless of what age he claims, he must be more than seventy-five. . . ."

Della Street straightened. With a quick twist of her lithe body, she turned to face Perry Mason. She was frowning. "It might interest you to know," she said, "that someone is shadowing your cat-loving client."

Perry Mason shoved back his chair as he got to his feet, strode across the office. He braced himself with one arm on the window ledge, the other around Della Street's waist. Together, they stared down at the street.

"See?" he said. "That man with the light felt hat. He darted out of a doorway. . . . See, he's getting into that car."

"One of the new Pontiacs," Mason said speculatively. "What makes you think he was following Ashton?"

"The way he acted. I'm certain of it. He jumped out of the doorway. . . . See, the car's barely crawling along —just to keep Ashton in sight."

Ashton hobbled around the corner, to the left. The car followed him, apparently crawling in low gear.

Mason, watching the car in frowning speculation, said, "A million dollars in cash is a whale of a lot of money."

2

MORNING SUN, STREAMING IN THROUGH THE WINDOWS OF
Perry Mason's private office, struck the calf-skin bindings
on the shelved law books and made them seem less grimly
foreboding.

Della Street, opening the door from her office, brought
in a file of mail and some papers. Perry Mason folded the
newspaper he had been reading, as Della Street seated
herself, pulled out the sliding leaf of the desk, and held
her fountain pen poised over an open notebook.

"Lord, but you're chockful of business," Perry Mason
complained. "I don't want to work. I want to let down
and play hookey. I want to do something I shouldn't. My
Lord, you'd think I was a corporation lawyer, sitting at a
desk, advising banks and probating estates! The reason
I specialized in trial law was because I didn't like the
routine, and you're making this business more and more
of a job and less and less of an adventure.

"That's what I like about the practice of law—it's
an adventure. You're looking behind the scenes at human
nature. The audience out front sees only the carefully re-
hearsed poses assumed by the actors. The lawyer sees
human nature with the shutters open."

"If you *will* insist on mixing into minor cases," she
said acidly, with that degree of familiarity which comes
from long and privileged association in an office where
conventional discipline is subordinated to efficiency,
"you'll have to organize your time so you can handle your
work. Mr. Nathaniel Shuster is in the outer office waiting
to see you."

Perry Mason frowned. "Shuster?" he said. "Why, he's

a damned jury-briber—a pettifogger. He poses as a big trial lawyer, but he's a bigger crook than the people he defends. Any damn fool can win a case if he has the jury bribed. What the devil does *he* want?"

"He wishes to see you in regard to a letter you wrote. His clients are with him—Mr. Samuel C. Laxter and Mr. Frank Oafley."

Abruptly Perry Mason laughed. "The caretaker's cat, eh?" he asked.

She nodded.

Mason pulled the file of mail over toward him.

"Well," he said, "as a matter of professional courtesy, we won't keep Mr. Shuster waiting. We'll take a quick run through this important stuff and see if there are any telegrams to be sent out."

He looked at a folder, and frowned. "What's this?" he asked.

"Quotations from the N.Y.K. Line on a deluxe single stateroom on the *Asamu Maru*—stops at Honolulu, Yokohama, Kobe, Shanghai and Hongkong."

"Who made the inquiry?"

"I did."

He pulled a letter from the pile of mail, stared at it, and said, "The Dollar Steamship Company—quotations on a deluxe single stateroom on the *President Coolidge*—Honolulu, Yokohama, Kobe, Shanghai, Hongkong and Manila."

Della Street continued to look demurely at her notebook.

Perry Mason laughed, and pushed the pile of mail away.

"We'll let it wait," he said, "until after we've disposed of Shuster. You sit right there and if I nudge your knee, start taking notes. Shuster's a pretty slippery customer. I wish he'd have his teeth fixed."

She raised her eyebrows in silent inquiry.

"Franklin teeth," he told her, "and they leak."

"Franklin teeth?" she asked.

14

"Yes, air-cooled, you know. If there's anything in re-incarnation, he must have been a Chinese laundryman in a prior existence. Every time he snickers, he sprays his audience, like a Chinese laundryman sprinkling clothes. He has a fondness for shaking hands. Personally I don't like him, but you can't insult him. I suppose the situation calls for some show of professional courtesy; but, if he tries to slip anything over on me, I'm going to forget the ethics of the situation and kick him out."

"The cat," she said, "must feel flattered—so many busy attorneys putting in their time deciding whether he's going to get his muddy feet on a bedspread."

Perry Mason laughed outright. "Go ahead," he said, "rub it in! Oh, well, I'm in for it now. Shuster will try to egg his clients into a fight, and I'll either have to back up or play into his hands. If I back up, he makes his clients believe he's browbeaten me into submission, and charges them a good fee. If I don't back up, he tells them their whole inheritance is involved and soaks them a per-centage. That's what I get for running that bluff about a forfeiture of the inheritance."

"Mr. Jackson *could* talk with them," she suggested.

Perry Mason grinned good-naturedly. "Nope, Jackson isn't accustomed to having his face sprinkled. I've met Shuster before. Let's get them in."

He lifted the telephone, said to the girl at the desk, "Send Mr. Shuster in."

Della Street made one last appeal, "Oh, *please,* Chief, let Jackson handle it. You'll get into an argument, and the first thing we'll know, you'll be putting in all of your time fighting over a cat."

"Cats and corpses," Mason remarked. "If it isn't one it seems to be another. I've been fighting over corpses for so long, a good live cat will be a welcome diversion from . . ."

The door opened. A blonde with wide blue eyes said in a lifeless voice, "Mr. Shuster, Mr. Laxter, Mr. Oafley."

The three men pushed the doorway into the room. Shuster, small-boned and active, was in the lead, bustling about like a sparrow peering under dead leaves. "Good morning, Counselor, good morning, good morning. Going to be warm today, isn't it?" He bustled across the room, hand outstretched. His lips twisted back, disclosing a mouthful of teeth, between each of which was a well-defined space.

Mason, seeming to tower high above the little man, extended a reluctant hand and said, "Now let's get these people straight. Which is Laxter and which is Oafley?"

"Yes, yes, yes, of course, of course," Shuster said. "This is Mr. Laxter—Mr. Samuel C. Laxter. He's the executor of the will—a grandson of Peter Laxter."

A tall man with dark skin, smoldering black eyes and hair which had been carefully marcelled, smiled with that oily affability which speaks of poise rather than sincerity. A large cream-colored Stetson hat was held in his left hand.

"And this is Frank Oafley. Frank Oafley is the other grandson, Counselor."

Oafley was yellow-haired and thick-lipped. His face seemed unable to change its expression. His eyes had the peculiar watery blue tint of raw oysters. He had no hat.

He said nothing.

"My secretary, Miss Street," Perry Mason remarked. "If there's no objection, she'll be here during the conference and take such notes as I may wish."

Shuster chuckled moistly. "And if there *is* any objection, I suppose she'll stay here anyway, eh? Ha, ha, ha. I know you, Counselor. Remember, it isn't as though you were dealing with someone who didn't know you. I know you well. You're a fighter. You're to be reckoned with. It's a matter of principle with my clients. They can't knuckle under to a servant. But they've got a fight on their hands. I told them you were a fighter, I warned them. They can't say I didn't warn them!"

"Sit down," Mason said.

Shuster nodded to his clients, indicating the chairs which they were to take. He sank in the big overstuffed leather chair himself and seemed almost lost in the space of it. He crossed his legs, pulled down his cuffs, adjusted his tie, beamed at Mason and said, "You can't make it stick. It's a matter of principle with us. We'll fight to the last ditch. But it's a serious matter, all right."

"What's a serious matter?" Mason asked.

"Your contention about that being a condition in the will."

"And what's the matter of principle?" Mason inquired.

"Why," Shuster remarked, showing surprise, "the cat, of course. We can't stand it. But, more than that, we can't stand to have this caretaker start dictating. He's too officious already. You understand, when a person can't discharge his hired help, it doesn't take long for that help to get completely out of hand."

"Has it ever occurred to you," Mason asked, letting his eyes shift from Shuster's face to the faces of the two grandchildren, "that you folks are making a mountain out of a molehill? Why don't you let poor Ashton keep his cat? The cat won't last forever and Ashton won't either. There's no reason for spending a lot of money on lawyers, and . . ."

"Not so fast, Counselor, not so fast," Shuster broke in, sliding forward on the smooth leather of the chair until he sat on the very edge of it. "It's going to be a hard fight; it's going to be a bitter fight. I've warned my clients of that. You're a resourceful man. You're a sly man. If you don't mind the expression, I'll say you're a cunning man. Lots of us would take that as a compliment; I take that as a compliment myself. Lots of times my clients say, 'Shuster is cunning.' Do I get sore? I don't! I say that's a compliment."

Della Street glanced at Perry Mason, her eyes showing

amusement. Mason's face was momentarily becoming more granite-hard.

Shuster went on, speaking rapidly, "I warned my clients that Winifred was going to try to break the will. I knew that she'd try it by every means in her power, but she couldn't claim the grandfather was of unsound mind, and there's no question of undue influence. So she had to get something she could tie to, and she picked on Ashton and his cat."

There was anger in Mason's voice. "Look here, Shuster, cut out this flimflamming. All I want is to have the caretaker left with his cat. Your clients don't need to spend any money fighting. The amount that it's costing just to have this conference would more than pay for all the bedspreads the cat could soil in ten years."

Shuster's head bobbed up and down eagerly. "That's what I've told them all along. Counselor. A poor compromise is better than a good lawsuit. Now, if you're willing to compromise, we are."

"On what basis?" Mason inquired.

Shuster recited his proposed compromise with a glibness which showed much rehearsal. "Winifred signs an agreement that she won't contest the will. Ashton signs a paper that he knows that the will is genuine; that it was executed by the old man when he was of sound and disposing mind and memory, and then Ashton can keep his cat."

Mason's voice was edged with irritation. "I don't know anything about Winifred," he said. "I've never met her and haven't talked with her. I can't ask *her* to sign anything."

Shuster glanced triumphantly at the two clients. "I told you he was clever," he said. "I told you it was going to be a fight."

"Winifred doesn't enter into it," Mason said. "Now let's come down to earth and talk sense. All I'm interested in is this damned cat."

18

There was a moment of silence, broken by Shuster's moist chuckle.

Sam Laxter, glancing at the growing rage of Mason's features, took a hand in the conversation. "Of course, you'll admit you threatened to invalidate my inheritance. I know that wouldn't have come from Ashton. We've been expecting Winifred to contest the will."

There was something smoothly ingratiating in his tone, a suave smirking of the vocal cords which made his voice seem like the smile of a courtesan.

"All I want," Mason said, "is to have that cat left alone."

"And you'll have Winifred sign a complete waiver?" Shuster asked.

Mason faced him. "Don't be a damn fool," he said. "I'm not representing Winifred. I haven't anything to do with her."

Shuster rubbed his hands gleefully. "We couldn't settle on any other basis. It's a matter of principle with us. Personally, *I* don't think that's a condition in the will, but it's open to controversy."

Mason got to his feet, like an angry bull turning to face a yapping terrier.

"Now listen," he said to Shuster, "I don't like to lose my temper unless someone's paying for it, but you've gone far enough."

Shuster chuckled. "Clever!" he said. "Very clever. Cunning."

Mason took a step toward him. "You know damn well I'm not representing Winifred. You know that the letter of mine meant exactly what it said, but you knew you couldn't kid your clients into paying big fees over a cat, so you dragged in this will-contest business. You laid this egg, and you've brought your clients in to see it hatched. Not knowing Winifred and not representing her, I naturally can't get her signature to anything. You've frightened your clients into believing they've got to get Winifred's signature to a release. That's laying the foundation for a nice fat fee for you."

Shuster came up out of his chair. "That's slander!" he screamed.

Mason face the two grandsons. "Listen," he said, "I'm not your guardian. I'm not going to break my neck trying to save your money. If you two want to give that cat a home, say so now; that's all there'll be to it. If you don't I'll make Shuster earn his fees by dragging you into the damnedest fight you've ever been in. I'm not going to be used as a bugaboo to frighten you two into sticking a fat fee on Shuster's desk and have him do nothing but rub his hands in order to earn it. . . ."

"Have a care! Have a care!" Shuster shouted, literally dancing about in his indignation. "You can't talk that way. That's a violation of professional ethics. I'll report you to the Grievance Committee. I'll sue you for slander."

"Report, and be damned," Mason said. "Sue and be doubly damned. Take your clients and get out of here. By two o'clock this afternoon you either notify me that cat stays in the house, or you're going to have a fight on your hands—all three of you. And remember one thing about me—when I start fighting I don't hit where the other man's expecting the punch. Now don't say I didn't warn you. Two o'clock this afternoon. Get out."

Shuster pushed forward. "You can't fool me for a minute, Perry Mason. You're using this cat as a blind. Winifred wants to contest the will, and . . ."

Perry Mason took two quick steps towards him. The little lawyer danced away, turned and scuttled for the doorway. He pulled it open and shot through it.

"We'll fight!" he called back over his shoulder. "I'm just as tough a fighter as you are, Perry Mason."

"Yes," Perry Mason sighed, "you act like it."

Samuel Laxter hesitated for a moment, as though about to say something, then turned and walked out of the office, followed by Oafley.

20

Perry Mason met Della Street's smiling eyes with a grin. "Go on," he said; "say, 'I told you so.'"

She shook her head. "Fight that little shyster off his feet!" she said.

Mason looked at his watch. "Ring up Paul Drake and ask him to be here at two thirty."

"And Ashton?" she asked."

"No," he told her. "Ashton's got enough to worry about. I think this is going to be a matter of principle all around."

3

THE CLOCK ON PERRY MASON'S DESK SHOWED TWO thirty-five. Paul Drake, head of the Drake Detective Agency, sat crosswise in the big leather chair, his knees draped over one arm, the small of his back propped against the other. His mouth turned up at the corners, giving an expression of droll humor to his face. It was as though he were on the point of breaking into a smile. His eyes were large, protruding, and glassy.

"What's the grief this time?" he asked. "I didn't know there'd been another murder."

"It isn't a murder, Paul; it's a cat."

"A *what?*"

"A cat, a Persian cat."

The detective sighed and said, "All right, then, it's a cat. So what?"

"Peter Laxter," Mason said, "probably a miser, had a house in the city that he wouldn't live in. He stayed in his country place at Carmencita. The place burned up, and Laxer burned up with it. He left three grandchildren:

Samuel C. Laxter and Frank Oafley, who inherit under his will, and a granddaughter, Winifred Laxter, who was left out in the cold. His will contained a provision that Charles Ashton, his caretaker, was to be given a perpetual job during his lifetime. Ashton had a cat. He wanted to keep the cat with him. Sam Laxter told him to get rid of the cat. I sympathized with Ashton, wrote Laxter a letter and told him to leave the cat alone. Laxter went to Nat Shuster. Shuster saw a chance to horn in on a big fee, so he sold Laxter on the idea I was trying to break the will; demanded a lot of impossible conditions from me in order to effect a settlement, and when I didn't agree to them because I couldn't, he made the most of my refusal. I presume he's collected a fat retainer."

"What do you want?" Drake inquired.

"I'm going to break that will," Mason said grimly.

The detective lit a cigarette and said, in his slow drawl, "Going to break the will over a cat, Perry?"

"Over a cat," Mason admitted, "but really I'm going to break Shuster, as well as the will. Shuster's been setting himself up as a big-time criminal lawyer. I'm tired of it. He's a shyster, a suborner of perjury and a jury-briber. He's a disgrace to the profession, and he gets us all into disrepute. My God, Paul, whenever he has a client he not only tries to get that client off, but he deliberately frames evidence, so it will point to some innocent party, in order to make his own case look better. He's been boasting around town that if he ever runs up against me, he's going to show just how smart he is. I'm sick of him."

"Have you got a copy of the will?" Drake asked.

"No, not yet. I'm having a copy made from the probate records."

"Has it been admitted to probate?"

"I understand it has. It can be contested, however, after probate as well as before."

"Where do I come in?"

"First, find Winifred. Then dig up everything you can

22

about Peter Laxter, and everything you can about the two grandchildren who inherit the property."

"Shall I go at it in the routine way, or do you want action?" Drake asked.

"I want action."

Drake's glassy eyes surveyed Perry Mason in expressionless appraisal. "There must be a lot of money in cats," he remarked.

Mason's face was grave. "I'm not certain but what there is going to be a chance to make some money, Paul. Evidently Peter Laxter was a miser. He didn't trust too much in banks. Shortly before his death, he cashed in securities to the tune of about a million dollars. After his death, the heirs couldn't find the million."

"Suppose it burnt up in the house with him?" Drake asked. "He'd have had it in currency, you know."

"It may have," Mason admitted. "Again, it may not. When Ashton left my office, some man was shadowing him —a man who was driving a new green Pontiac."

"Know who this chap was?"

"No, I saw him from the window. I couldn't see his face. I saw a light felt hat and a dark suit. The Pontiac was a sedan. Of course, there may be nothing to it; again, there may be. At any rate, it's going to be a swell break for Winifred Laxter, because I'm going to smash that will for her. Shuster has been talking about what he was going to do to me if he ever got in court against me, and I'm going to give him a chance to make good."

"You can't make Shuster sore by fighting," the detective said. "That's what he wants. You fight to get results for your clients; Shuster fights to collect fees from his."

"He can't collect fees if his clients have lost their money," Mason said. "A prior will leaves everything to Winifred. If I break this will, the other will stand up and take its place."

"Going to have Winifred as your client?" Drake asked.

23

Mason shook his head, said doggedly, "I've got a cat for a client. I may want Winifred as a witness."

Drake slid his legs over the smooth leather of the chair, got to his feet.

"Knowing you as I do," he said, "I presume that means you want *lots* of action."

Mason, nodding grimly, said, "And I want it fast. Get me information on every angle you can uncover, property, soundness of mind, undue influence, everything."

As Drake closed the exit door behind him, Jackson gave a perfunctory knock and entered the office bearing several typewritten sheets of legal-sized paper.

"I've had a copy of the will made, and have gone over it carefully," he said. "The provision about the cat is rather weak. It certainly isn't a condition relating to the vesting of the inheritance, and it may not even be a charge upon the estate. It's probably just the expression of a wish on the part of the testator."

Mason's face showed disappointment. "Anything else?" he asked.

"Apparently Peter Laxter drew the will himself. I understand he practiced law for several years in some eastern state. It's pretty much of an iron-clad job, but there's one peculiar paragraph in it. We might be able to do something with that paragraph in a contest."

"What is it?" Mason asked.

Jackson picked up the will and read from it: "During my lifetime I have been surrounded with the affectionate regard not only of those who were related to me, but those who apparently hoped that fortuitous circumstance would include them in my bounty. I have never been able to ascertain how much was intended to pave the way for an inheritance under my will. If the latter is the case, I am afraid my legatees are doomed to disappointment, because the extent of my estates will doubtless be disappointing to them. However, I have one thought to offer in the nature of a condolence and, at the same time, a suggestion. While those who waited impatiently for my passing merely in order to share in my estate are doomed to disappointment, those who had a genuine affection for me are not."

Jackson ceased reading and looked owlishly across at Perry Mason.

Mason scowled and said, "What the devil is he getting at? He disinherited Winifred, and he left all of his property to two grandchildren, share and share alike. There's nothing in this paragraph which could change that."

"No, sir," Jackson agreed.

"He secreted something like a million dollars in cash shortly before his death, but even if that is discovered, it would still pass as a part of his estate."

"Yes, sir."

"Unless," Mason said, "he'd made a gift of some sort before his death. And in that event, the property would be owned by the person to whom it had been given."

"It's a peculiar provision," Jackson remarked noncommittally. "He might have made a gift in trust, you know."

Mason said slowly, "I can't help thinking of the sheaf of currency Charles Ashton had in his pocket when he offered me a retainer. . . . However, Jackson, *if* Peter Laxter gave Ashton money . . . well, there's going to be one hell of a fight over it—trust or no trust."

"Yes, sir," Jackson agreed.

Mason, nodding slowly, picked up the telephone which connected with Della Street's office, and, when he heard her voice on the wire, said, "Della, get hold of Paul Drake and tell him to include Charles Ashton in his investigations. I want particularly to find out about Ashton's financial affairs—whether he has any bank account; whether he's filed any income tax return; whether he owns any real property; whether he has any money out at interest; how much he's assessed for on the assessment roll, and anything else Paul can find out."

"Yes, sir," Della Street said. "You want that information in a hurry?"

"In a hurry."

"The Dollar Line said they'd hold a reservation until tomorrow morning at ten thirty," Della Street remarked in tones of cool efficiency, and then slid the receiver back on the hook, terminating the connection, leaving Perry Mason grinning into a dead transmitter.

4

THE OFFICE WORKERS HAD LONG SINCE GONE HOME. Perry Mason, his thumbs tucked in the armholes of his vest, paced the floor steadily. On the desk in front of him was a copy of the Last Will and Testament of Peter Laxter.

The telephone rang. Mason scooped the receiver to his ear, and heard Paul Drake's voice saying, "Have you had anything to eat?"

"Not yet. I don't care much about eating when I'm thinking."

"How'd you like to listen to a report?" the detective asked.

"Swell."

"It isn't complete yet, but I've got most of the high spots."

"All right, suppose you come in."

"I think I can work it to better advantage if you'll join me," Drake said. "I'm down on the corner of Spring and Melton Streets. There's a waffle joint down here and we can have a bite to eat. I haven't had any dinner and my stomach thinks I'm on a hunger strike."

Mason frowningly regarded the will on his desk.

"Okay," he said, "I'll come down."

He switched out the lights, took a cab to the place Drake had indicated, and stared into the detective's pop-eyes. "You look as though you had something up your sleeve, Paul. There's a cat-licking-the-cream expression on your face."

"Is there? I could use a little cream."

"What's new?"

"I'll tell you after we eat. I refuse to talk this stuff on an empty stomach. . . . My God, Perry, snap out of it. You'd think this was another murder case, the way you're prowling around on it. It's just a case involving a damned cat. I'll bet you didn't get over fifty dollars out of it as a fee, did you?"

Mason laughed, and said, "Ten, to be exact."

"There you are," Drake remarked, as though addressing an imaginary audience.

"The fee has nothing to do with it," Mason said. "A lawyer has a trust to his client. He can set any fee he pleases. If the client doesn't pay it, the lawyer doesn't need to take the business; but if a client pays it, it doesn't make any difference whether it's five cents or five million dollars. The lawyer should give the client everything he has."

"You couldn't practice law on that sort of theory unless you were a damned individualist, Perry. . . . Here's the waffle joint. Come on in."

Mason stood in the doorway, looking dubiously into the lighted interior. A young woman, with dark hair, laughing eyes, and full, red lips, was presiding over a battery of waffle irons. The only customer in the place paid his check. She rang up the money in the cash register, flashed him a bright smile, and started wiping off the counter.

"I don't think I want a waffle," Mason said.

27

The detective, taking him by the arm, gently pushed him through the door, saying, "Sure, you want a waffle."

They seated themselves at the counter. Dark eyes flashed to their faces as the full, red lips gave a quick smile.

"Two waffles," Drake said, "stripped with bacon."

The young woman's hands became a blur of swift efficiency as she poured waffle dough and spread strips of bacon on a hot plate.

"Coffee?" she asked.

"Coffee," Drake said.

"Now?" she asked.

"Now."

She drew two cups of coffee, placed them, with a little pitcher of cream at each plate. She produced paper napkins, arranged silverware, put down glasses of water and butter.

Drake raised his voice, while steam simmered up from the waffle irons.

"Do you think you can bust Pete Laxter's will, Perry?"

"I don't know," Mason admitted. "There's something queer about that will. I've been stewing over the thing for three hours."

"Seems funny that he'd have disinherited his favorite grandchild," the detective went on in a loud voice. "Sam Laxter went in for bright lights, and dissipation. The old man didn't like it. Oafley is a secretive, non-social duck. The old man didn't care much for him. He's too damned negative."

The young woman behind the counter turned the bacon, flashed them a swift glance.

"It takes a lot to bust a will, doesn't it?" Drake persisted.

"An awful lot," Mason admitted wearily, "if you try to break it on the ground of undue influence, or unsoundness of mind. But I'm telling you, Paul, I'm going to break that will."

28

A plate banged down on the counter explosively. Mason raised perplexed eyes to encounter a flushed countenance, straight determined lips, blazing black eyes. "Say," the girl said, "what kind of a game is this? I'm making my own way without asking odds of anyone, and you came . . ."

Paul Drake waved a hand with the studied nonchalance of one who is creating a sensation, but wishes to make it appear it is all in the day's work.

"Perry," he said, "meet Winifred."

Mason's face showed such unmistakably genuine surprise that the indignation faded from Winifred Laxter's eyes. "Didn't you know?" she asked.

Mason shook his head.

She pointed to the sign on the outside of the place. "You should have known from the sign 'WINNIE'S WAFFLES.' "

"I didn't read the sign," Mason said. "My friend brought me in here. What was the idea, Paul, trying to make a grandstand, or pull a rabbit from the hat, or something?"

Drake, caressing his coffee cup with the tips of his fingers, gave a slow smile. "I wanted you two to get acquainted. I wanted my friend here to see how you ran the place, Miss Laxter. Most people would think an heiress couldn't turn to running a waffle kitchen."

"I'm not an heiress."

"Don't be too sure," Drake told her. "This is Perry Mason, the lawyer."

"Perry Mason," she repeated slowly.

Her eyes widened slightly.

"Heard of him?" Drake asked.

"Who hasn't?" she said, and colored.

"I wanted to ask you some questions about your grandfather," Mason said. "I employed Mr. Drake to locate you."

She opened the waffle iron, took out two crisply brown waffles. Moving with swift efficiency, she poured melted

29

butter on the waffles, set out a pitcher of syrup, handed each a waffle and strips of golden-brown bacon on a side dish.

"A little more coffee?" she asked.

"No, this will be fine," Mason assured her.

He put syrup on the waffle, cut into it, and his face showed surprise as he conveyed a piece to his mouth.

Paul Drake, at his side, chuckled and said, "I don't know what the case is worth to you, Perry, but these waffles are a pretty good fee in themselves."

"Where did you learn how to make these waffles?" the lawyer wanted to know.

"I studied cooking, and Grandpa used to like these waffles. When I found myself out on my own, I figured it would be a good plan to make waffles. Things are rather quiet now, but an hour ago there was a rush, and after the theater, there'll be another big rush. Then, of course, there's a big trade in the morning."

"Who handles the morning trade?" Mason asked.

"I do."

"And the after-theater trade?"

She nodded. "I'm working for myself, not employing anyone, so there's no law to keep me from working as long as I want to."

Drake nudged Mason's leg under the table and said, out of the side of his mouth, "Get a load of the bird looking in the window."

Mason raised his eyes.

Nat Shuster, his lips twisted back from his separated teeth, was jerking his head up and down in an effusive salutation. As soon as he realized Mason had seen him, he walked on past the window.

Mason saw the puzzled expression on Winifred Laxter's face.

"Know him?" he asked.

"Yes. He's a customer. Been eating here for two or three days now. He had me sign a paper tonight."

Mason slowly placed his knife and fork by the side of his plate. "Oh," he said, "he had you sign a paper, did he?"

"Yes. He said he was a friend and that he knew I'd want to help carry out Grandfather's intentions; that even if I hadn't been remembered in the will, he knew that I'd be broad-minded enough to realize Grandpa could do what he wanted to with his property; that unless the other two grandchildren could cut some red tape, they'd have to wait quite a while to get everything cleaned up, but I could cut some of the red tape and help them out if I'd sign a paper."

"What sort of a paper was it?"

"I don't know. It was something that said I knew Grandpa wasn't crazy, that I was satisfied with the will and wouldn't do anything to contest it. . . . But of course I wouldn't have done that anyway."

Drake looked at Perry Mason significantly.

"Did he pay you anything?" Mason asked.

"He insisted on giving me a dollar. He walked out and left it on the counter. I laughed at him and told him I didn't want anything at all; but he said I'd have to take the dollar to make it legal. He was very nice. He said he liked the waffles and was going to advertise the place among his friends and send me a lot of customers."

Perry Mason started in once more on his waffle. "Yes," he said slowly, *"he would."*

Winifred Laxter rested her hands on the shelf supporting the battery of waffle irons. "I take it," she said, "I've been trimmed. Is that right?"

Mason looked searchingly into her eyes. Drake was the one who answered the question. He nodded and said, "In a big way."

Winifred leaned closer to them. "Okay. Now let *me* tell *you* something. I don't care. I knew Sam Laxter had sent that fellow in here, and had a pretty good idea he was a lawyer. I knew he was trying to get me to sign away

31

something, and I knew he was doing that because he was afraid I could make trouble.

"Now, I don't know what *you* two are in here for, but probably you're trying to line me up so you can start a lawsuit, so let's come out in the open and understand each other. Then you can enjoy eating your waffles a lot more.

"Grandfather wasn't a fool. He knew what he was doing. He decided to leave his property to the two boys. That's swell. It suits me right down to the ground. We, all three of us, had been living with him for years. We'd grown accustomed to having him pay our bills. We didn't worry about money. We didn't care whether there was a depression, unemployment, or panic. Grandpa had his money, and he had it in cold cash. He dished it out to us generously.

"What was the result? We were out of touch with the world. We didn't know what was going on and we didn't care. We were young people who might just as well have been retired and living in an institution for the aged and infirm.

"I had a couple of boy friends who were rushing me to death. I couldn't decide which I liked the better. They were both perfectly swell. Sometimes I thought I liked one; sometimes I thought I liked the other. Then Grandfather died. I was disinherited. I had to get out and get to work. I picked up this business and began to learn about life. I've seen more people, made more contacts, had more fun living and working in this place than I ever had being the pampered pet of a rich granddad. And I'm finished with all of the petty jealousies and intrigue of the two grandsons who were afraid I was going to get all of the property. One of my boy friends decidedly lost interest in me as soon as he found out I wasn't going to have a million dollars or so in my own name. The other one is tickled to death because he wants to support me.

"Now then, figure that out, and see if you think I'm going to walk into court, drag out a lot of dirt about

32

Grandpa and the other two grandchildren, and either wake up with a headache or with a slice of property that I don't want."

Perry Mason slid his coffee cup across the counter.

"Give me another cup of coffee, Winnie, and I'll send all of *my* friends in here."

Her flashing eyes stared steadily into the lawyer's for a moment; then, recognizing a kindred spirit, she broke into a light laughter and said, "I'm glad you understand. I was afraid you wouldn't."

Paul Drake cleared his throat. "Look here, Miss Laxter, it's all right for you to feel that way, but don't forget you may not *always* feel that way. Money is hard to get. You've been tricked into signing something we could set aside. . . ."

Winifred handed Perry Mason a full coffee cup, and said to him significantly, "Tell your boy friend what it's all about, will you?"

Mason interrupted Paul Drake by placing a hand on Paul's arm, digging in with his powerful fingers. "Paul, you don't get the sketch. You're too damned commercial. Why not forget about money and laugh at life? It isn't the future that counts; it's the present. It isn't what you save; it's what you make, and the way you make it."

Winifred nodded. The detective shrugged his shoulders, and said, "It's your funeral."

Perry Mason finished his waffle, eating slowly and appreciatively. "You're going to make a success," he said, as he pushed back his empty plate.

"I've already made a success; I'm finding myself. The bill is eighty cents."

Mason handed her a dollar bill. "Put the change under the plate, if you will, please," he said, grinning. "How did you and Ashton get along?"

"Ashton's a great old crab," she laughed, manipulating the cash register.

Mason remarked with studied carelessness, "Too bad he's going to lose his cat."

Winifred paused, the change drawer open, her hand held poised over it. "What do you mean, he's going to lose his cat?"

"Sam won't let him keep the cat."

"But he has to under the will. He has to keep Ashton employed as a caretaker."

"But not the cat."

Dismay showed on Winifred's face. "Do you mean to say he isn't going to let Ashton keep Clinker?"

"That's it."

"But he can't put Clinker out."

"He says he's going to poison him."

Mason nudged Drake surreptitiously, started toward the door.

"Wait a minute," she called. "We've got to do something about that. He can't get by with that. Why, that's outrageous!"

"We'll see what we can do," Mason promised.

"But look here. You must do something. Perhaps I can do something. Where can I reach you?"

Perry Mason gave her one of his cards, and said, "I'm Ashton's lawyer. If you think of anything that will help, let me know. And don't sign any more papers."

The door from the street opened. A young man of medium build smiled at Winifred Laxter, then regarded Perry Mason with a level, appraising stare, shifted his eyes to Paul Drake and suddenly became hostile.

He was a head shorter than the tall detective, but he pushed up in front of him belligerently, stared at him steadily with gray eyes that didn't so much as flicker. "Say," he demanded, "what's *your* game?"

Drake remarked casually, "Just eating waffles, Buddy. Don't quarrel with the cash customers."

"He's all right, Doug," Winifred said.

"How do you know he's all right?" the young man retorted, without taking his eyes from Paul Drake. "He hunted me up this afternoon with a stall about going into the contracting business and wanting to have someone who knew architecture work with him. I hadn't talked with him five minutes before I found out he didn't know a single thing about contracting. I think he's a detective."

Drake, smiling, said, "You're a better detective than I am a contractor. You've guessed right. So what?"

The young man turned to Winifred. "Shall I throw him out, Winnie?" he asked.

She laughed. "It's all right, Doug. Shake hands with Perry Mason, a lawyer. You've heard of him. This is Douglas Keene, Mr. Mason."

The young man's expression changed. "Perry Mason," he said. "Oh. . . ."

Mason's hand found Keene's right hand and pumped it up and down. "Glad to know you, Keene," Mason said. "Shake hands with Paul Drake."

As Mason released his grip of Keene's hand, Drake grabbed it. "Okay, Buddy," he said, "no hard feelings. It's all in the day's work."

The steady gray eyes surveyed the two men thoughtfully. The first diffidence gave place to a very evident determination.

"Let's find out if it's all right," he said. "I've got something to say about this. Winifred and I are engaged. She's going to marry me. If I could support her I'd marry her tomorrow, but I can't support her and I won't let her support me. I'm an architect, and you know it takes a while for a young architect to get started. You just don't begin making money right away. But the country needs architects today more than ever. With credit inflated and more and more young families and more and more babies, it's only a question of time before I'll be sitting pretty."

Mason surveyed the youthful enthusiasm of the young man's face and nodded.

35

Paul Drake said, "Yeah . . . a couple of years." He said it tonelessly.

"And don't think I'm waiting for business to pick up, either," Keene said. "I'm working in a service station, and darned glad to get the job. Today the big boss was through. He stopped at the service station without anyone knowing who he was. And when he left he gave me his card and a pat on the back for the way I was handling the trade."

"Good boy," Mason told him.

"I'm just telling you fellows this," Keene said, "so you'll know where I stand, because I'm going to find out where *you* stand."

Mason glanced over at Winifred Laxter. Her eyes were absorbed in Douglas Keene. Her face was flushed with pride.

Keene took a step backward, so that he was between both men and the door.

"Now then," he said, "I've put my cards on the table and you chaps are going to put yours on the table. Peter Laxter died. He didn't leave Winifred a cent. So far as I'm concerned, I'm glad he didn't. She doesn't need his money. She's better off now than she was when she was living with him.

"I'm going to support her. I don't want any of her grandfather's money and she doesn't need any of her grandfather's money, but I don't like the idea of you birds trying to slip something over on her."

Mason's hand dropped to the young man's shoulder. "We're not trying to slip anything over on her," he said.

"What are you hanging around here for, then?"

"I want to get information," Mason said, "so I can represent a client."

"Who's the client?"

Mason grinned. "Believe it or not, but the client's a cat."

"A what?"

Winifred interrupted. "It's Charlie Ashton, Doug—you know, the boys have to keep him on as caretaker, but Sam has threatened to poison the cat, and Mr. Mason's representing Ashton, trying to fix things up so he can keep the cat."

Keene's jaw set grimly. "Do you mean to say that Sam Laxter threatens to poison Clinker?"

She nodded.

"Well, I'll be damned," Keene said slowly. He turned to Perry Mason. "Listen," he said, "I was going to keep out of that, but if Sam's pulling stuff like that, ask him what became of the Koltsdorf diamonds."

Winifred said sharply, "Doug!"

He swung to face her. "Don't stop me," he said. "You don't know what I know. I know stuff about Sam that's going to come out. No, don't worry, Winnie, *I'm* not going to bring it out; I'm going to keep out of it. It's Edith DeVoe. She . . ."

Winifred interrupted him firmly. "Mr. Mason is only interested in the cat, Doug."

Keene laughed, a quick, nervous laugh. "I'm sorry. Guess I got pretty well worked up. I can't stand the idea of anyone poisoning an animal, and when it comes down to brass tacks, Clinker is worth a dozen Sam Laxters. Oh, well, I'll keep out of it."

Paul Drake casually seated himself on one of the stools. "What's going to come out about Sam Laxter?" he asked.

Mason dropped his hand to the detective's shoulder. "Wait a minute, Paul. These people have shot square with us; let's shoot square with them."

He turned to Winifred. "Do you want to give us any information?" he asked.

She shook her head. "I want to keep out of it and I want Doug to keep out of it."

Mason took Drake's arm and literally pushed him

along the passageway between the booths on one side and the stools on the other. "Come on, Paul," he said.

As the outer door closed behind them Winifred's eyes flashed them a smile. She waved her arm.

"What did you do that for?" Drake protested. "That fellow knows something. He's been talking with Edith DeVoe."

"Who's Edith DeVoe?"

"She's the nurse who lived there in the house. I had a hunch she might know something."

Mason, staring moodily up and down the street, said, "If I catch Shuster hanging around here, I'm going to punch his face. Can you imagine the damn shyster going in and taking advantage of the kid and getting her to sign a paper like that?"

Drake said, "It's his style. What can you do now? You haven't got any client who can bust the will. That will's just as good as gold, isn't it?"

"I've got a cat for a client," Mason said grimly.

"Can a cat contest a will?"

Mason's face showed the determination of a born fighter. "Damned if I know," he said. "Come on, we're going to see Edith DeVoe."

"But you can't contest a will unless you're representing an interested party. Two of the interested parties take under the will and the other one has signed away her rights," the detective protested.

"I've told you before," Mason said, "that I never hit where the other man's expecting the punch."

5

IN THE TAXICAB, THE DETECTIVE GAVE PERRY MASON A
few pertinent bits of information. "There's something off
color about your caretaker, Charles Ashton," he said.
"He was riding with Peter Laxter, his employer, and they
were in an automobile accident. It busted Ashton up
pretty badly. He tried to collect damages and couldn't.
The driver of the other car wasn't insured and didn't have
a dime. Ashton made quite a squawk, trying to get something, said he hadn't saved a dime."

"That's nothing unusual," Mason remarked. "It's a
regular sales talk. He might have had a million dollars
salted away and still have said the same thing."

Drake went on in the mechanical tone of voice of one
who is primarily interested in facts rather than in their
interpretation. "He had a bank account at one of the
banks. As nearly as we can find out, it was the only bank
account he ever had. He deposited his salary there. He'd
saved something like four hundred dollars. After the
accident, he spent it all, and still owes some to a doctor."

"Wait a minute," Mason interposed, "didn't Peter
Laxter take care of his expenses in that automobile accident?"

"No, but don't jump at conclusions on account of it.
Ashton told one of his friends that Laxter would take
care of him all right in the long run, but Laxter thought
he'd stand a better chance recovering damages if he could
show that the money for the doctors and hospital bills had
been paid out of his own savings."

"Go ahead," Mason said. "You're leading up to something. What is it?"

"Shortly before the house burned, Laxter started cashing in. I can't find how much, but it was plenty. Three days before the house burned down, Ashton rented two large-size safety deposit boxes. The boxes were rented by Charles Ashton and in his name, but he told the clerk in charge that he had a half-brother who was to be given access to the boxes at any time. The clerk told him his half-brother would have to come in and register for signature. Ashton said the half-brother was sick in bed and couldn't move, but couldn't he take out a card and have the half-brother sign. He said he'd guarantee the signature, indemnify the bank against any claim, and all that sort of stuff. The bank gave him a card for his half-brother's signature. Ashton went out and came back in an hour or so with the signature on the card."

"What was the name?"

"Clammert—Watson Clammert."

"Who's Clammert?" Mason asked. "Is it a phony?"

"No," Drake said, "he's probably Ashton's half-brother. That is, he was; he's dead now. He wasn't registered in the city directory, but I took a chance, inquired at the motor vehicle department and found Clammert had a driving license. I got the address, chased him down and found that Watson Clammert had died within twenty-four hours after affixing his signature to that card."

"Anything fishy about the death?" Mason asked.

"Absolutely nothing. He died of natural causes. He died in a hospital. Nurses were in constant attendance, but—and here's the phony part—he'd been in a coma for days prior to his death. He hadn't regained consciousness."

"Then how the devil," Mason asked, "could he have signed his name on that card?"

Drake said tonelessly, "I'll bite, how could he?"

"What else about him?" Mason asked.

"Apparently he and Ashton are chips off the same block. Ashton went for years without seeing him or speaking to him. It wasn't until Ashton heard that Clammert was

40

dying in the charity ward of a hospital that he came to help him out."

"How did you get this stuff?" Mason asked.

"Ashton talked quite a bit to one of the nurses. She got a kick out of him. He was so bitterly vindictive and yet so bighearted. He'd heard Clammert was sick and broke, so he hobbled around, making a canvass of the hospitals until he found Clammert lying unconscious and near death. He dug down in his pocket and did everything he could, hired specialists, got special nurses and haunted the bedside. He left instructions with the nurse to see that Clammert had everything money could buy. Of course, the nurse knew he was dying and the doctors knew it, but, naturally, they kidded Ashton along, telling him there was perhaps one chance in a million, and Ashton told them to take that chance.

"But just to show you what a cantankerous cuss you've got for a client, he stipulated that when Clammert recovered consciousness, he was never to know who his benefactor had been. Ashton told the nurses they quarreled years ago and hadn't seen each other since—and what do you think they quarreled about?"

Mason said irritably, "I'll bite, Little Peter Rabbit, what did Ruddy the Lame Fox and Goofy the Sleeping Beauty quarrel about?"

The detective grinned and said, "A cat."

"A cat?" Mason exclaimed.

"That's right—a cat by the the name of Clinker—it was just a kitten then."

"Oh, hell," Mason said disgustedly.

"As near as I can figure out," Drake went on, "from the time Ashton discovered his half-brother until Clammert died a couple of days later, Ashton had spent something like five hundred dollars in hospital and doctors' bills. He paid everything out in cash. The nurse said he had a big sheaf of bills he carried in his wallet. Now, then, where the hell did Charles Ashton get that money?"

Mason made a grimace. "Shucks, Paul, I didn't want you to dig up facts that would put *my* client in a spot; I wanted you to dig up something that would put Sam Laxter in a spot."

"Well," Drake remarked in his dry, expressionless voice, "they're some of the pieces in the puzzle picture. I'm hired to get the pieces; you're hired to put them together. If they're going to make the wrong kind of picture when they're put together, you can always lose some of the pieces so no one else can find them."

Mason chuckled, then said thoughtfully, "Why the devil did Ashton want it so Clammert could go to that safety deposit box?"

"Well, the only thing I could think of," Drake said, "was that if Clammert got well Ashton intended to give him money but didn't intend to have any personal contact, so he arranged to give Clammert a key to a safety deposit box into which he'd put money from time to time and Clammert could take it out."

"That doesn't make sense," Mason said, "because Clammert would have to sign his name to get access to the box and the signature that Ashton turned in as being that of Clammert couldn't have been made by Clammert because Clammert was unconscious."

"Okay," Drake said, "you win. That's what I meant when I said the facts were the pieces in the puzzle. I get them and you put them together."

"Did anyone using Clammert's name ever go to the safety deposit boxes?" Mason asked.

"No, Clammert's never been near the box. Ashton went to it several times. He went to it yesterday, and he went to it today. While the clerks didn't want to talk about it, I gathered the impression they thought Ashton had pulled out a wad of dough from those safety boxes either yesterday or today, or both."

"How do they know what a man takes out?"

"Ordinarily they don't, but one of the clerks saw Ashton stuffing currency into a satchel."

Perry Mason laughed. "In most cases," he said "we can't find out any facts at all until after we've gone through a lot of preliminary work. In this case they pour into our laps."

"Did your client tell you about the Koltsdorf diamonds?" Drake wanted to know.

"Gosh," Mason remarked, "I feel like the interlocutor at a minstrel show. No, Mr. Drake, Mr. Ashton did not tell me about the Koltsdorf diamonds. What about the Koltsdorf diamonds? . . . Now, Paul, that's your cue to tell me about the Koltsdorf diamonds."

The detective chuckled. "The Koltsdorf diamonds are about the only jewels Peter Laxter ever fell for. Lord knows how he came by them. They were some of the stones smuggled out of Russia by the old aristocracy. Peter Laxter showed them to a few friends. They were large, brilliant diamonds."

"What about them?"

"Some of this other stuff," Drake said, "such as the currency, bonds, and all that, might have burnt up when the house was burned. It wouldn't have been possible to find even a trace of them. But the Koltsdorf diamonds haven't been found."

"Diamonds in the wreckage of a burnt house could hide pretty well," Mason said dryly.

"They've taken that wreckage to pieces with a fine-tooth comb, sifted ashes and done all sorts of things. But the diamonds can't be located. A distinctive ruby ring which Peter Laxter always wore on his left hand was found on the body, but no diamonds."

"Tell me the rest of it," Mason demanded. "Has Ashton shown up with those diamonds?"

"No, not that I've been able to find out. But he's done other peculiar things that are just as incriminating. For instance, shortly before the fire, Laxter had been dicker-

43

ing for a piece of property. He'd taken Ashton out with him to look the property over. A couple of days ago, Ashton called on the owner of that property and made an offer. The offer was for cash on the nail."

"It was refused?"

"Temporarily, yes, but I think the deal's still open."

Mason, frowning thoughtfully, said, "Looks like I'm stirring up a mare's nest. Laxter *might* have cached his property and Ashton *might* have had an inside track. In that event he probably wouldn't feel obligated to hand Sam Laxter the coin on a silver platter. Guess we're due for a talk with Ashton."

Drake said tonelessly, "The two grandchildren have been pretty wild, particularly Sam. Oafley's the quiet, unsociable sort. Sam went in for speedy automobiles, polo ponies, women, and all that sort of stuff."

"Where'd the money come from?"

"From the old man."

"I thought the old man was a miser."

"He was tighter than a knot in a shoelace except with his grandchildren; he was very liberal with them."

"How much was he worth?"

"No one knows. The inventory of the estate . . ."

"Yes," Mason said, "I checked over the inventory of the estate. Apparently the only things that were left were the frozen assets. The other stuff hasn't been discovered yet."

"Unless Ashton discovered it," Drake commented.

"Let's not talk about that," Mason said. "I'm interested right now in cats."

"The day before the fire there was a hell of a fight out at the house. I can't find out exactly what it was, but I think this nurse can tell us. I've talked with the servants. They froze up. I hadn't got around to the nurse yet. . . . Here's her apartment."

"What's her name—Durfey?"

"No—DeVoe—Edith DeVoe. According to the reports

44

I get, she isn't a bad looker. Frank Oafley was pretty much interested in her when she was taking care of the old man, and he's been seeing her off and on since."

"Intentions honorable?" Mason asked.

"Don't ask me; I'm just a detective—not a censor of morals. Let's go."

Mason paid off the cab. They rang a bell, and, when a buzzer had released the door catch, entered the outer door and walked down a long corridor to a ground floor apartment. A red-haired woman with quick, restless eyes, swift, nervous motions, and a well-modeled figure which was set off to advantage by her clothes, met them at the door of the apartment. Her face showed disappointment. "Oh," she said, "I was expecting . . . Who are you?"

Paul Drake bowed, and said, "I'm Paul Drake. This is Mr. Mason, Miss DeVoe."

"What is it you want?" she asked. Her speech was very rapid. The words seemed almost to run together.

"We wanted to talk with you," Mason said.

"About some employment," Paul Drake hastened to add. "You're a nurse, aren't you?"

"Yes."

"Well, we wanted to talk with you about some work."

"What sort of a position?"

"I think we could talk it over better if we stepped inside," Drake ventured.

She hesitated a moment, looked up and down the corridor, then stepped back from the door and said, "Very well, you may come in, but only for a few minutes."

The apartment was clean and well cared for as though she had just finished a careful housecleaning. Her hair was perfectly groomed. Her nails were well kept. She wore her clothes with the manner of one who is wearing her best.

Drake sat down, relaxing comfortably, as though he intended to stay for hours.

Mason sat on the arm of an overstuffed chair. He looked at the detective and frowned.

"Now this employment may not be exactly the kind of a job you had in mind," Drake said, "but there's no harm talking it over. Would you mind telling me what your rates are by the day?"

"Do you mean for two or three days, or. . . ."

"No, just one day."

"Ten dollars," she said crisply.

Drake took a billfold from his pocket. He extracted ten dollars but didn't at once pass it over to the nurse.

"I have one day's employment," he said. "It won't take over an hour, but I'd be willing to pay for a full day."

She wet her lips with the tip of a nervous tongue, glanced swiftly from Mason to Drake. Her voice showed suspicion. "Just what is the nature of this employment?" she asked.

"We wanted you to recall a few facts," Drake said, folding the ten dollar bill about his fingers. "It would take perhaps ten or fifteen minutes for you to give us an outline, and then you could sit down and write out the facts you'd told us."

Her voice was distinctly guarded now.

"Facts about what?"

The detective's glassy eyes watched her in expressionless appraisal. He pushed the ten dollar bill toward her. "We wanted to find out all you knew about Peter Laxter."

She gave a start, staring from face to face in quick alarm, and said, "You're detectives!"

Paul Drake's face registered the expression of a golfer who had just dubbed an approach shot.

"Let's look at it this way," he said. "We're after certain information. We want to get the facts—we don't want anything except facts. We're not going to drag you into anything."

She shook her head vehemently. "No," she said. "I was

46

employed by Mr. Laxter as a nurse. It wouldn't be ethical for me to divulge any of his secrets."

Perry Mason leaned forward and took a hand in the conversation. "The house was burned, Miss DeVoe?"

"Yes, the house was burned."

"And you were in it at the time?"

"Yes."

"How did the house burn—rather quickly?"

"Quite quickly."

"Have any trouble getting out?"

"I was awake at the time. I smelled smoke and thought at first it was just smoke from an incinerator. Then I decided to investigate. I put on a robe and opened the door. The south end of the house was all in flames then. I screamed, and, after a few minutes . . . Well, I guess perhaps I shouldn't say anything more."

"You knew the house was insured?" Mason asked.

"Yes, I suppose so."

"Do you know whether the insurance has been paid?"

"Why, I think it has. I think it's been paid to Mr. Samuel Laxter. He's the executor, isn't he?"

"Was there someone in that house you didn't like?" Mason asked. "Someone who was particularly obnoxious to you?"

"Why, whatever makes you ask such a question as that?"

"Whenever a fire occurs," Mason said slowly, "which might result in the loss of life and in which a person actually was killed, the authorities usually make an investigation. That investigation isn't always completed at the time of the fire, but when it *is* made it's always advisable for the witnesses to tell what they know."

She thought that over for several seconds, during which her eyes blinked rapidly.

"You mean that if I shouldn't make a statement I might be under suspicion of having set the fire to trap someone whom I didn't like? Oh, but that's *too* absurd!"

47

"I'll put it to you another way," Mason said. "Was there someone in the house whom you *did* like?"

"Just what do you mean by that?"

"Simply this: You can't be thrown with people for some time under the same roof without forming attachments, certain likes and dislikes. Let's suppose, for example, there was some person whom you didn't like and some person whom you did. We're going to get the facts about that fire. We're going to get them from *someone*. If we should get them from you, it might be better all around than if we happened to get them from the person whom you didn't like, particularly if that person should try to fasten guilt upon the person you *did* like."

She seemed to stiffen in the chair. "You mean that Sam Laxter has accused Frank Oafley of setting that fire?"

"Certainly not," Mason said. "I am purposely refraining from making *any* statement of facts. I'm giving out no information. I came to get it."

He nodded to the detective. "Come on, Paul," he said. He got to his feet.

Edith DeVoe jumped from her chair, almost ran between Mason and the door.

"Wait a minute, I didn't understand just what you wanted. I'll give you all the information I have."

"We'd want to know quite a few things," Mason said dubiously, as though hesitating about returning to his chair, "not only about the fire, but about the things which preceded it. I guess we'd better get the information somewhere else after all. We'd want to know all about the lives and personal habits of the people who lived in the house, and you, being a nurse . . . I guess perhaps we'd better leave you out of it."

"No, no, don't do that! Come back here. I'll tell you everything I know. After all, there's nothing that's confidential, and if you're going to get the facts I'd prefer that you get them from me. If Sam has even intimated Frank

48

Oafley had anything to do with that fire, it's a dirty lie by which Sam hopes to save his own bacon!"

Mason sighed, then, with apparent reluctance, returned to his chair, sat once more on the arm and said, "We're willing to listen for a few minutes, Miss DeVoe, but you'll have to make it snappy. Our time is valuable, and . . ."

She broke into swift conversation: "I understand all that. I thought at the time there was something funny about the fire. I told Frank Oafley about it and he said I should keep quiet. I screamed and tried to arouse Mr. Laxter—that's Peter Laxter—the old man. By that time the flames were all over that end of the house. I kept screaming, and groped my way up the stairs. It was hot there and smoky, but there weren't any flames. The smoke bothered me a lot. Frank came after me and pulled me back. He said there was nothing I could do. We stood on the stairs and yelled, trying to arouse Mr. Laxter, but we didn't get any answer. Lots of black smoke was rolling up the stairs. I looked back and saw some flames just breaking through the floor near the bottom of the stairs and I knew we had to get out. We went out through the north wing. I was almost suffocated with smoke. My eyes were red and bloodshot for two or three days."

"Where was Sam Laxter?"

"I saw him before I saw Frank. He had on pajamas and a bathrobe, and he was yelling 'Fire! Fire!' He seemed to have lost his head."

"Where was the fire department?"

"It didn't get there until the place was almost gone. It was very isolated, you know—the house."

"A big house?"

"It was too big!" she said vehemently. "There was too much work in it for the help they employed."

"What help was employed?"

"There was Mrs. Pixley; a girl named Nora—I think her last name was Abbington—I can't be certain; and then there was Jimmy Brandon—he was the chauffeur. Nora

49

was sort of a general maid-of-all-work. She didn't live at the place, but came every morning at seven and stayed until five in the afternoon. Mrs. Pixley did all the cooking."

"And Charles Ashton, the caretaker—was he there?"

"Only occasionally. He kept the town house, you know. He'd drive in at times when Mr. Laxter would ask him. He'd been there the night of the fire."

"Where did Peter Laxter sleep?"

"On the second floor, in the south wing."

"What time did the fire take place?"

"Around one thirty in the morning. It must have been about quarter to two when I woke up. The house had been burning for some time then."

"Why were you employed? What was wrong with Mr. Laxter?"

"He'd been in an automobile accident, you know, and it had left him quite nervous and upset. At times he couldn't sleep and he had a dislike of drugs. He wouldn't let the doctor give him anything to make him sleep. I'd been a masseuse, and I massaged him when he had those nervous fits. It relaxed him. A bath in a tub of hot water, with the water running over his body, then a massage, and he could relax and sleep. And he had some heart complications. Sometimes I had to give him hypodermics—heart stimulants, you know."

"Where was Winifred the night of the fire?"

"She was asleep. We had some trouble getting her up. I thought for awhile the smoke had got her. Her door was locked. The boys nearly broke it down before they were able to wake her up."

"Where was she? In the north wing or the south wing?"

"Neither. She was in the center of the house, on the east."

"How about the two boys—where did they sleep?"

"They were in the center of the house, on the west."

"And the servants?"

50

"All of them were in the north wing."

"If you were there as a nurse for Mr. Laxter, and he was having heart trouble, why didn't you sleep where you would be near him in case he was taken with a spell?"

"Oh, but I did. You see, he had an electric push button installed in his room, so that all he needed to do was to signal me and I could signal back, to let him know I was coming."

"How did you signal back?"

"A button that I pressed."

"That rang a bell in his room?"

"Yes."

"Why didn't you ring that the night of the fire?"

"We did. That was the first thing I did. I ran back and rang the bell repeatedly. Then, when we didn't hear from him, I started up the stairs. The fire must have burnt through the wires."

"I see. There was a lot of smoke?"

"Oh, yes, the central part of the house was simply filled with smoke."

"What was the trouble about the day before the fire?"

"What do you mean?"

"There'd been a row over something, hadn't there?"

"No . . . not exactly. There'd been some trouble between Peter Laxter and Sam. I don't think Frank was mixed up in it."

"Was Winifred drawn into it?"

"I don't think so. It was just an argument between the old man and Sam Laxter. Something about Laxter's gambling."

"Have you any idea how the fire started?" Mason asked.

"Do you mean did someone set it?"

Mason said slowly and impressively, "You've dodged the issue long enough, Miss DeVoe—*tell us what you know about the fire!*"

She took a quick breath. Her eyes faltered for a

moment. "Is there any way a person could start a fire by feeding exhaust fumes into a furnace?" she asked.

Drake shook his head. "No," he said, "not exhaust fumes. Come on down to earth and . . ."

"Wait a minute, Paul," Perry Mason interrrupted, "let's find out just what she means when she refers to exhaust fumes being put into a furnace."

"It isn't important unless a fire could be started that way," she countered evasively.

The lawyer, flashing a warning glance at the detective, nodded his head gravely and said, "Yes, I think perhaps a fire could be started that way."

"But it would have to be started several hours after the fumes were put into the furnace?"

"Just *how* were they put into the furnace?" Mason inquired.

"Well, it's this way: The garage was built into the house. It held three cars. The house was on a slope, and the garages were on the southwest corner, down the slope. I guess when they built the house there was that extra room under the hill and the architects just decided to put garages in there, instead of having separate buildings or . . ."

"Yes," Mason agreed hurriedly, "I understand exactly what you mean. Tell me about the exhaust fumes."

"Well," she said, "I'd been out for a walk and I was coming back to the house when I heard the sound of a car running in the garage. The garage door was closed, but the motor kept running. I thought someone must have gone away and left his motor running without knowing it, so I opened the door—that's a little door in the side—not the big sliding door that you open to let the cars out—and switched on the lights."

Mason leaned toward her. "What did you find?" he asked.

"Sam Laxter was sitting in there in his car, with the motor running."

52

"The motor of his car was running?"

"Yes."

"Running slowly, as though it were idling?"

"No, it was running rapidly. I would say the motor was being raced. If it had been running slowly, I couldn't have heard it."

"How did that get exhaust fumes into the furnace?" Paul Drake inquired.

"That's the peculiar thing. I just happened to notice that there was a tube running from the car to the heating pipe. The furnace was a gas furnace which supplied hot air. It was in a basement in the back of the garage."

"How did you know the tube from the exhaust led into the pipe?"

"I saw it, I tell you! I saw a tube from the exhaust running along the floor and then up into a pipe. You see the pipes from the furnace—that is some of them—ran up through the garage."

"Did Sam Laxter know you'd seen the tube running from the exhaust?" the lawyer asked.

"Sam Laxter," she said very emphatically, "was drunk. He could hardly stand. He switched off his motor and spoke roughly to me."

"What did he say?" Mason asked.

"He said, 'Get the hell out of here. Can't a man ever have any privacy without you snooping around?' "

"What did you say?"

"I turned on my heel and left the garage."

"Didn't say anything to him?"

"No."

"Did you switch out the lights when you went out?"

"No, I left the lights on so he could find his way out."

"How did you know he was drunk?"

"From the way he was sprawled all over the seat and the tone of his voice."

Mason's eyes narrowed into thoughtful slits. "See his face clearly?" he asked.

She frowned for a moment, and said, "Why, I don't believe I saw his *face*. He wears a big cream-colored Stetson, you know, and when I switched on the lights the first thing I saw was this Stetson hat. I walked over toward the side of the car. He was slumped down over the wheel and when I came up beside the car, he hung his head. . . . Come to think of it, I didn't see his face at all."

"Did you recognize his voice?"

"The voice was thick—you know the way a man's voice sounds when he's been drinking."

"In other words," Mason said, "if it came to a show-down in court, you couldn't swear positively that it was Sam Laxter who was in that car, could you?"

"Why, of course I could. No one else around the house wore that sort of a hat."

"Then you're identifying the hat instead of the man."

"What do you mean?"

"Anyone could have put on that hat."

"Yes," she said acidly, "they *could* have."

"It may be important," Mason said, "and if you had to testify, you'd be cross-examined ruthlessly."

"You mean I'd have to testify about how the fire started?"

"Something like that. How do you know it wasn't Frank Oafley who was sitting in there behind the wheel?"

"I *know* it wasn't."

"How?"

"Well, if you want to know, because I'd been out with Frank Oafley. We'd been walking, and I'd left him at the corner of the house. He went around toward the front and I came up toward the back. That took me past the garages. That was when I heard the sound of the motor running."

"How about the chauffeur—what was his name—Jim Brandon?"

"That's right."

"Could it have been the chauffeur?"

"Not unless he was wearing Sam Laxter's hat."

"Whom else have you told about this?" Mason asked.

"I've told Frank."

"You usually call him by his first name?" Mason asked.

She turned her eyes quickly from Mason's, then, after a moment, raised them to stare defiantly at him. "Yes," she said. "Frank and I are very close friends."

"What did he say when you told him about it?"

"He said there was no way exhaust fumes could start a fire; that I'd just make trouble if I said anything about it, and to keep quiet."

"Whom else did you tell?"

"I told Winifred's boy friend—not Harry Inman—but the other one."

"You mean Douglas Keene?"

"That's right—Douglas Keene."

"Who's Harry Inman?"

"He was a boy who was rushing her. I think she favored him, but, as soon as he found out she wasn't going to get any money, he dropped her like a hot potato."

"What did Douglas Keene say when you told him?"

"Douglas Keene said he thought it was evidence of the greatest importance. He asked me a lot of questions about where the different pipes led, and wanted to know if the pipe into which the tube was running ran up to Peter Laxter's bedroom."

"Did it?"

"I think it did."

"Then what?"

"He advised me to tell the authorities what I'd seen."

"Did you do it?"

"Not yet. I was waiting for . . . a friend. . . . I wanted to get his advice before I did anything which would cause trouble."

"What time was this that you encountered Sam Laxter in the garage?"

"About half past ten, I guess."

"That was several hours before the fire."

"Yes."

"Do you know whether Sam came in the house immediately after that?"

"No, I don't. I was so angry when he made that crack I walked out to keep from slapping him."

"But he must have returned to the house before the fire because he was in pajamas and robe when you were aroused by the fire."

"Yes, that's so."

"And he was fully clothed when you saw him there in the car?"

"I think so, yes."

"Now, you say that you turned on the lights?"

"Yes. Why?"

"The lights in the garage were off?"

"Yes."

"The door was closed?"

"Yes."

"Then the last person driving a car into that garage must have closed the door behind him, is that right?"

"Yes, of course."

"And the light switch was near the small door."

"Within a few inches of it. Why?"

"Because," Mason said slowly, "if Laxter had driven his car into that garage, he must necessarily have left the car, gone to the garage door, closed it, switched off the lights and then returned to his own car. After all, one doesn't drive cars into garages through closed doors."

"Well, what of it?"

"If he was so drunk he couldn't shut off the motor, but was just sprawled over the wheel, letting the motor run, it would hardly seem possible he'd have been able to get up, close the garage doors, switch out the lights and return to his car."

She nodded slowly.

"I hadn't thought of that."

"You're expecting this friend who is going to advise you what to do?"

"Yes, he's due at any minute."

"Would you mind telling me his name?"

"I don't think that needs to enter into it."

"Is it Frank Oafley?"

"I refuse to answer."

"And you aren't going to tell the authorities about this unless your friend tells you to?"

"I'm not going to commit myself on that. I'm not putting myself entirely in this friend's hands. I'm only asking him for advice."

"But you feel that in some way the fire was started through the exhaust fumes?"

"I'm not a mechanic; I don't know anything about automobiles. I don't know anything about gas furnaces. But I do know there's a flame in that gas furnace all the time, and it seemed to me if the mixture in the carburetor had been rather rich and some gasoline fumes had been thrown into the furnace, they might have exploded and started a fire."

Mason yawned ostentatiously, glanced at Drake and said, "Well, Paul, I guess that isn't going to help us much. There's no way those exhaust fumes could have started a fire."

She looked from one to the other with disappointment on her face.

"Are you sure?"

"Positive."

"Then why was the hose running from the exhaust to the pipe in the heating outfit?"

Mason countered with another question. "There was only one light in the garage?"

"That's right—a very brilliant light which hung in the center of the garage."

"Don't you suppose it's possible what you saw was a rope instead of a hose?"

"Absolutely not—it was some sort of flexible tubing— that is, the outside of it looked like flexible rubber tubing, and it ran from the exhaust of Sam Laxter's car to a hole which had been cut in the heating pipe. It's a big heating pipe, you know, covered with asbestos. The hot air goes up through there, into Pete Laxter's bedroom and sitting room."

Mason nodded thoughtfully. "Tell you what I'll do," he said, "I'll look around a little bit and if you decide to tell your story to the authorities I may be able to help you get in touch with some of the members of the homicide squad who aren't quite as skeptical and hard-boiled as Sergeant Holcomb."

"I'd like that," she said simply.

"Well," Mason told her, "we'll think it over and give you a buzz, if we get any new ideas. In the meantime, you can let us know what your friend advises you to do. If you decide to tell the authorities, let us know."

She nodded slowly. "Where can I reach you?"

Mason took Drake's arm and, by a gentle pressure, pushed him toward the door. "We'll call you back later on tonight. Simply swell of you to have talked with us," he told her.

"It wasn't an ordeal at all," she said, smiling. "I was glad to tell you all I knew."

In the corridor, the detective looked at the lawyer.

"Well," Mason said, chuckling, "the cat stays."

"So I gathered," Drake observed. "But I don't see just how you're going to play your cards."

Mason led the detective to the end of the corridor, lowered his voice almost to a whisper.

"When next I see my esteemed contemporary, Nat Shuster, I'll ask him to read Section 258 of the Probate Code, which provides, in effect, that no person convicted of murdering a decedent shall be entitled to succeed to any portion of the estate, but the portion that he would be entitled to shall go to the other heirs."

"Let's see if we figure the mechanics of this thing the same way," Drake said.

"Sure we do," Mason answered. "It's dead open and shut. The hot-air gas furnace had a lot of pipes leading to different rooms in the house. Each of those pipes had a damper, so that heat could be shut off from the rooms which weren't in use. Sam Laxter committed murder by a very simple process. He drove his car into the garage, clamped flexible tubing to his exhaust pipe, tapped a hole in the pipe which sent hot air to Peter Laxter's bedroom, and closed the damper back of the place where he'd brought the tubing into the pipe. Then he sat in his car, running the motor. Deadly monoxide gas from the automobile exhaust went through the flexible tube into the heating pipe, and was carried into Peter Laxter's bedroom.

"Notice the diabolical cleverness of the thing: He had only to let his motor run in order to bring about a painless death in a room many feet removed from the motor behind locked doors. Then he set fire to the house. Carbon monoxide is normally found in the blood of persons who have expired in burning buildings. It was a beautiful case of murder, and apparently the only witness is this red-headed nurse who caught him in the act, and the only reason she's alive today is that Sam Laxter thinks she doesn't realize the significance of what she saw. Or perhaps he doesn't know she saw the tube leading from the exhaust to the pipe."

The detective pulled a stick of chewing gum from his pocket, and said, "What do we do next?"

"We get in touch with the district attorney," Mason replied. "He's always claimed that a criminal lawyer uses his intelligence to keep murderers from paying the penalties of their crime. Now I'm going to fool him by showing him a perfect murder case I've uncovered, where his own men have fallen down on the job."

"It seems like such a thin skeleton of evidence on

which to hang a murder accusation," the detective objected.

"There's nothing thin about it," Mason retorted. "Notice that the time was about quarter past ten at night. It had been dark for several hours. The garage doors were closed. Sam Laxter pretended he'd been drunk when he brought his car into the garage. But he must have left the car, gone to the sliding doors, closed them, and then climbed back in the car and kept the motor running. He must have attached the flexible tubing to his exhaust pipe and then must have arranged to feed it into the pipe which ran to his grandfather's room. Then all he had to do was to start the motor. Probably he didn't need to keep it running very long. If I remember my forensic medicine correctly, the exhaust gas of motor cars produces carbon monoxide at the rate of one cubic foot per minute per twenty horsepower. The average garage can be filled with deadly fumes in five minutes from running an ordinary automobile. Exposure to an atmosphere containing as little as two-tenths of one percent of the gas will cause a fatal result in time. The post mortem indications are a bright, cherry-red blood. The gas affects the blood so so that it can't distribute oxygen to the tissues, and these indications are customarily found in the blood of one who has died in a burning house.

"We'll hand it to Samuel C. Laxter for being damned clever. If it hadn't been for the fortuitous circumstances of that nurse happening on him, he'd have committed a perfect murder."

"You're putting this whole thing in the hands of the district attorney?" Drake ventured, his eyes rolling toward Perry Mason, his face utterly devoid of expression.

"Yes."

"Hadn't you better find out just where *your* client stands in this thing first?"

Mason said slowly, "No, I don't think so. If my client has done wrong, I'm not going to try and shield him. I'm employed to see that he keeps his cat, and, by God, he's going to keep that cat. If he's found money that belongs to the estate and has embezzled it, that's an entirely different matter. And don't overlook the fact that Pete Laxter *may* have made a valid gift of that money to Ashton before his death."

"Baloney," the detective remarked. "Pete Laxter didn't expect to die; therefore, there was no reason for him to give away his money."

"Don't be to too certain," Mason said, "He had some reason for turning his property into cash. But let's quit speculating about that, Paul. The main thing in handling a lawsuit is to keep the other man's client on the defensive; not to get yours in a position where he has to do a lot of explaining. However, I'll give Ashton a buzz and tell him that I think his cat is safe."

The detective laughed. "Talk about using a ten-guage shotgun to kill a canary," he said: "we certainly are getting into a lot of ramifications in order to keep a cat alive."

"And," Mason said, "in order to show Nat Shuster that he can't cut corners with me and get away with it. Don't forget that angle, Paul."

"There's a public telephone in the drugstore around the corner," Drake said.

"Okay, Paul, let's telephone Ashton and telephone the district attorney."

They strolled around the corner. Mason dropped a dime in, dialed the number listed under the name of Peter Laxter, and asked for Charles Ashton. It took several minutes before he heard Ashton's rasping voice on the telephone.

"This is Perry Mason talking, Ashton. I don't think you need to worry any more about Clinker."

"Why not?" Ashton asked.

"I think that Sam Laxter is going to have his hands full," Mason explained. "I think he'll be kept quite well occupied. Don't say anything just yet to any of the servants, but I think there's a possibility Sam Laxter may be summoned to the district attorney's office to answer some questions."

The caretaker's voice was harshly strident. "Can you tell me what about?"

"No. I've told you everything I can. Just keep it under your hat."

There was growing uneasiness manifest in the tones of Ashton's voice. "Wait a minute, Mr. Mason. I don't want you to go too far in this thing. There are some reasons why I don't want the district attorney messing around asking questions."

Mason's tone was one of finality. "You employed me to see your cat wasn't poisoned. I'm going to do just that."

"But this is something else," Ashton said. "I want to see you about it."

"See me tomorrow then. In the meantime, give Clinker a dish of cream with my compliments."

"But I must see you, if the district attorney's going to start an investigation."

"Okay, see me tomorrow, then," Mason told him, and hung up. He made a wry grimace as he turned from the telephone booth and faced the detective.

"These damn cat cases," he said, "are more bother than they're worth. Let's go hunt up the district attorney."

"Sound as though he had a guilty conscience?" Drake asked.

Mason shrugged his shoulders. "My clients never have guilty consciences, Paul. And, after all, don't forget my real client is the cat."

Drake chuckled and said, "Sure, I understand, but just as a side line I sure would like to know where Ashton got that money. . . . Listen, Perry, it's starting to rain. I'd prefer to use my car if we're going places."

Mason, thumbing through the telephone directory for the residence number of the district attorney, said, "Sorry, Paul, we're going places, but you won't have a chance to get your car—we'll be moving too fast. . . . I'll get out my convertible. We can use that."

Drake groaned. "I was afraid of that. You drive like hell on wet roads."

6

THERE WAS SOMETHING SUGGESTIVE OF A HUGE BEAR about Hamilton Burger, the district attorney. He was broad of shoulders, thick of neck, and, when he moved, his arms had that peculiar swinging rhythm which speaks for a network of perfectly coördinated muscles rippling under the skin.

"You know, Mason," he said, "I'm anxious to coöperate with you whenever coöperation is possible. I've told you before, and I'll tell you again, that I've a horror of prosecuting an innocent man; but I'll also tell you that I don't like to have anyone use me for a cat's-paw."

Mason sat silent. Paul Drake, sprawled in a chair, his long legs thrust out in front of him, kept his glassy eyes fixed on the toes of his shoes, and managed to look bored.

Burger started pacing the floor, his manner nervous. He flung his head around in a half turn as a bear might sniff the wind, and said, "You're a good lawyer, Mason."

Perry Mason sat quiet.

Burger pivoted on his heel, started walking in the other direction. He said, flinging the words over his shoulder, "But you're a better detective than you are a lawyer. When you turn your mind to the solution of a crime, you ferret out the truth. That doesn't keep you from defending guilty clients."

Mason said nothing.

Burger took one more turn; then stopped abruptly, swung to face Mason, leveled his forefinger and said, "If the people in my office thought that I was going to act on information you had given me, they'd think you were making a cat's-paw of me."

"That," Mason retorted, "is the reason I came to you personally instead of going to your assistants. Here's an opportunity for you to clean up something, and prove that what appeared to be an accidental death was in fact a murder. I'm not asking favors. I'm giving you an opportunity. You can take it or leave it. I'm interested in this thing because of a cat; and if you want to know, I'm making exactly ten dollars as a fee."

Burger pulled a cigar from his waistcoat pocket, tore at the end of it with his teeth, scraped a match along the bricks of the fireplace, and puffed the cigar into smoke. He sighed and said, "All right, Dr. Jason happens to be visiting me this evening. I'm going to call him in. If the thing sounds reasonable to him, we're going to make a whirlwind investigation. I'll know whether I want to go ahead or run for cover by the time the publicity breaks."

Perry Mason lit a cigarette.

"Excuse me just a moment," Burger said. "I'll call Dr. Jason, and I'll telephone Tom Glassman, my chief investigator, and have him come up right away."

As the door closed behind the district attorney, Paul Drake rolled his expressionless eyes toward Perry Mason. The detective's face was wearing its habitual expression of droll humor. "I notice you didn't tell him anything about the peculiar and sudden rise to affluence of your client, Charles Ashton."

"I'm only concerned with reporting such facts as may point to a murder," Mason remarked.

Drake turned his eyes back to stare at his toes.

"If I were a district attorney, I'm not so certain that I'd play along with you, Perry," he remarked.

"Whenever a man plays ball with me, he gets a square deal," Mason insisted.

"Yeah, but God help him if he ever tries to steal second," Drake said lugubriously.

The door of the room opened, and Dr. Jason, a tall, rather thin man with brown eyes which were unusually piercing, surveyed the two men.

"Good evening, Mason," he said. "I don't think I know Mr. Drake."

Drake slowly doubled up his knees, arose from the chair, extended a languid hand.

"Glad to know you, Doctor," he said. "I've heard a lot about you from Perry Mason. I always remembered what he said about you when you'd been examining one of his clients on a sanity test."

"Indeed?" Dr. Jason inquired.

"Mason said that when you started worming your way into a man's consciousness, you were as persistent as the head of a wild oat working up a man's sleeve."

Dr. Jason laughed. "I only wish he'd say that publicly. It would be the best advertisement I could have. It doesn't exactly coincide with what he said about me to the jury in his last case."

District Attorney Burger, indicating chairs, puffed nervously on his cigar. "Doctor," he said, "I have a problem. A house burns; a man's body is found. Apparently he has burned to death in his bed. There was no suggestion of anything sinister in that death. Now, then, witnesses appear who can testify that a man, who might have profited very materially by the death of this person, was in a garage, with a flexible tube running from the exhaust pipe of his automobile to a hole cut in the pipe of a hot air furnace which led to this man's room. The fire may well have been of incendiary origin. Is it possible that sufficient carbon monoxide gas could have been introduced into the room in this way to have brought about the man's death?"

"Quite readily possible," Dr. Jason admitted, his eyes shifting from Drake to Mason.

"The man would have died in his sleep?"

"It is very likely. Carbon monoxide is a very insidious poison. There are numerous instances of persons who have been working in closed garages where motor cars were running and who died without being able to reach the outer air."

"How could you tell if a person died of carbon monoxide poisoning?"

"There are several methods. One of the most usual is to notice the color of the blood. It is a bright, cherry-red."

"And, if a person was burned to death, could you detect the presence of carbon monoxide?"

"Wait a minute," Dr. Jason said slowly. "You are overlooking something. If a person burnt to death, we would have every reason to expect that carbon monoxide would be present in his lungs. In fact, it might well be that the person had suffocated from monoxide incidental to the fire."

"In that case, Doctor, would it be possible to tell from an examination of the body whether the man had been murdered by this method before the house was fired?"

Dr. Jason's glittering eyes stared searchingly at Perry Mason. "How long before the fire was the monoxide introduced into this man's room by means of the automobile exhaust?"

"Probably two or three hours."

Dr. Jason nodded slowly. "I think," he said to Hamilton Burger, "that we could tell from an inspection of the body. It would, of course, depend somewhat upon the condition of the body after the fire. I would say that it would be quite possible to make this determination. Blisters, which are formed by heat when the tissues are able to react, usually vary greatly from evidences of heat applied after death."

"In other words, we should exhume the body?" Burger inquired.

Dr. Jason nodded.

Burger got to his feet with a peculiar lunging motion, as though about to charge some obstacle. "Well," he said, "if we're going to tackle this thing, we may as well make a good job of it. I'll get an order permitting us to exhume the body."

7

RAIN SEEPED SILENTLY DOWN FROM THE MIDNIGHT SKY, dripped in mournful cadences from the glistening leaves of the trees, gave forth hissing noises as the drops struck against the hot hoods of the gasoline lanterns which illuminated the scene.

A grassy slope studded with marble headstones stretched from a circle of vivid illumination into a mysterious border of dripping darkness.

There was no wind.

Hamilton Burger, a big overcoat covering his broad shoulders, the wide collar turned up about his ears, was plainly impatient. "Can't you fellows speed it up a little bit?" he asked.

One of the shovelers cast him a resentful glance. "There ain't room enough for any more men," he said, "and we're working at top speed. We're almost there, anyhow."

He wiped a perspiring forehead with a soggy coat sleeve, and fell once more to rapid shoveling. A moment later the blades of one of the shovels gave forth a peculiar sound as it struck something solid.

"Take it easy," the other shoveler cautioned. "Don't let him rush you. We've got to get the dirt from around the edges before we can raise it up. Get ropes on the handles, and then these fellows that are just standing around can get some exercise."

Burger ignored the sarcastic comment, to lean forward and look down into the oblong hole.

Perry Mason lit a cigarette and stamped his soggy shoes. Paul Drake, sidling up to him, said, "Won't your face be red if the medico says the guy really burned to death?"

Mason shook his head impatiently.

"All I did was to report facts. Personally, I think they're going at this thing backwards. If they'd get Edith DeVoe and then drag Sam Laxter in for questioning they'd stand more chance of getting somewhere."

"Yeah," Drake said, "but then Burger would be out in the open investigating Peter Laxter's death. He's afraid that's just what you want him to do, so he'll sort of sneak up on the case from the back way and convince himself he's got a case before he makes any overt moves. He's played with you before, you know. He's a burnt child who dreads the fire."

"Well," Mason said disgustedly, "he's too damn cautious. This case is going to slip through his fingers if he isn't careful. He may dread the fire, but he can't cook dough into cake without using fire, and even then he can't eat his cake and have it too."

Tom Glassman, chief investigator for the district attorney, blew his nose violently. "What's good to keep from taking cold at a time like this, Doc?" he asked.

Dr. Jason said, unsympathetically, "Staying in a warm bed. . . . They *would* have to pick a rainy night to do this. The man's been buried for days, but no one takes any interest in him until it starts to rain."

"How long will it take you to tell what you want after examining the body?"

"It may not take very long. It will depend somewhat on the extent to which the body was charred by heat."

"Bring out that coil of rope," one of the men in the grave ordered, "and get ready to pull. We can get the rope around the handles now."

A few moments later, with everyone straining on ropes, the coffin jerked, and started its uneven journey upward.

"Pull steady on them ropes, now; don't get it tilted up at one end, and take it easy."

The coffin reached the surface. Boards were shoved under it. Then the coffin slid along the wet, muddy boards until it rested on the firm ground.

One of the men produced a cloth and wiped the soil from the top of the coffin. A screwdriver made its appearance. After a moment, the lid of the coffin was swung back and a voice said, "Okay, Doc, it's all yours."

Dr. Jason stepped forward, leaned over the coffin, gave an exclamation, and tugged a flashlight from his pocket.

The men shuffled around in a circle, but, as yet, no one had picked up the gasoline lantern, so that the interior of the coffin was plunged in shadow.

"What's the verdict, Doctor?" the district attorney inquired.

Dr. Jason's pocket flashlight illuminated the interior of the coffin. His fingers moved the charred body.

"It's going to be hard to tell. The man's been burned to a crisp. I'll have to look for some place where clothing protected the skin somewhat."

"How about monoxide?"

"No need testing for that. It would be present anyway."

"Well, can you go ahead with your examination?"

"You mean here?"

"Yes."

"It would be difficult, and the conclusion wouldn't be final."

"Can you make a good guess?"

Dr. Jason sighed resignedly, started working with the

screwdriver. "I'll answer that question in a few minutes," he said.

One of the men held a lantern. Dr. Jason, showing his resentment against the weather, his disapproval of the entire procedure, removed the top from the coffin. "Bring that light over here—no, not so close—don't let the shadow fall on the inside. That's right—stand about there. . . . Oh, don't be so damned squeamish!"

He fumbled about in the interior of the coffin, took a sharp knife from his pocket. The sound of the blade ripping through cloth sounded startlingly distinct above the steady drip of the misty rain. After a moment he straightened, and nodded to Hamilton Burger. "You wanted a guess?" he asked.

"That's right, a guess—the best you can make, of course."

Dr. Jason dropped the lid back into position. "Go ahead with your investigation," he said.

Hamilton Burger stood staring moodily down at the coffin, then he nodded and turned on his heel. "Okay," he said, "let's go. You ride with us, Mason. Paul Drake can follow in your car. You take charge of the body, Doctor."

Mason followed Burger to the district attorney's car. Tom Glassman drove. The men were grimly silent. The windshield wipers swung back and forth in monotonous tempo, their steady throbbing sounding above the purr of the motor and the whine of the tires.

"Going out to Laxter's place?" Mason asked at length.

"Yes," Burger answered, "up to the place where they're living now—the city house I believe they call it. I want to ask some questions."

'Going to make any accusations?" Mason inquired.

"I'm going to ask some pretty direct questions," Burger admitted. "I don't think I'll make any definite accusations. I don't want to divulge just what we're trying to get at until I'm ready to do so. I'm not going to ask anything about the tube which ran from the exhaust until after

I've laid a pretty good foundation. I think it would be better, Mason, if you and your detective weren't present when we asked the questions."

"Well," Mason said, "if you feel that we've done all we can, I know where there's a nice soft bed, a piping hot toddy, and . . ."

"Not yet," Burger interrupted. "You've started this thing, and you're going to stick around until we see whether we've drawn a blank."

Mason sighed and settled back against the cushions. The car made time through the deserted streets, climbed a winding road which ran up a hill. "That's the place up there," Burger announced—"the big place. Try not to use a flashlight unless you have to, Tom. I'd like to get a look at that garage before we alarm anyone."

Glassman eased the car in close to the curb, stopped it and shut off the motor. There was no sound, save for the beating of rain on the roof of the car.

"So far so good," he said.

"Got skeleton keys?" Burger asked.

"Sure," Glassman said. "You want me to get that garage open?"

"I'd like to take a look at the cars, yes."

Glassman opened the door, climbed out into the rain and turned a flashlight on the padlock which held the garage doors. He produced a bunch of keys from his pocket, and, after a moment nodded to Burger, and pulled back the sliding door of the garage.

The men opened the door of the garage.

"Be careful," Burger cautioned, "not to slam those doors shut. We don't want to alarm anyone until after we've looked the place over."

There were three cars in the garage. Glassman's flashlight flickered over them in turn. Mason stared with narrowed eyes at a new green Pontiac sedan. Burger, seeing the expression on his face, inquired, "Have you discovered something, Mason?"

71

Perry Mason shook his head.

Glassman's flashlight explored the registration certificates. "This one's in the name of Samuel C. Laxter," he said, indicating a custom-built sports coupe with spare tires mounted in fender wells on either side. It was a powerful, low-hung car of glistening enamel and chrome steel.

"Sure built for speed," Burger muttered. "Turn your flashlight down here on the muffler, Tom."

Glassman swung the beam from his flashlight to the exhaust pipe, and Burger bent over to examine it. He nodded slowly. "Something's been clamped around here," he said.

"Well, let's go have a talk with Mr. Samuel Laxter and see what he has to say for himself," Glassman suggested.

Perry Mason, leaning nonchalantly against the side of the garage, tapped a cigarette on his thumb nail, preparatory to lighting it. "Of course, I don't want to interfere, but there's just the possibility you might find that flexible tubing if you looked hard enough."

"Where?" Burger asked.

"Some place in the car."

"What makes you think it's there?"

"The fire," Mason pointed out, "originated at a point in or near Laxter's bedroom. The garage was some little distance from that. They managed to save the automobiles that were in the garage. That bit of flexible tubing was a damaging piece of evidence which Laxter wouldn't ordinarily have left where it could be discovered. Of course, he may have hidden it afterwards, but there's a chance it's somewhere in the car."

Glassman, without enthusiasm, pulled the trigger which raised the back of the rumble seat, climbed into the car, and started exploring with his flashlight. He raised the front seat, opened the flap pocket, prowled around in the back of the car.

"There's a compartment here that's locked," Burger pointed out.

"For golf clubs," Glassman explained.

"See if one of your keys will fit it."

Glassman tried his keys, one after another, then shook his head.

"See if you can't pull that piece out in the back of the front seat and see down into it."

The car springs swayed as Glassman's heavy body moved around. Then he said in a muffled voice, "There's something down here that looks like a long vacuum sweeper tube."

"Jimmy the door open," Burger ordered, his voice showing excitement. "Let's take a look."

Glassman pried the lock, saying as he did so, "This isn't a very neat job. It's going to lead to an awful squawk if we're wrong."

"I'm commencing to think we're right," Burger remarked grimly.

Glassman reached in his hand and pulled out some twelve feet of flexible tubing. On one end were two adjustable bands which tightened with bolts and nuts. The other end contained a mushroom-like opening of soft rubber.

"Well," Burger said, "we'll get Laxter out of bed."

"Want us to wait in here?" Mason inquired.

"No, you can come up to the house and wait in the living room. It may not be very much of a wait. Pulling him out of bed like this, he may confess."

The big house sat well upon a hill. The garage was some distance from the house, having been excavated from the earth. Cement steps led up to a graveled walk. A private driveway from the garage swung up a more gentle incline, and circled the house, serving both as a driveway by which cars might be brought to the front door, as well as a service road by which fuel and supplies might be delivered to the back of the house.

The men climbed the stairs, moving silently in a compact group. At the top of the stairs, Burger paused. "Listen," he said, "what's that?"

From the misty darkness came the sound of a metallic clink, and, a moment later, it was followed by a peculiar scraping noise.

"Someone digging," Mason said in a low voice. "That's the noise made by a spade striking a loose rock."

Burger muttered, "By George, you're right. Mason, you and Drake keep back of us. Tom, you'd better have your flashlight ready, and put a gun in the side pocket of your coat—just in case."

Burger led the way forward. The four walked as quietly as possible, but the graveled walk crunched underfoot. Glassman muttered, "We can do better on the grass," and pushed over to the side of the walk. The others followed him. The grass was wet, the soil slightly soggy, but they were able to move forward in complete silence.

There were lights in the house which showed ribbons of illumination around the edges of the windows. The man who was digging kept plugging away.

"From behind that big vine," Glassman said.

It needed no comment from him to point the direction. The vine was agitated by a weight thrust against it. Drops of rain cascaded down from the leaves, were caught in a shaft of light coming from an uncurtained diamond-shaped pane of glass in one of the doors and transformed into a golden spray.

The shovel made more noise.

"Scraping dirt back to fill up the hole," Mason remarked.

The beam from Glassman's flashlight stabbed through the darkness.

A startled figure jumped back and thrashed about in the vine, which, under the illumination of Glassman's flashlight, resolved itself into a climbing rosebush. Glassman said, "Come out, and be careful with your hands. This is the law."

"What are you doing here?" asked a muffled voice.

"Come on out," Glassman ordered.

The figure showed itself first as a black blotch in the midst of the glistening leaves, the wet surfaces of which reflected the illumination of the flashlight. Then, as it broke through the vine, Perry Mason caught a glimpse of the man's face and said to Burger, "It's Frank Oafley."

Burger moved forward. "What's your name?" he asked.

"I'm Oafley—Frank Oafley. I'm one of the owners of this place. Who are you and what are you doing here?"

"We're conducting a little inquiry," Burger said. "I'm the district attorney. This is Tom Glassman, my associate. What were you digging for?"

Oafley grunted, pulled a telegram from his pocket and held it out to the district attorney. The beam of the flashlight illuminated the telegram, a torn coat-sleeve, a scratched, dirt-covered hand.

"You frightened me with that flashlight," he said. "I jumped right into the middle of those thorns. But it's all right. I was pretty well scratched up anyway. I guess my clothes are a wreck."

He looked down at his suit and laughed apologetically.

The four men paid no attention to him, but studied the telegram, which read:

THE KOLTSDORF DIAMONDS ARE HIDDEN IN ASHTONS CRUTCH STOP MORE THAN HALF OF YOUR GRANDFATHERS MONEY IS BURIED JUST UNDER THE LIBRARY WINDOW WHERE THE CLIMBING ROSEBUSH STARTS UP THE TRELLIS WORK STOP THE SPOT IS MARKED BY A LITTLE STICK STUCK IN THE GROUND STOP IT ISNT BURIED DEEP STOP NOT OVER A FEW INCHES

The telegram was signed simply "A FRIEND."

Glassman said in a low voice, "Looks like a genuine telegram. It cleared through the telegraph office."

75

"What did you find?" Burger asked.

Oafley, stepping forward to answer him, caught sight of Mason for the first time. He stiffened and said, "What's this man doing here?"

"He's here at my request," Burger said. "He's representing Charles Ashton, the caretaker. I had some questions I wanted to ask Ashton, and I wanted Mason to be along. Did you find anything where you were digging?"

"I found the stick," Oafley said, pulling a small stake from his pocket. "That was sticking in the ground. I dug clean through the loam and down to gravel. There wasn't anything there."

"Who sent the telegram?"

"You can search me."

Burger said in a low voice to Glassman, "Tom, take the key number of that message, get on the telephone and have the telegraph company dig up the original. Find out all you can about it. Get the address of the sender."

"Did you come out because of that telegram?" Oafley asked. "It's a rotten night. I shouldn't have gone out and dug, but you can realize how I felt after I got that message."

"We came out in connection with another matter," Burger said. "Where's Sam Laxter?"

Oafley seemed suddenly nervous. "He's out. What did you want to see him about?"

"We wanted to ask him some questions."

Oafley hesitated for a moment, then said slowly, "Have you been talking with Edith DeVoe?"

"No," Burger said, "*I* haven't."

Mason stared steadily at Oafley. "*I* have," he said.

"I knew *you* had," Oafley told him. "It's a wonder you wouldn't mind your own business."

"That'll do from you," Burger said. "Come on in the house. What's this about the Koltsdorf diamonds being hidden in Ashton's crutch?"

"You know just as much about it as I do," Oafley said sullenly.

"Sam isn't in?"

"No."

"Where is he?"

"I don't know—out on a date I guess."

"Okay," Burger said. "Let us in."

They climbed up to the tiled porch. Oafley produced a bunch of keys and opened the door. "If you'll excuse me a minute, I'll wash some of this mud off and slip on another suit of clothes."

"Wait a minute," Glassman said. "There's a million bucks involved, Buddy. We aren't doubting your word any, but we'd better frisk you and see . . ."

"Glassman," Burger warned, "Mr. Oafley isn't to be handled that way."

He turned to Oafley. "I'm sorry Mr. Glassman used exactly those words, but the thought is something which has occurred to me, and will doubtless occur to you. There's a large sum of money involved. Suppose the person who sent that telegram should claim you had been in the garden and found some or all of that money?"

"But I didn't find any. If I had, it would have been mine—half of it, anyway."

"Don't you think it might be better to have some corroborative evidence?" Burger asked.

"How could I get that?"

"You could submit to a voluntary search."

Oafley's face was sullen. "Go ahead," he said, "and search." They searched him.

Burger nodded his satisfaction. "It's just a check," he said, "on the situation. Perhaps you'll be glad later on you coöperated with us."

"I'll never be glad, but I'm not raising any very strenuous objections, because I can appreciate your position. May I go get my clothes changed now?"

Burger slowly shook his head. "Better not. Better sit down and wait. You'll dry out quickly."

Oafley sighed. "Well," he said, "let's have about four fingers of whiskey apiece. You look as though you chaps might have been out in the rain. Bourbon, rye or Scotch?"

"Whichever you come to," Mason said, "just so it's whiskey."

Oafley flashed him a speculative glance, rang a bell.

A man with a livid scar across his right cheekbone, which gave to his face a peculiar expression of leering triumph, appeared in a doorway. "You rang?" he asked Oafley.

"Yes," Oafley said. "Bring some whiskey, James. Bring some Scotch and soda and some of the Bourbon."

The man nodded, withdrew.

"Jim Brandon," Oafley said in an explanatory tone. "He acts both as chauffeur and butler."

"How was he hurt?" Burger inquired.

"Automobile accident, I believe. . . . You're Mr. Burger, the district attorney?"

"Yes."

Oafley said slowly, "I'm sorry that Edith DeVoe said what she did."

"Why?"

"Because that fire wasn't started by the fumes from an automobile exhaust. It's impossible on the face of it."

Glassman said, "Where's your telephone?"

"There in the hallway. I'll show you . . . or James will show you."

"Never mind. You sit there and talk with the Chief. I'll find it all right."

Burger said, "Did you ever hear of carbon monoxide poisoning, Mr. Oafley?"

"Of course I have."

"Do you know that carbon monoxide is generated by an automobile engine when it's running?"

78

"But what's carbon monoxide got to do with it? It isn't an inflammable gas, is it?"

"It's a deadly gas."

Something in the grim finality of Burger's voice sent Oafley's eyebrows arching.

"Good God!" he exclaimed. "You don't mean that? . . . Why, it's unthinkable! . . . Why, I can't believe . . ."

"Never mind what you can or cannot believe, Mr. Oafley. We want certain information. We stopped in the garage on the way up, and looked through Sam Laxter's machine. We found a long, flexible tube."

Oafley said without surprise, "Yes, Edith said she saw it quite distinctly."

"Just where is Sam Laxter now?"

"I don't know. He went out."

"How did he go out? His car's in the garage."

"Yes," Oafley said, "*his* car is. He didn't want to take it out and get it wet. The chauffeur drove him uptown in the Pontiac, then brought the Pontiac back. I don't know how Sam will come back, unless the Chevvy is uptown somewhere."

"The Chevvy?"

"Yes. It's a service car. Ashton usually drives it. We keep it for hauling things and running errands."

"You have a car?" Burger asked.

"Yes, the Buick in the garage is mine."

"And the big Pontiac?"

"That's the car my grandfather bought shortly before his death."

"The cars were saved when the house burned?"

"Yes, the garage was in the corner. It was one of the last things to go."

"In other words, the fire was started at some point removed from the garage?"

"It must have been started near grandfather's bedroom."

"Have you any ideas as to how it was started?"

"Not one. . . . Look here, Mr. Burger. I would much

prefer that you talked with Sam about this. My position is rather delicate. After all, Sam's related to me. Frankly, I had heard Edith DeVoe's story before, but I hadn't given it any attention. The carbon monoxide was, of course, a new thought to me. I simply can't believe it's possible. There must be some explanation."

Glassman entered the room carrying the telegram in his left hand. He stood in the doorway and made his report. "It's a genuine telegram all right. It was telephoned in. It was to be signed 'A Friend,' but the telephone number of the sender was Exposition 6-2398. The phone's listed under the name of Winnie's Waffle Kitchen."

Mason got to his feet and said, "Baloney!"

"That will do, Mason," Burger told him. "You keep out of this."

"Like hell I will," Mason retorted. "You can't boss me, Burger. Winifred Laxter never sent that telegram."

Oafley stared at Tom Glassman. "Why," he said, "Winnie wouldn't send a telegram like that. There's some mistake."

"She sent it, all right," Glassman insisted.

"The hell she sent it!" Mason exploded. "It's a cinch to send a telegram over the telephone in someone else's name."

"Yeah," Glassman remarked. "*Your* clients always have someone conspiring against them."

"She isn't my client," Mason said.

"Just who is your client?"

Mason grinned, and remarked, "I think it's a cat."

There was a moment of silence. The noise of an automobile engine could be heard as a car climbed the incline. Headlights flashed for a moment against the window, then a horn blared its imperative summons. Jim Brandon, entering the room with a tray on which were whiskies and glasses, also syphons of soda, hurriedly set the tray down and started for the door as the horn blared again.

"That's Mister Sam," he said.

Burger caught the man's sleeve as he hurried past. "Don't be in too big a hurry," he suggested.

Glassman strode through the corridor, jerked open the front door just as the horn sounded again. "Go on out, Jim," he said, "and see what's wanted."

Jim Brandon switched on a porch light, stepped out to the porch. Sam Laxter called, "Jim, I've had a bit of an accident. You come and put the car away."

Burger pulled aside some drapes. The brilliant light from the porch illuminated a somewhat antiquated Chevrolet, with a broken windshield, a dented fender, and smashed bumper. Sam Laxter was climbing from the driver's seat. His face was cut. His right arm was bandaged with a bloody handkerchief.

Burger started for the door. Before he reached it, headlights again illuminated the drizzling night. A smoothly purring automobile swung into view, circled the driveway and came to a stop. The door of a big sedan opened. A slender figure jumped to the driveway, turned and ran excitedly toward the house, saw Sam Laxter and came to a surprised stop.

Perry Mason chuckled, and said to Burger, "We have with us none other than our esteemed contemporary, Mr. Nathaniel Shuster. During the course of the next half hour you can endeavor to discover whether he followed Sam Laxter because he knew you were going to be here or merely put in an accidental appearance."

Burger, muttering an exclamation of disgust, strode to the porch.

Shuster called, in a voice which was shrill with excitement, "Have you heard about it? Have you heard about it? Do you know what they're doing? Do you know what happened? They got an order to dig up your grandfather's body. They went out in the cemetery and dug it up."

Sam Laxter's blood-stained countenance showed surprised consternation. Frank Oafley, standing near Burger, said, "What the devil's this?"

"Take it easy," Glassman warned.

"I just found out about the order. I've made an investigation. They dug the body up already. Do you want me to take legal steps to . . ."

His voice trailed away into silence as he caught sight of Burger's figure standing in the light of the porch.

"Come in, Shuster," Burger said. "You'll get wet standing out there."

Rain glistened on Sam Laxter's face. The cut on his cheek dripped blood, unheeded. His lips were twisting with emotion. "What's the big idea?" he asked.

"I'm just making an investigation," Burger said, "and I wanted to ask you a few questions. Have you any objection?"

"Certainly not," Laxter replied, "but I don't like the way you're going about this thing. What was the idea digging up . . ."

"Not a question! Not a question!" Shuster shouted. "Not unless I am present, and not unless I tell you you should answer."

"Oh, bosh, Shuster!" Laxter said. "I can certainly answer any question the district attorney wants to put to me."

"Don't be foolish," Shuster screamed. "It's not an investigation by the district attorney; it's stirred up by that busybody, Mason. It's all over this damned cat. Don't answer them. Don't answer anything. The first thing you know, you'll be outside in the cold, and then what? All your inheritance gone. Mason sitting in the saddle. Winifred inheriting your property. The cat laughing . . ."

"Shut up, Shuster," Burger said. "I'm going to talk with Sam Laxter, and I'm going to talk with him without having to put up with a lot of your insane interruptions. Come in the house, Laxter. Do you need a doctor to dress those wounds?"

"I don't think so," Laxter said. "I skidded and hit a telephone pole. It shook me up a bit and I've got a bad cut on the right forearm, but it only needs washing with a good antiseptic and a clean bandage. I may have a doctor look at it later, but I won't keep you waiting."

Shuster ran toward him. "Please!" he said. "I beg of you! I implore you! Don't do it!"

"Shut up," Burger said once more, taking Sam's arm as Sam walked up the steps toward him.

Laxter and Burger entered the house, closely followed by Glassman. Shuster slowly climbed the stairs, moving like an old man whose every step was an effort.

Mason watched the three men cross the living room and disappear through a door. He entered the living room and sat down. Drake pulled a cigarette from his pocket, sat crosswise on an overstuffed chair and said, "Well, that's that."

Jim Brandon stood in the doorway and said to Shuster, "I don't know if you're supposed to come in or not."

"Don't be silly," Shuster told him, and then lowered his voice, saying something which was inaudible to Mason and the detective. Brandon also lowered his voice. The two men engaged in a conversation conducted in a low monotone.

The telephone rang repeatedly. After several minutes, a fat woman with sleep-swollen eyes came shuffling down the corridor, wrapping a bathrobe about her. She picked up the telephone, said "Hello" in a drowsy, uncordial voice, then, her face showing surprise, she said, "Oh, yes, Miss Winifred. . . . Why, I could call him. He's asleep, of course. . . . Tell him to have Mr. Mason call you at once at . . ."

Perry Mason crossed toward the telephone. "If that's someone asking for Mr. Mason," he said, "I'm here and will talk on the telephone."

The woman handed him the receiver. "It's Miss Winifred Laxter," she said.

Mason said "Hello" and heard Winifred's voice, hysterical with excitement. "Thank God I was able to reach you. I didn't know where to get you so I called for Ashton to leave a message for you. Something terrible has happened. You must come at once."

Mason's voice was guarded. "I'm rather occupied here at present. Could you tell me generally what has happened?"

"I don't know, but Douglas is in serious trouble. . . . You know Douglas, you met him . . . Douglas Keene."

"And what has happened to him?"

"I don't know, but I must see you at once."

"I'll leave here," Mason told her, "within ten minutes. That's the best I can do. There's another matter here I'm interested in. Where will I find you?"

"I'll be at the waffle place. There won't be any lights on—just open the door and come in."

Mason said crisply, "Okay, I leave here in ten minutes."

Mason hung up the receiver as Shuster, leaving Brandon at the door, crossed the hallway with quick, nervous strides. He grabbed the lapel of Mason's coat.

"You can't do it!" he said. "You can't get away with it! It's outrageous. I'll have you brought up before the Grievance Committee. It's pettifogging."

Mason placed the flat of his hand against the man's chest, pushed him out at arm's length and said, "You should go in the lecture business, Shuster. No one could ever accuse you of delivering a dry lecture."

Mason pulled a handkerchief from his pocket, wiped his face. Shuster jumped about as excitedly as a terrier barking at a steer. "You knew you couldn't break the will; that will is as good as gold. So what did you do? You started in trying to frame up a murder charge on my clients. You can't make it stick! You and your caretaker are going to find yourselves in plenty of trouble. Plenty of trouble! You hear me? You . . ."

He broke off as District Attorney Burger, accompanied by Tom Glassman, reentered the room. Burger's features were puzzled. "Mason," he said, "do you know anything about diamonds your client Ashton has?"

Mason shook his head. "We can ask him," he suggested.

"I think we want to talk with him," Burger said. "Apparently he's mixed up in this thing."

Mason nodded.

Shuster said, "A damned outrage! A frame-up! Mason cooked this up in order to bust the will."

Mason's smile was tolerant as he remarked, "I told you, Shuster, that I always hit in an unexpected place."

"Do you wish me to call the caretaker?" the flabby woman in the wrapper asked, as Oafley, in bathrobe and slippers, shuffled into the room.

"Who are you?" Burger inquired.

"The housekeeper," Oafley interposed. "Mrs. Pixley."

"I think we'll go and interview the caretaker without giving him previous notice," Burger announced.

"Look here," Mason said. "In view of the circumstances, don't you think it would be fair to let me know just what it is you're after?"

"Come along," Burger said, "and you'll find out, but don't interrupt to ask questions or give advice."

Shuster darted around the table. "You've got to watch him," he warned. "He's hatched up this whole business."

"Dry up," Tom Glassman said over his shoulder.

"Go on," Burger said to Mrs. Pixley; "show us the way."

The woman moved along the hallway, her bedroom slippers slopping against her heels as she walked. Paul Drake fell into step beside Perry Mason. Oafley dropped behind, for a word with Shuster. Burger held Sam Laxter's arm.

"Funny-looking character—the housekeeper," Drake remarked in a low voice. "All soft except her mouth and it's hard enough to make up for everything."

"Underneath that softness," Mason said, his eyes appraising the woman's figure, "is a great deal of strength.

Her muscles are cased in fat, but she's plenty husky. Notice the way she carries herself."

The woman led the way down a flight of stairs to a basement. She opened a door, crossed a cement floor, paused in front of another door, and said, "Shall I knock?"

"Not unless it's locked," Burger told her.

She turned the knob of the door and stepped to one side, pushing open the door.

Mason couldn't see the interior of the room but he could see her face. He saw light from the inside of the room strike her features. He saw the flabby flesh of her face freeze in an expression of wild terror. He saw the hard lips sag open, and then heard her scream.

Burger jumped forward. The housekeeper swayed, flung up her hands, and her knees sagged as she slid to the floor. Glassman jumped through the door into the caretaker's room. Oafley caught the housekeeper by the armpits. "Steady," he said. "Take it easy. What's the trouble?"

Mason pushed past them into the room.

Charles Ashton's bed was by an open window in the basement. The window opened almost directly at street level. It had been propped open with a stick, the opening being some four or five inches, just enough to enable a cat to slip through easily.

Directly beneath the window was the bed, covered with a white counterpane and on this white counterpane was a series of muddy cat tracks, tracks which covered not only the spread, but appeared on the pillow as well.

Lying in the bed, his face an unpleasant thing to behold, was the dead body of Charles Ashton. It needed but one look at the bulging eyes and protruding tongue to enable these experts in homicide to realize the manner in which the man had died.

Burger whirled to Glassman.

"Keep the people out of this room," he warned. "Get the homicide squad on the telephone. Don't let Sam

86

Laxter out of your sight until this thing has been cleaned up. I'll stay here and look around. Get started!"

Glassman whirled, thrust his shoulder against Perry Mason. "On your way," he said.

Mason left the room. Glassman slammed the door shut. "Let me get to the telephone. Oafley, don't try to leave the place."

"Why should *I* try to leave the place?" Oafley demanded indignantly.

"Don't make any statements! Don't make any statements! Don't make any statements!" Shuster pleaded hysterically. "Keep quiet! Let me do the talking. Can't you understand? It's a murder! Don't talk with them. Don't have anything to do with them. Don't . . ."

Glassman stepped forward belligerently. "You can either keep your face closed," he said, "or I'll button up your lips so they'll stay shut for a while."

Shuster scuttled away from him like a squirrel climbing a tree, chattering continuously. "No statement. No statement at all. Can't you understand that I'm your lawyer? You don't know what these people have said about you. You don't know what accusations they've made. Keep quiet. Let me do the talking for you."

"There's no necessity for such talk," Oafley said to Shuster. "I'm just as anxious to help clean this thing up as the officers are. You're hysterical. Shut up!"

The party climbed the stairs. Perry Mason, dropping behind, put his lips close to Paul Drake's ear. "Stick around, Paul," he said, "and see what happens. Get an eyeful if you can and an earful if you can't."

"You're ducking?" Drake asked.

"I'm ducking," Mason said.

At the head of the stairs leading from the cellar, Glassman hurried toward a telephone. Perry Mason turned to the right, crossed a kitchen, unlocked a door, crossed a screened porch, descended a flight of stairs, and found himself in the rainy night.

8

THE ELECTRIC SIGN BEARING THE LEGEND "WINNIE'S Waffles" was dark. A night light burned over the door. Perry Mason tried the knob. The door opened. Mason closed the door behind him, walked down the passageway between counter and booths, until he came to a swinging open door. The room was dark. He heard the sound of a woman sobbing. Mason said, "Hello," and a light switch clicked. A table lamp, with a rose silk shade, gave soft illumination.

A single bed sat against the wall. There were two chairs, a table and a bookcase made by the simple expedient of nailing the wooden cases in which canned goods came into tiers and giving them coats of enamel. The homemade bookcase was well filled with books. A corner of the room had been curtained off to form a closet. A door stood partially open and through it Mason could see the gooseneck connection of a shower. A few framed pictures hung on the wall, and the place, despite the cheapness of its furnishings, had a comfortable, homelike atmosphere. On the table, turned so it faced the bed, was a large framed photograph of Douglas Keene.

Winifred Laxter sat on the bed. Her eyes were red from tears. A big Persian cat sprawled contentedly at her side, its head resting against her leg. It was purring audibly. As the light switched on, the cat turned with that peculiar writhing motion common to felines, and stared at Perry Mason with bright, hard eyes. Then it closed its eyes, stretched out its forepaws, yawned, and once more began to purr.

"What's the trouble?" Mason asked.

The girl indicated the telephone with a little hopeless gesture, as though that gesture explained everything. "And I thought I could laugh at life," she said.

Mason drew up a chair and sat down. He recognized that she was near hysteria, and made his voice casual. "Nice cat."

"Yes, it's Clinker."

Mason raised his eyebrows.

"Doug went out and got it."

"Why?"

"Because he was afraid Sam would poison it."

"When?"

"Around ten o'clock. I sent him."

"Did he talk with Ashton?" Mason asked, making his voice sound elaborately casual.

"No. Ashton wasn't there."

"Mind if I smoke?"

"I'd like one myself. You must think I'm an awful baby."

Mason took a cigarette case from his pocket, gravely proffered her one and held a match to the end of the cigarette, when she had placed it between her lips.

"Not at all," he said, lighting his own cigarette. "Pretty lonesome here, isn't it?"

"It hadn't been; it will be."

"Tell me about it any time you're ready," he invited.

"I'm not ready yet." Her voice was stronger now, but there was still that overtone of near hysteria. "I've been sitting here in the dark too long, thinking, thinking . . ."

"Quit thinking," he said. "Let's just talk. What time did Douglas Keene leave Ashton's place?"

"Around eleven I think. Why?"

"He was there about an hour?"

"Yes."

"Waiting for Ashton to come in?"

"I believe so."

"And then he brought the cat here to you?" Mason asked.

"Yes."

"Let's see—when did it start raining? Before eleven or after eleven?"

"Oh, earlier than that—around nine, anyway."

"Can you tell exactly what time it was when Douglas brought you the cat? Have you any way of fixing it definitely?"

"No. I was cooking waffles for the after-theater trade. Why are you asking me all these questions?"

"I was just trying to make conversation," Mason remarked casually. "You feel as though I'm too much of a stranger to confide in me right now. I'm trying to put you at your ease. Did one of the servants let Douglas in?"

"You mean to the town house? No. I gave Doug my key. I didn't want Sam to know I was taking the cat. Grandfather had given me a key to the house. I'd never turned it back—in fact, I guess there was no one to turn it back to."

"Why didn't you let Ashton know you'd taken the cat? Won't he be worried?"

"Oh, but he knew Doug was coming after Clinker," she said.

"How did he know?"

"I telephoned him."

"When?"

"Before he went out."

"What time did he go out?"

"I don't know, but I talked with him over the telephone and we decided, everything considered, that it might be best for me to keep Clinker for a while. He said he'd be there when Doug arrived, and told me to give Doug my key so Sam wouldn't know."

"But Ashton wasn't there when Douglas arrived?"

"No. Doug waited an hour. Then he took the cat and left."

Mason, leaning back in the chair, studied the cigarette smoke which spiraled upward.

"Clinker always sleeps on Ashton's bed, doesn't he?"

"Yes."

"Any other cats there?"

"Around the house you mean?"

"Yes."

"No. I should say not. Clinker would chase any cat away. He's insanely jealous, particularly of Uncle Charles."

"Uncle Charles?" he asked.

"I sometimes call the caretaker Uncle Charles."

"Rather a peculiar character, isn't he?"

"Peculiar, but he's a fine man when you get to know him."

"Honest?"

"Of course, he's honest."

"Something of a miser, isn't he?"

"He would be if he had anything to save, I guess. He's been around Grandpa so long. Grandpa was always suspicious of banks. When the country went off the gold basis Grandpa nearly died. He'd been hoarding gold, you know. But he went down and turned his gold in and took paper money. It was quite a blow to him. He was upset for weeks."

"He must have been a peculiar chap."

"He was—very peculiar—and yet very lovable. He had a great sense of right and wrong."

"His will wouldn't seem to indicate that."

"No," she said, "I think under all the circumstances, it was the best thing that could have happened. I think I was pretty much hypnotized by Harry."

"Harry?" Mason asked.

"Harry Inman. He was rushing me to death. He seemed one of those straight-forward, clean-cut, sincere young men, and . . ."

"He wasn't?" Mason prompted as her voice faded away.

"He most certainly was not. As soon as he found out I

wasn't going to get anything under the will, he fell all over himself taking back everything he'd said. I think he was afraid at the last minute I'd try to marry him in order to have someone to look after me."

"He has money?"

"He has a good position. He's making around six thousand a year, in an insurance office."

"Douglas Keene stuck by you, eh?" Mason asked, bringing the subject casually around to the young man whose framed picture stood on the table facing the bed.

"I'll say he stuck by me. He was a brick. He's the most wonderful boy in the world. I never realized just how much there was to him—you know, words don't mean anything—anyone who can talk can use words. Some people can use them better than others. Many insincere people, who have the gift of expressing themselves, can sound more sincere than those who are perfectly loyal."

Mason nodded, waited for her to go on talking.

"I wanted to see you about Douglas," she said. "Something awful has happened and Douglas is afraid I might get involved in it. He's mixed in it himself some way—I don't know just how."

"What's happened?" Mason asked.

"A murder," she told him, and began to sob.

Mason moved over to the bed, sat down beside her and put his arm around her shoulders. The cat looked up at him appraisingly, flattened its ears slightly, then slowly relaxed, but did not resume purring.

"Now take it easy," Mason told her, "and give me the facts."

"I don't know the facts; all I know is that Douglas rang up. He was frightfully excited. He said there'd been a murder and that he wasn't going to let me get dragged into it; that he was going to skip out and that I'd never see him again. He said that I was to say nothing, and answer no question about him."

"Who was murdered?"

"He didn't say."

"How did he think you might be dragged into it?"

"Just through knowing him, I guess. It's all too silly. But I think it's all mixed up with Grandfather's death."

"When did he telephone you?"

"About fifteen minutes before I telephoned you. I tried to locate you every place I could think of—your office and your apartment. When I couldn't get any answer I decided to call Uncle Charles. He'd told me you'd telephoned him something about Sam and the district attorney, and I thought he might hear from you again."

"Did you," Mason asked, "know that your grandfather was murdered?"

She stared at him with wide eyes. "Grandfather? No."

"Did it impress you there was anything peculiar about the manner in which the house burned?"

"Why, no. The fire seemed to have centered right around Grandpa's bedroom. It was a windy night and I thought they blamed the fire on defective electric wiring."

"Let's come back to the cat for a minute," Mason said. "He's been with you ever since around eleven o'clock?"

"Yes—shortly after eleven, I guess it was."

Perry Mason nodded, picked up the cat and held it in his arms.

"Clinker," he said, "how would you like to go for a nice ride somewhere?"

"What do you mean?" Winifred asked him.

Perry Mason, holding the cat, stared steadily at her, and said slowly, "Charles Ashton was murdered sometime tonight. I don't know yet exactly what time. He was strangled, probably after he'd gone to bed. There were muddy cat tracks all over the counterpane and over the pillow; there was even a track on his forehead."

She got to her feet, staring at him with wide eyes. Then she opened bloodless lips and tried to scream.

No sound came.

Perry Mason dropped the cat to the bed, took Winifred in his arms, stroked her hair. "Take it easy," he told her. "I'm going to take the cat with me. If anyone comes to question you, refuse to answer, no matter what the questions are."

She slid from his arms to sit on the bed. It was as though her knees refused to support her weight. There was panic in her face. "He didn't do it," she said. "He couldn't have. I love him. He wouldn't hurt a fly!"

"Can you buck up," Mason asked, "until I can get rid of this cat?"

"What are you going to do with it?"

"I'll find a home for it—some place where we can keep it until things blow over. You see what it means having the cat tracks on the bedspread. It means the cat was there after the murder was committed."

"But it's impossible," she said.

"Of course it's impossible," he told her, "but we've got to make other people see that it's impossible. The question is, can you be brave enough to help me?"

She nodded silently.

Perry Mason picked up the cat and started for the door.

"Listen," she told him, as he put his hands on the knob of the door, "I don't know if you understand, but you must defend Douglas. That's why I telephoned you. You must find him and talk with him. Douglas isn't guilty of murder. You understand what I mean?"

"I understand," he told her gravely.

She came to him and put her hands on his shoulders. "He's clever enough so the officers will never find him. . . . Oh, don't look at me like that. I know you think they can find him, but you don't realize how clever Douglas is. The officers will never, never catch him. And that means he'll be a fugitive as long as he lives unless you clear things up. . . . And I know what it'll mean as far as I'm concerned. They'll figure that he's going to get in touch with me. They'll watch my mail; they'll tap my telephone; they'll do everything, trying to trap Douglas."

He nodded and patted her shoulder with his free hand, holding the big Persian cat in his left arm.

"I haven't much," she said. "I'm building up a good business here. I can make my living, and I can make more than my living. I'll pay you by the month. I'll give you anything that I make. You can have the business and I'll run it for you without any salary except just what I need to eat, and I can live on waffles and coffee, and . . ."

"We'll talk that over later," Mason interrupted. "The thing to do now is to find out where we stand. If Douglas Keene is guilty, the thing for him to do is to plead guilty, and plead whatever extenuating circumstances there may be."

"But he's not guilty. He isn't; he can't be."

"All right, if he isn't, then the thing for you to do is to get rid of this damned cat. Otherwise, *you'll* be tied up with the murder. Do you understand?"

She nodded silently.

"I've got to have a box or something to carry the cat in."

She ran to the closet and picked up a big hatbox. She jabbed her finger through the pasteboard top, making little breathing holes.

"I'd better put him in," she said, "he'll understand if I do it. . . .Clinker, this man is going to take you with him. You must go with him and be a nice cat."

She put the cat in the box, stroked it for a moment or two, then gently put on the cover. She whipped a piece of string about the cover, tied it, and handed the box to Perry Mason.

The lawyer, holding the hatbox by the string, smiled reassuringly at her, and said, "Stay right here. Remember, don't answer questions. You'll hear from me after a while."

She held open the door of the bedroom. Mason walked to the outer door, opened it, and pushed his way out into the wind and rain. The cat in the box stirred uneasily.

Mason put the hatbox on the seat of the convertible coupe, climbed in behind the wheel and started the motor. The cat meowed a faint protest.

Mason spoke to the cat reassuringly, drove the car for several blocks, then swung in close to the curb by an all-night drugstore. He parked the car, got out, and picking up the hatbox, walked into the drugstore, where the clerk eyed him curiously.

Mason put the box down on the floor of the telephone booth and dialed the number of Della Street's apartment. After a few moments, he heard her voice, thick with sleep.

"Okay, kid," he said, "snap out of it. Put cold water on the face, throw on a few clothes, and be ready to open the door of your apartment when I give you a ring. I'm coming out."

"What time is it?"

"Somewhere around one o'clock."

"What's happened?" she asked.

"I can't tell you about it over the telephone."

Her voice showed that she was now fully awake. "Good Lord, Chief, I thought you only worked all night on murder cases. Now you're doing it on a cat case. How in the world can you get into trouble with a cat?"

"I do," he said cryptically, "I can; I have," and, chuckling, hung up the receiver.

DELLA STREET, WITH A ROBE THROWN OVER SILK pajamas, sat on the edge of her bed and watched Perry Mason untying the cord around the hatbox.

"Getting me out of bed at one o'clock in the morning to show me the latest in hats?" she inquired.

The lawyer, sliding the string off the cover, said, "It simply shows how easy it is to become accustomed to environment. He was raising hell in the telephone booth."

He pulled the cover from the box. Clinker got to his feet, arched his back in a long stretch, yawned, sniffed the air, raised his forepaws to the edge of the hatbox, and leapt out onto the bed. He sniffed Della Street inquiringly, then curled into a fluffy ball by the side of her leg.

"If you're going in for a collection," she said, "it might be easier to use postage stamps. They take up less room."

She ran her fingers around the cat's ears.

"I think that's something of a compliment," Mason told her, "the way he takes to you. As I remember it, there are few people he likes."

"Going to use him as a playmate for the caretaker's cat?" she asked.

"He *is* the caretaker's cat."

"Why not leave him with the caretaker, then?"

"The last time I saw the caretaker, he was dead. His face wasn't pretty. There were muddy cat tracks all over his bed."

She stiffened to attention. "Who did it?" she asked.

"I don't know."

"Who do the police think did it?"

"I don't know. I don't think they do, yet."

"Who will they think did it by the time they get that far?"

"Several people might be interested in the caretaker. There's some evidence indicating the caretaker had something like a million dollars in currency in his possession. Some of it may have been locked in a safety deposit box; again, the safety deposit box may have been a blind. People will do a lot for a million dollars. Then there are some rather valuable diamonds. Ashton may have had them. I've located the green Pontiac that followed Ashton from our office. It's in the garage at Peter Laxter's town house."

"Whom do we represent?"

"The boy friend of a girl who runs a waffle parlor."

"Any retainer?"

"Do you like waffles?" he countered.

Her eyes showed anxiety. "Look here, Chief, you're not going to get mixed up in a murder case without first getting a fee?"

"I guess I've done it."

"Why don't you sit in your office and wait for clients to come to you after they get arrested, and then go into court and defend them? You're always out on the firing line, taking chances. How did you get this cat?"

"It was given to me."

"By whom?"

"The waffle girl. But we're supposed to forget that."

"You mean you want me to keep the cat here?"

"That's it."

"Under cover?"

"As much as you can. Or, if you have some friend who can keep it, it might be better than to have it here. The police may be looking for it. I have an idea the cat is going to figure in that murder."

"Please," she pleaded, "don't jeopardize your professional standing mixing into this case. Let it go. Sail on

98

that liner for the Orient. After someone gets arrested go ahead and defend him if you want to, but don't get involved in the case itself."

There was something maternal and tender in her eyes.

Perry Mason reached out, possessed himself of her right hand, and patted it.

"Della," he said, "you're a good kid. But the stuff you want just isn't in the cards. I could get a swell rest on that liner to the Orient for just about three days, and then the inactivity would drive me crazy. I want to be working at high speed. I'm going to get ten times as much kick out of this as I would out of a trip to the Orient."

"You're going to handle the case?"

"Yes."

"And you think this young man you're representing will be accused of the murder?"

"Probably."

"He hasn't paid you any retainer?"

Mason shook his head, and then said impatiently, "To hell with the money! If a man's accused of murder and has money, I want a big slice of it as a fee. If people who are living their lives the best they can get into trouble and are accused of committing crimes of which they're innocent, I want to give them a break."

"How do you know this chap is innocent?"

"Only from the impression he made on me when I met him."

"Suppose he's really guilty?"

"Then we'll find out all about the extenuating circumstances and either make him plead guilty and get the lightest sentence we can for him, or else let him get some other lawyer."

"That's not an orthodox way of practicing law," she pointed out, but there was no reproach in either her eyes or her voice.

"Who the hell wants to be orthodox?" Mason grinned.

She matched his grin, got to her feet. "I worry over you

as a mother worries over a wayward child. You're a combination of a kid and giant. I know you're going to mix into something devilish, and I feel like saying, 'Don't go near the water.' "

Mason's grin broadened. "Maternal, eh? By looking up the application blank which you filled out when you applied for your job I could find out just how much my junior you really are. I would say it was about fifteen years."

"Being gallant?" she inquired. "By looking up the records in connection with your admission to practice before the courts, I could tell just how much you're trying to flatter me."

He moved toward the door. "Take good care of the cat," he said. "Don't lose him. His name's Clinker. He may wander away if he gets the chance. We may be able to use him later."

"Will the police look for him here?"

"I don't think so. Not right away. Things aren't hot enough yet. . . . Are you going to tell me not to go near the water?"

She shook her head. There were both pride and tenderness in her smile. "No," she said; "just don't get in over your head."

"I haven't even got my feet wet, yet," he told her, "but something seems to tell me I'm going to."

He gently closed the door, walked down the corridor to the street, and drove to Edith DeVoe's apartment.

The outer door of the apartment house was locked. Mason pushed his finger against the button opposite Edith DeVoe's apartment, held it there for several seconds. There was no answer. He took a key container from his pocket, selected a skeleton key, hesitated for several seconds, then tried Edith DeVoe's bell once more. When there was no answer, he inserted the key in the lock, and, after a moment, clicked the bolt back and entered the apartment house. He walked down the corridor to Edith

100

DeVoe's apartment and tapped gently on the door. When there was no answer, he stood for a moment in frowning concentration, then tried the knob of the door. The knob turned, the door opened, and he stepped into a dark room.

"Miss DeVoe," he said. There was no answer.

Perry Mason switched on the light.

Edith DeVoe lay sprawled on the floor.

The window which opened on the alleyway was not entirely shut. It was open some two or three inches at the bottom. The bed had not been slept in, and the body was attired in pajamas of very thin silk. Near the body lay a piece of wood some eighteen inches long. One end was splintered, and near the other end was a tell-tale red stain.

Perry Mason, closing the door carefully behind himself, stepped forward and peered down at the body. There was a wound in the scalp near the back of the head.

The piece of wood which lay near the body had evidently been used as a club. The edges were neatly sawed. The wood was highly polished, and about an inch and a half in diameter. A fingerprint appeared very plainly imprinted in the red stain at the upper part of the wood. The varnish at the lower end was blistered.

Mason looked swiftly about the apartment. He stepped to the bathroom. It was empty, but a blood-stained towel lay on the washstand. He walked to the fireplace. There were ashes in the grate, and it was still warm. Mason looked at his watch. It was one thirty-two. Rain had drifted in through the opening in the window. The sill was glistening with moisture, and some of the water had dripped down to the hardwood floor beneath the sill.

Mason dropped to his knees beside the sprawled figure and felt for a pulse, listening for breathing.

He arose, crossed to the telephone, placed a handkerchief around the receiver so he would leave no fingerprints and called police headquarters. Speaking rapidly, in a mumbling undertone, he said, "A woman is dying from a blow on the head. Send an ambulance."

When he was certain that his message had been understood, he gave the address in the same mumbling undertone and hung up.

Mason polished the doorknob with his handkerchief, rubbing both inside and outside surfaces; then he switched off the lights, stepped into the corridor, pulled the door shut behind him, and started for the front exit of the apartment house.

As he passed an apartment, he heard a man laugh, the sound of clinking chips, and a moment later, that peculiar purring noise which is made by the corners of a deck of cards being riffled in a shuffle.

Mason walked on down the corridor. As he reached the lobby, he heard an automobile pull up to the curb. He hesitated for a moment, standing just back of the street door; then he opened the door a crack and peered out.

Hamilton Burger had just stepped to the sidewalk, and had his back turned to Perry Mason, watching Tom Glassman get out of the car.

Mason stepped back, gently closed the door behind himself, turned and walked down the corridor. He paused at the door where he had heard chips rattling and knocked.

Mason heard the sound of a chair being scraped along the floor, then complete silence from the other side of the door. He knocked again, and, after a moment, the door opened a crack, and a man's voice said, "Who is it?"

Mason smiled affably. "I'm in the adjoining apartment," he said, "and your poker game is keeping me awake. How about getting some sleep, or, if the limit isn't too high, letting me in. I don't care one way or another."

The man hesitated a moment. A booming masculine voice from the interior of the room called, "Open the door and let him in. We can use another player."

The door opened and Mason entered the room. Three men were grouped around a table. The atmosphere of the room was close and stuffy. A vacant chair marked where the man who stood at the door had been seated.

"What's the limit?" Mason asked, taking care to close the door.

"Fifty-cent limit, except in jack-pots, and then it's a dollar."

Mason took twenty dollars from his wallet. "Could you fellows use twenty dollars of outside money?" he asked.

"Could we," grinned the man with the booming voice. "It would be like manna from heaven. Sorry we kept you awake. Didn't know you could hear us."

"That's all right. I'd rather play poker than sleep, anyway. Mason is my name."

"Hammond's mine," said the man who had admitted him.

The others introduced themselves.

Mason drew up a chair, took chips, and heard men walking down the corridor toward Edith DeVoe's apartment. Some fifteen minutes later, when he was twelve dollars and thirty cents ahead of the game, he heard the low moan of a siren, and shortly afterwards, the clang of an ambulance bell.

The players looked at each other in dismay.

"Guess we'd better cash in," Mason said, "and get the evidence out of sight."

One of the men looked at him accusingly. "You aren't by any chance a detective, are you?"

Mason laughed good naturedly. "No chance," he said. "I don't think they're coming here, boys. It sounds as though there's something down the corridor that's interesting them; probably a man beating up his wife."

The men paused to listen. They could hear the sound of steps shuffling along the corridor. Hammond took his coat from the back of the chair, thrust his arms into it and said, "Okay, boys. Let's call it quits until next week. It's time to break up, anyway."

Mason stretched and yawned as he cashed in his chips.

"Think I might as well go out now and get a waffle and a cup of coffee," he observed.

"I have a car out here. How about giving you a lift?"

Mason nodded. They left the apartment together. Two police cars and an ambulance were drawn up in front of the curb.

Mason's companion showed curiosity. "Wonder what's going on here. Looks as though someone had been hurt."

"It might be a good time to duck out of here," Mason said. "I don't mind putting in my nights sleeping, or playing poker, but I hate like hell to put in my spare time answering the questions asked by a lot of dumb cops."

His companion nodded. "My car's around the corner. Let's go."

10

PERRY MASON UNLOCKED THE DOOR OF HIS PRIVATE office and switched on the lights. He looked at his wristwatch, crossed to the telephone, dialed the number of the Drake Detective Agency and was informed by the night operator that Paul Drake was not in and had not telephoned. Mason left his name and instructions for Drake to get in touch with him, and hung up the telephone. He hooked his thumbs in the armholes of his vest and started pacing the office, his head thrust forward in thought.

After a few minutes, fingertips tapped gently on the panels of the corridor door. Perry Mason opened it, and Drake grinned a greeting.

Mason carefully closed the door behind the detective, offered a cigarette, and took one himself. "Get the dope, Paul?" he asked.

"Pretty much of it."

"What happened after I left?"

"Lots of detail stuff. They quizzed Shuster. He wouldn't tell who tipped him off the body had been exhumed, so I rang up Shuster's secretary, and told her I was in a jam on a murder charge and had to see Shuster right away."

"How did you locate her?"

"That's a cinch. Shuster is one of those criminal attorneys who gets calls at all hours of the day and night. The telephone directory carries his office number and says in the event there is no answer at that number to call another one. The other number is the number of his secretary's apartment."

"I see. Did you learn anything from her?"

"Just this—she was expecting Shuster to telephone any minute. She said that someone had given him a hurry-up call about an hour before I telephoned. She didn't know the exact nature of the case he'd gone out on, but understood it was a murder case."

"Then it wasn't a tip on this body digging."

"Apparently not."

"But he knew about it by the time he arrived at the house."

"Exactly," Drake said.

Mason, holding his thumbs in the armholes of his vest, drummed silently on his chest with the tips of his fingers. "In other words, Paul, you mean that *after* Shuster had received that mysterious telephone call he went out and contacted someone who wanted him to rush to Laxter's house."

Drake said, "Why not? Stranger things have happened. You don't think that Shuster just put in an appearance because he thought his clients should know the body had been exhumed, do you?"

"Probably not," Mason said thoughtfully.

"Shuster is cunning," Drake cautioned. "Don't underestimate him."

"I won't," Mason said slowly. "What else do you know, Paul?"

"Lots."

"Spill it."

"Did you know that Frank Oafley and Edith DeVoe were married?"

Perry Mason paused in his pacing back and forth across the office. His eyes were thoughtfully attentive.

"Four days ago," Drake said, "they took out an application for a marriage license. Then they got a marriage license today. One of my men happened to pick it up. We make it a point to file the vital statistics of marriages, births, deaths and divorces, alphabetically. Then we check through them whenever we start an investigation."

Mason said slowly, "You did a good job that time, Paul. How did they keep it quiet?"

"They gave phony residences. Oafley went to an apartment house, rented a bachelor apartment for a few days, and gave that as his address when he took out a marriage license as F. M. Oafley."

"Sure it's the same one?"

"Yes, one of my operatives checked up with a photograph."

"How do you know they're married?"

"I'm not absolutely certain, but I think they got married tonight."

"What makes you think so?"

"Oafley was calling a minister and arranging to meet him at a certain place. The housekeeper kicked through with that information—to me, not to the officers."

"Has Oafley admitted it yet?"

"No, he didn't let out a peep. He said he went out to 'see a friend,' and Burger let it go at that."

"Did you find out the name of the minister?"

"Milton's the name. I got his telephone number, but I don't know the initials. We can get the address from the directory."

Mason resumed his pacing of the room, his head thrust thoughtfully forward.

"The trouble with Shuster, Paul," he said, "is that he always wants to help the police find the 'guilty' party. If they leave Shuster alone, that guilty party is always someone other than Shuster's client.

"Both of Shuster's clients have good alibis in this case, Paul."

"Meaning what?"

"Sam Laxter wasn't near the house all the evening. He showed up after the police had arrived. Frank Oafley was away until about eleven, and then he came in. Ashton was killed right around ten thirty."

"How do they fix the time?"

"A lot of ghoulish stuff that autopsy surgeons specialize in. They know what time he ate dinner, and they can tell the extent to which digestion had progressed."

Mason reached for his hat.

"Come on, Paul, we're going places."

"Where?"

"Just places."

Drake pulled his hat down lower on his forehead, tossed his half-smoked cigarette into a cuspidor. Together the men rode down in the elevator.

"One thing about your cases," Drake said, "a person never gets too much sleep."

Mason led the way to the sidewalk. "Got a car here, Paul?"

"Yes."

"We're going to 3961 Melrose Avenue. I've put my car away."

The detective repeated the address musingly, then said, "That's where Douglas Keene lives."

"Correct. Are the police investigating him?"

"Not particularly. They're just rounding up names and addresses, and I made notes. Boy friend of Winnie's, isn't he? There was another one named . . . Let me see. . . ."

He thumbed through the pages of his notebook and said, "Inman—Harry Inman."

"Check," Mason said. "Let's go. We'll take your car."

"Okay," the detective said, "my car's carefully picked so it won't attract attention. It isn't distinctive, if you know what I mean."

"I take it," Mason said, grinning, "there are a million cars in this state. One hundred thousand of them are new —two hundred thousand of them are almost new—and this is . . ."

"One of the seven hundred thousand," the detective finished, opening the door of a dilapidated, nondescript car.

Mason climbed in. Drake wormed under the steering wheel, and started the motor.

"The police going to be interested in this chap?" Drake inquired.

"That's a chance we've got to take."

"Under those circumstances," the detective announced, "we park the car a block or two away and walk the rest of the distance."

Mason nodded moodily. "And pray that we're not interrupted while we're searching the room."

"We going to break in?" Drake inquired with a sidelong glance.

"We'll try not to break anything," Mason replied.

"Meaning, I take it, that you want me to bring along a house-breaking kit."

"Something of the sort, yes."

"I've got one in the car, but where will we be if the police catch us?"

Mason said, "It's Douglas Keene's place, and he's a client of mine although he may not know it. I'm going to enter his rooms for the purpose of protecting his interests. Burglary, you understand, lies in the unlawful entering of a place with a felonious purpose."

"These fine distinctions are too much for me," Drake

108

admitted. "I'm just leaving it up to you to keep us out of jail. I figure I can take any chances you can take. Come on, let's go."

Paul Drake's car was decidedly inconspicuous in color, model and design. Mason sighed resignedly as it jolted into motion. "Keene figure as a suspect on anything?" Drake asked.

"That's why we're going out there—we want to beat everyone to it."

"You mean that he will enter into the picture later on?"

Mason failed to answer the question, and Drake said, with a grin, "I take it that means that what I don't know won't hurt me," and devoted himself to driving the car.

After some fifteen minutes, he slid the car in close to the deserted curb, looked up and down the street, switched off the lights and locked the car. "Two blocks to walk," he observed. "That's close enough to leave the machine on this sort of a job."

"With a real burglary, I take it, you'd have left it a mile away," Mason said.

Drake nodded his head emphatically. "And then stayed parked behind the steering wheel," he agreed. "You lawyers take too many chances with the law to suit me."

"I'm not a lawyer," Mason grinned, "except as a sideline. I'm an adventurer."

The men walked briskly side by side, saying nothing, but their eyes were restless as they kept a watch for prowl cars of radio officers. They turned the corner, walked three quarters of a block, and Drake nudged the attorney's elbow. "This is the place."

"The outer door should be easy," Mason said casually.

"Nothing to it," Drake agreed optimistically. "They're made to open with a pass-key. Almost anything will work them. Anyone coming?"

"No one in sight."

"Okay, hold your coat so it conceals the beam of this flashlight."

Drake played the beam of a small flashlight on the door, produced keys from his pocket.

A moment later the lock clicked back, and the men entered the apartment house.

"What floor?" Drake asked.

"The third."

"What's the apartment?"

"308."

"Better take the stairs."

They walked up the stairs with silent feet. On the third corridor Drake cast professional eyes over the locks on the doors.

"Spring locks," he observed.

He found 308, paused before it and whispered, "How about a knock?"

Mason shook his head.

Drake whispered. "We can rush things by pushing back the catch."

Mason said laconically, "Rush things, then."

There was a fine crack between the door and the jamb. The detective, taking a cowhide tool kit from his pocket, extracted an instrument which looked very much like the long, thin spatula knife used by artists and druggists. "Hold the flashlight, Perry."

Mason held the flashlight. Drake was inserting the steel, when Mason suddenly gripped his wrist. "What's that?" the lawyer asked in a whisper.

Drake looked at the peculiar markings on the woodwork under the tip of Mason's pointing finger. "Someone's beat us to it," he said. "They may be in there now."

Both men stared at the place where the wood had been slightly crushed under the pressure of a steel instrument. "A bungling job," Drake volunteered.

"Let's go on in," Mason told him.

Drake said, "You're the doctor," and inserted the blade. He manipulated it for a moment. The lock clicked back.

"Turn the knob and open the door, Perry," the detective said, still holding the latch back.

Perry Mason turned the knob, and they entered the room.

"Lights?" Drake inquired.

Mason nodded and clicked on the electric lights.

"A good place not to leave any fingerprints, Paul," he suggested.

Drake looked at him with an expression which intensified the droll humor of his features. "Are *you*," he asked, "telling *me*?"

Mason looked about the room.

"Bed hasn't been slept in," he said.

"It's turned down," Drake pointed out, "and the pillow is mussed up."

"Just the same, it hasn't been slept in. There's nothing that's harder to simulate than the type of wrinkle which is produced in a sheet from long contact with a body."

Drake inspected the bed, and nodded.

The apartment was a typical bachelor's apartment. Ash trays were littered with cigarette stubs. There were a whiskey bottle, a dirty glass, a couple of soiled collars, and a tie clasp on the bureau. Half a dozen neckties were hooked over the mirror support. A closet door was half open, showing several suits hanging from a rod. Drawers in a dresser were partially open.

Mason opened the drawers and stared thoughtfully at them.

"Suitcase," he said, "packed in a hurry." He scooped out handkerchiefs, socks, shirts and underwear. "Let's take a look in the bathroom, Paul."

"What are you looking for?" Drake asked.

"I don't know; I'm just looking."

Mason opened the bathroom door, then suddenly recoiled.

Drake, looking over his shoulder, gave a low whistle

111

and said, "If he's your client, you'd better plead him guilty."

Someone, working with the frenzy of panic, had evidently tried to remove traces of blood from clothing in the bathroom, and the job had not been thoroughly done. The washbowl was spattered with red. Water had been turned in the bathtub and had not been drained. It was colored a peculiar reddish brown. A pair of trousers had been washed and hung up to dry over the metal rod which supported the shower curtain. A pair of shoes had been washed, evidently with soap and water, and the washing had been insufficient. Stains still remained in the leather.

"We'll take a look in the closet," Mason said.

They walked back to the closet. Drake's flashlight illuminated the dark corners, showed a pile of dirty clothes. Drake pulled clothes from the top of the pile and then paused as the beam of the flashlight illuminated blood-spattered garments.

"Well," he said, "that's that."

Mason kicked the clothes back in the corner.

"Okay, Paul, we're finished here."

"I'll say," the detective agreed. "What's the technical definition of what we're doing here?"

"That," Mason said, "depends on whether I define it or whether a district attorney does. Come on, let's get going."

They left the apartment, switching out the lights, and pulling the spring lock shut behind them.

"Let's hunt up that preacher," Mason suggested.

"He won't come to the door," Drake objected, "and let us in just to answer questions—not at this hour of the morning. He'll be more than likely to call the police."

"We'll use Della," Mason said, "and let him think it's an elopement."

He had Drake drive to a restaurant where there was a telephone, and called Della Street's apartment. He heard her sleepy voice coming over the wire.

"Getting to be a habit with me, waking you up like this," he said. "How would you like to elope?"

There was a quick, gasping intake in her breath.

"I mean," Mason explained, "make a person *think* you're eloping."

"Oh," she said tonelessly. "Like that, eh?"

"That's the sketch," Mason told her. "Get on some things and we'll be out there. It'll be a new experience for you. You're going to drive in a car that'll send ripples up and down your backbone every time you hit a bump in the street, so don't worry about taking a shower; you can be massaged into wakefulness."

Paul Drake was yawning prodigiously as Mason hung up the telephone.

"The first night is always the hardest," he said; "after that I get accustomed to going without sleep on your cases. Some day, Perry, we're going to get caught and go to jail. Why the hell don't you sit in your office and let cases come to you the way other lawyers do?"

"For the same reason a hound doesn't like to follow a cold scent," Mason said. "I like my cases served up while they're hot."

"I'll say they're hot!" the detective agreed. "Some day we'll both get our fingers burnt."

11

PERRY MASON PUSHED HIS FINGER AGAINST THE DOORBELL. Della Street nudged Paul Drake and said, "Say something and laugh. We're all too serious for an elopement. You'd look more natural with a shotgun. Stand over here closer to me, Chief. He'll probably turn on a porch light and look out."

Drake remarked lugubriously, "Why should people laugh at a marriage? Marriage is a serious business."

Della Street moaned. "I should have known better than to stage an elopement with a couple of confirmed bachelors. You're so darned afraid some fish might steal the bait, you don't dare let your line get near the water."

Perry Mason stepped close to Della Street, put his arm around her and drew her close to him. "The trouble with us is, we haven't even got a line," he said.

A light in a hallway clicked on. Della Street kicked Paul Drake in the shin with the heel of her shoe and said, "Hurry up and laugh."

She broke into a peal of light, merry laughter, as a porch light flooded the trio with dazzling brilliance.

The detective gave a grimace of pain, rubbed his shin, and said mirthlessly, "Ha, ha."

The door opened some two or three inches. A safety chain snapped taut. A man's eyes stared out at them cautiously.

"Reverend Milton?" asked Perry Mason.

"Yes."

"We wanted to see you . . . about . . . a marriage."

The man's eyes showed extreme disapproval. "It's no time to be getting married," he said.

Mason took a wallet from his pocket, took out a five-dollar bill, then another five-dollar bill, then a third, and a fourth. "I'm sorry," he remarked, "that we awakened you."

After a moment, Milton slipped off the safety chain, opened the door and said, "Come in. Have you a license?"

Mason stood to one side while Della Street entered the hallway; then he and Drake crowded in. Drake kicked the door shut. Mason moved so he was between the inner door to the hallway and the man who wore dressing gown, pajamas and slippers.

"You received a call tonight from a chap by the name of Oafley," Mason said.

"What has that to do with this marriage?" Milton demanded.

"That's the marriage we came to see you about."

"I'm sorry. You got in here under false representations. You said you wished to be married. I don't care to answer any questions whatever about Mr. Oafley."

Perry Mason arched his eyebrows in surprise, then frowned and said belligerently, "Look here, what are you talking about—getting in here by false representations?"

"You said you wanted to be married."

"I said no such thing," Mason retorted. "We told you that we wanted to see you about *a* marriage. It was Oafley's marriage to Edith DeVoe."

"You didn't say that."

"Well, we're saying it now."

"I'm very sorry, gentlemen, but I have nothing to say."

Mason looked significantly at Paul Drake, nodded his head toward a wall telephone which was near the hall door and said, "Okay, Paul, call Police Headquarters."

Drake strode to the telephone. Milton made a grimace, wet his lips nervously with the tip of his tongue, and said in surprise, "Police Headquarters?"

"Certainly," Mason said.

"Who are you?" Milton demanded.

"*That* man," the lawyer remarked, indicating Drake by a nod of his head, "is a detective."

"Look here," Milton said nervously, "I don't want to get into any trouble over this thing."

"I didn't think you did. . . . Wait a minute, Paul. Don't call Headquarters right away. It may be this man's innocent."

"Innocent!" Milton blazed. "Of course, I'm innocent. I performed a marriage ceremony and that's all."

Mason's face showed utter incredulity. "And didn't know the woman had a husband living?" he asked.

"Of course, I didn't know the woman had a husband living. What are you insinuating? Do you mean to intimate that I'd perform a bigamous marriage knowing that it was bigamous?"

Milton's voice rose in quavering indignation.

Della Street stepped forward, slipped her arm through his and said soothingly, "It's all right. Don't lose your temper. That isn't what the Chief meant."

"The Chief?" Milton remarked, his eyes bulging.

"Oh, I'm sorry," Della Street remarked. "I shouldn't have said that."

"Just who are you and what do you want?" Milton asked.

"I'll answer your second question first. We want to know exactly what time you performed a marriage ceremony between Edith DeVoe and Frank Oafley."

Milton was now only too willing to talk.

"The parties were very anxious to keep the ceremony secret, but I didn't suspect it was a bigamous marriage. I received a call at approximately nine o'clock, asking me to come to a certain address. The party who called me on the telephone stated that it was a matter of the greatest importance, but didn't say what it was. He did say, however, that I would be very well compensated. I went to the address. I found Mr. Oafley, whom I had met previously, and a young woman who was introduced as Miss Edith DeVoe. They had a marriage license, properly issued, and, as a minister of the Gospel, I solemnized a marriage."

"Were there witnesses?"

"There were some men next door who were engaged in a little . . . er . . . gathering. I think perhaps they were playing cards. Mr. Oafley stepped to the door and asked them to witness the marriage ceremony."

"What time was the ceremony performed?"

"About ten o'clock."

"When did you leave there?"

"Twenty minutes later. There was quite a bit of good-natured chaffing. The men were very nice, very cordial, very . . . well, er, convivial. There was a little party. . . . Of course, I didn't touch anything myself, and I can't say that I approved of the spirit of the occasion, but, nevertheless, they were interesting people, and it was impossible to leave immediately."

"You mean they drank a toast to the health of the bride and groom?"

"To the health of the bride, the health of the groom, to my health."

"Do you know exactly what time you left?"

"No, it was around ten fifteen, perhaps a few minutes later than that."

"Were you well paid?" Perry Mason asked.

"Very well paid; very well paid, indeed."

Mason said slowly, "How long had you known Frank Oafley?"

"He has been in my church on several occasions."

"A regular member?"

"No. Not a regular member. I wouldn't class him as such, but he has been there, and I have met him."

"He introduced you to the young woman?"

"Yes. And the apartment was in her name, 'Edith DeVoe.' "

"Did they tell you why they were anxious to have the marriage kept secret?"

"No, they didn't. I understood there was some question of opposition on the part of relatives. I think the young woman was a nurse, and Mr. Oafley is, I believe, of rather a wealthy family. However, I paid little attention to that. I performed the marriage ceremony and . . ."

"Kissed the bride, I presume," Mason interrupted with a laugh.

The Reverend Milton failed to see any ground for humor in the remark. He said very seriously, "As a matter of fact, I did not. The bride kissed me as I was leaving."

Mason nodded to Paul Drake, reached for the knob of the outer door. "That's all," he said.

"Was the marriage bigamous?"

"In view of what you tell me," Mason said, "I don't think it was. But I was checking up on it. You know, marriages that are performed under such circumstances are always open to suspicion."

The trio slipped hastily through the door into the night, leaving Milton blinking after them in bewildered appraisal. Then he slammed the door shut, and they heard the clink of the safety chain as it was slid into position, and the rasp of the bolt.

"I'm a lawyer," Mason remarked, "and darn seldom even bother to lock my door. This chap is supposed to have all sorts of faith in human nature, and he barricades himself behind a lot of thief-proof doodads."

"I know," Della Street said with a nervous giggle, "but brides don't have to follow *you* to the door to kiss you."

Mason chuckled.

"What's next?" Paul Drake asked.

"If we can survive the ordeal of another journey in that car of yours, we're going to see Winnie."

"You know where to find her at this hour of the night?" Drake asked.

"Yes. She lives back of the waffle place."

"We don't want to make a racket there. There'll be a merchants' patrol and . . ."

"We'll telephone her and tell her we're coming," Mason said. "That is, I'll tell her I'm coming. I'll introduce you two after we get there."

"Has it ever occurred to you," Drake asked slowly, "that this marriage ceremony was taking place at just about the time Ashton was being murdered in his room, thereby giving both Oafley and Edith DeVoe iron-clad alibis?"

"A lot has occurred to me," Mason said, "that I'm not discussing right now. Let's go."

118

They piled into Drake's car. Mason stopped the car once to telephone Winifred he was coming, and then, when Drake had parked the car in front of the Waffle Kitchen, motioned them to silence as he placed them in the shadows near the doorway, while he stood in front of the plate-glass door, and pounded with his knuckles.

A moment later he saw a bit of diffused light come from the door at the end of the passageway, and then Winifred's supple figure, attired in a flowing silk negligee, glided toward him. She shot the bolt and opened the door.

"What is it?" she asked.

Mason said, "You know Paul Drake. He was with me the first time I came here, and this is Della Street, my secretary."

Winifred gave a little exclamation of dismay. "I didn't know I was to meet people," she said, "and I don't want anyone to know about . . ."

"That's all right," Mason told her. "No one knows anything at all. We want to talk with you."

He pushed the door open, then when his companions had entered, carefully closed it. Winifred led the way down the corridor to the bedroom, which apparently was just as Perry Mason had last seen it, except that the bed had been slept in.

"Where's Douglas Keene?" Mason asked.

She frowned, and said, "I told you all that I knew about him."

"I don't want you to think I'm betraying any confidences," Mason told her, "but it's necessary that these people know what's happening, because they've got to help us. Paul Drake is a detective who works for me, and Della Street is my secretary, who knows everything that goes on. You can absolutely trust their discretion. Now I want to know where Douglas Keene is."

She blinked her eyes rapidly, as though about to cry, but faced them steadily, saying, "I don't know where he is; all I know is he sent me a message saying that he was going to leave, where no one would ever find him."

"Let's take a look at the message."

She pulled back the pillow, and produced an envelope on the outside of which her name had been written. There was no other writing on the envelope, no address and no stamp. She opened the envelope and took from it a folded piece of paper. After a moment's hesitation, she handed the paper to Perry Mason.

Mason, standing near the center of the room, his feet spread wide apart, shoulders squared, read the message with expressionless features. When he had finished, he said, "I'm going to read this aloud," and then read in a monotone: " 'Darling: I am up against a combination of circumstances I can't beat. I lost my head and made a mistake, and I'll never have any opportunity to rectify that mistake. Please believe that I'm innocent of any crime, but you'll need lots of faith to hold that belief in the face of the evidence which will be presented. I am going out of your life forever. The police will never catch me. I am far too clever to walk into the traps which catch the ordinary fugitive from justice. I'll travel by plane, and no one will ever find me. Ashton had the Koltsdorf diamonds concealed in his crutch. He had hollowed out a hiding place for them. The diamonds are still there. Give the police an anonymous tip and let them trace the crutch. I shall always love you, but I am not going to drag your name through the mire of a murder trial. Try and make Ashton talk. He can tell a lot. Lovingly yours—Douglas.' "

Mason stared steadily at the letter for a while, then suddenly whirled to face Winifred Laxter.

"You didn't show me that note when I was here before," he said.

"No, I didn't have it."

"When did you get it?"

"It was slipped under the door."

"After I left?"

"Yes, I guess so. It must have been if you didn't see it there when you went out."

"You said Douglas had telephoned you."

"Yes."

"He didn't tell you this about the diamonds over the telephone?"

"No."

"How did he know where the diamonds were?"

"I don't know; I only know what's in the note."

"You love him?"

"Yes."

"Were engaged to him."

"We were going to be married."

"You didn't call him Douglas."

"What do you mean?"

"You had some pet name for him."

She lowered her eyes, and flushed.

"And," Mason went on, "when you didn't call him by that pet name, you still didn't call him Douglas—you called him Doug."

"Does that make any difference?" she countered.

"Simply this!" Mason said. "If Douglas had written that note to you, he'd have signed it 'Doug' or some pet name, and it would have been a lot more tragic. There'd have been some affectionate stuff in it, and he'd have told you good-by, and that he loved you. That note wasn't written for you; it was written for the public. That was a note that was given you to *show* people."

She was watching him with wide eyes, her lips compressed tightly together, as though she were trying to keep from whimpering or letting some damaging statement escape her.

"That note's a blind. Douglas telephoned you, and told you he was in a jam. He wouldn't leave without seeing you. He came to say good-by. You talked him into staying. You told him you'd employed me, and I was going to clear things up. You asked him to stay; he refused. You asked him if he wouldn't at least stay where you could keep in touch with him until after I'd made a complete investigation."

Her face gave no faintest flicker of expression, but she clenched her right fist, slowly brought it up until the muscles were pressing tightly against her lips.

"And so," Mason went on inexorably, "Douglas Keene agreed to stay within reach until the police had uncovered all of the facts, and I had tried to explain those facts in such a way as to establish his innocence. But you wanted to throw the police off the trail; so Douglas Keene left this note that you were to give to me, and later on intended to give to the newspaper reporters."

Mason pointed a rigid forefinger at her. "Speak up," he said; "don't lie to your lawyer. How the hell can I help you if you start concealing facts?"

"No," she said, "that's not true. That's . . . Oh!"

She dropped on the edge of the bed and started to cry.

Mason strode to the closet door, jerked it open, went to the room which contained the shower, opened the door, and looked about in that room. He frowned thoughtfully, shook his head, and said, "She's too wise to have him where the officers would be apt to look. Paul, get busy and see if there isn't a storeroom around here where boxes and stuff are kept."

Mason strode to the bed, jerked back the covers, felt of them and nodded. "Just one blanket," he said. "She's taken off some of the blankets to give him."

Della Street crossed to Winifred's side, put her arm around the girl's shoulder and said soothingly, "Can't you understand, dear, he's trying to help you? He's only being gruff because time is precious, and he must know the facts before he can plan his campaign."

Winifred slid her head over on Della Street's shoulder and began to sob.

"Won't you tell us?" Della asked.

Winifred shook her head, rolling it from side to side on Della Street's shoulder.

Mason strode out of the door to the corridor which ran between booths and lunch counter, peered about him, then crossed behind the lunch counter and started looking into the corners and down under the counter.

Paul Drake had explored a side passageway. Suddenly he gave a shrill whistle. "Here it is, Perry."

Winifred screamed, jumped to her feet, and ran the length of the passageway, her robe billowing out behind her. Mason, walking rapidly, covered the space almost as quickly as the running girl. Della Street, moving at a more leisurely pace, brought up the rear.

A door was open. It showed a litter of broken boxes, old barrels, some cans of paint, a few surplus stores, broken chairs and various odds and ends which had accumulated from the operation of the waffle kitchen. A space near one corner had been cleaned out, and broken packing cases and chairs piled in such a manner as to conceal it. On the floor were spread two blankets and a pillow made by stuffing papers into a flour sack. A sheet was pinned to the blanket.

Paul Drake's flashlight threw brilliant light into the corner, and held the square of note paper in the center of its beam.

"A note," he said, "pinned on that blanket."

Winifred made a dive for the note. Perry Mason's rigid right arm thrust in front of her held her back.

"Just a minute, sister," he said. "You take too many liberties with the truth. I'll read this one first."

The note was a scrawl, as though it had been penciled in the dark. It read:

"I can't do it, Winnie, dear. Probably they'd never find me. But if they did it would make it tough on

123

you. I'd feel that I was hiding behind you as a shield. Perhaps if things come out all right I'll get in touch with you. But I know they'll be watching you and watching your mail, so you won't hear anything from me for a while. Lots of love and kisses to you, sweetheart. Your own Doug."

Mason read the note out loud, folded it and said to Della Street, "Catch her, quick. She's going to faint."

Winifred sagged toward Della Street's protecting arm, then straightened. Her eyes were wan and pathetic. "I shouldn't have left him alone," she said. "I should have known he'd do that."

Perry Mason moved toward the door, kicked aside a broken packing case, walked down the passageway, entered Winifred's room, picked up a telephone and dialed a number. "I want to talk with District Attorney Burger," he said.

After a moment he said, "It's Perry Mason talking. I've got to see him on a matter of importance. Where can I reach him?"

The receiver made squawking noises, and Perry Mason, with an exclamation of disgust, hung up the receiver. He dialed another number, and said, "Police Headquarters? . . . Is Sergeant Holcomb where you can put him on the phone? . . . Hello, Sergeant Holcomb? This is Perry Mason. . . . Yes, I know it's late. . . . No, it isn't past my bedtime. If you're trying to be funny, you can skip it, and if you're wisecracking you can go to hell. I rang up to tell you that I personally will guarantee Douglas Keene will surrender to the police at five o'clock tonight. . . . No, not at Police Headquarters. That would give you a chance to pick him up en route, and claim he was a fugitive from justice. I'll telephone you from some place which I'll select. You can come there and pick him up. Don't try to keep the information from the newspapers, because I'm going to tell them. . . . Yes, I'll surrender him at five o'clock. . . ."

Winifred Laxter lunged toward the telephone. "No, no!" she screamed. "No! You can't. . . ."

Perry Mason pushed her away. "Five o'clock," he said, and hung up.

Della Street held one of the girl's arms. Paul Drake held the other. She was wrestling with them, her eyes fastened on Perry Mason's face with an expression of stark fear.

"You can't do it!" she screamed. "You mustn't. You . . ."

"I said I'd do it," Perry Mason said slowly, "and, by God, I will."

"You're selling us out."

"I'm selling no one out. You wanted me to represent him. All right, I'm going to represent him. The boy's made a fool of himself. He's just a kid. He got stampeded into running away. Someone's double-crossed him. I'm going to put him back on the right track.

"He'll read the newspaper. He'll read that I'm representing him. He'll read that I've personally guaranteed to surrender him into custody at five o'clock tonight. He'll know I'm acting for you. He'll come in and give himself up."

"Chief," Della Street pleaded, "suppose he *shouldn't* get in touch with you; suppose he should read that in the paper and still keep in hiding?"

Perry Mason shrugged his shoulders. "Come on," he said to Paul Drake. "We'd better get up to the office. Newspaper reporters are going to ask us questions."

He turned to Della Street. "You stay here until that girl gets quieted down. Don't let her have hysterics, and don't let her make a fool of herself. As soon as you can leave her, come up to the office."

Della Street, clicking her heels together, made a mock military salute. "Okay, Chief," she said.

She turned to Winifred Laxter. "Come on, baby, snap out of it."

"I'm s-s-s-snapped out of it," Winifred said, fighting back tears. "Mind your own d-d-d-damned b-b-b-business, and g-g-go on up to his office."

12

THE ELECTRIC LIGHTS GAVE A SICKLY PALE ILLUMINATION to Perry Mason's office. It was that hour of the morning when the concrete caverns of the city cliff dwellers appear to the greatest disadvantage. Outside was the freshness of early dawn, contrasting with the stale air of the office. It was some half hour before sunrise. There was only enough daylight to emphasize the inefficiency of the man-made substitute.

Perry Mason stretched out in his swivel chair, placed his heels on the corner of the desk, lighted a cigarette. "When the newspaper reporters come in, Della, keep them in the outer office and bring them in all at once."

She nodded. Her eyes showed worry.

Paul Drake moved over and sat on the edge of Perry Mason's desk.

"You and I," he said, "had better pool a little information."

Mason's eyes were expressionless. "Such as what?" he asked.

"My men tell me Edith DeVoe was killed. She was beaten over the head with a club. The club was part of a crutch which had been sawed up."

Perry Mason smoked in silence.

"Of course, I knew that you had something in mind

when you went up to Doug Keene's apartment. When I saw the blood-stained clothing, I knew it didn't come from the Ashton murder."

"But at that time," Mason asked, "you didn't know anything about the DeVoe murder?"

"Certainly not."

"That," Mason said, "might be a good thing to remember—in case you were questioned."

"Did you know about it?"

Mason stared steadily out of the window into the graying dawn.

After a few moments, when it became apparent he didn't intend to answer the question, Drake went on, "Do you know a man named Babson? He's an expert cabinetmaker. He does all sorts of woodwork, and, as a sideline, makes crutches."

Mason's face showed interest.

"A couple of weeks ago Ashton dropped into Babson's place. Ashton had his crutch made there. He wanted his crutch altered. He wanted a hole bored near the tip of the crutch, wanted it reenforced with metal tubing and lined with chamois skin. He wanted the metal threaded so that a cap could go on the end and the whole business be concealed under the rubber tip of the crutch."

Mason said slowly, "That's interesting."

"About three days ago," Drake went on, "Babson was questioned about that crutch business. A man who gave his name as Smith said he was representing an insurance company that was interested in Ashton's injuries. He wanted to know if Ashton had secured a new crutch or had any alterations made to the old one. Babson started to tell about the changes, then thought better of it and started questioning this man, Smith. Smith walked out."

"Got a description?" Mason asked tersely.

"Five foot eleven, age forty-five, weight a hundred and eighty pounds, light felt hat, blue suit, and a peculiar scar across the face. He was driving a green Pontiac."

"When did that report come in?" Mason asked.

"The night operator handed it to me when I went past the office. It had been on my desk for some little time. One of the boys turned it in in his report."

"Good work," Mason said. "How'd he happen to call on Babson?"

"You wanted a complete check-up on Ashton, so I told the boys to go the limit. Naturally, we were interested in the place where his crutch had been made."

"Well," Mason told him, "add one more name to your list—put a tail on Jim Brandon. Find out all you can about him. See if *he's* been flashing any ready money lately."

"Already done," Drake said laconically. "I put a couple of men on him as soon as I got the report. Now let me ask you a few questions."

"Such as what?" Mason inquired.

"Such as where you're going to stand in this thing. Did you have to telephone the police, promising to surrender that kid?"

"Sure I had to do it," Perry Mason said with a savage impatience. "Can't you get the sketch? He's either guilty as hell or else that was a plant. If it's a plant, he can't dodge it. He's got to face it. If he tries to run away, he's going to be picked up. If the police pick him up and he's running away, he's headed for the gallows. He'll stretch hemp in spite of anything I can do. If he's guilty and surrenders and stands up like a man, faces the music, pleads guilty and tells his story to the court, I can probably get him off with life imprisonment."

"But you're gambling that he isn't guilty?" Della Street asked.

"I'm gambling, with everything I've got, that he isn't guilty."

"That's just the point, Chief," Della Street protested in hot indignation. "You're gambling too much. You're staking your professional reputation backing the play of an emotional kid about whom you know nothing."

Perry Mason grinned at her, a grin which held no amusement, but was the savage grin of a fighter coming back into the ring to face a formidable adversary who has already inflicted terrific punishment. "Sure I am," he agreed. "I'm a gambler. I want to live life while I'm living it. We hear a lot about the people who are afraid to die, but we don't hear so much about the people who are afraid to live; yet it's a common failing. I have faith in Winifred, and I have faith in Douglas Keene. They're in a bad spot and they need someone to front for them, and I'm going to do it!"

Paul Drake's voice still held a note of pleading.

"Listen, Perry, it isn't too late to back out. You don't know anything about that kid. Look at the facts against him. He . . ."

"Shut up, Paul," Perry Mason said without rancor. "I know how the facts stack up just as well as you do."

"But why should *you* stake *your* reputation on the innocence of some kid when everything points to his guilt?"

"Because," Mason said, "I play a no-limit game. When I back my judgment, I back it with everything I have. I try not be wrong."

"A no-limit game makes for big winnings and big losings," Della Street pointed out.

Mason said impatiently, with a gesture which included both of them, "What the hell can a man lose? He can't lose his life because he doesn't own that, anyway. He only has a lease on life. He can lose money, and money doesn't mean one damn thing as compared with character. All that really counts is a man's ability to live, to get the most out of it as he goes through it, and he gets the most kick out of it by playing a no-limit game."

A buzzer sounded in the office as the door of the entrance office opened and closed. Drake nodded to Della Street. She rose and slid through the doorway into the outer office. Paul Drake lit a cigarette and said, "Perry, you're a cross between a boy and a philosopher, an impractical, hard-hitting visionary, a damned altruistic cynic, a credulous skeptic . . . and, dammit, how I envy you your outlook on life!"

Della Street opened the door and lowered her voice apprehensively. "Sergeant Holcomb is out there," she said, "with a whole flock of newspaper reporters."

"Did Holcomb bring the newspaper reporters?"

"No. I think he tried to beat them to it. They've been tagging along behind. He seems irritated."

Perry Mason grinned, blew a smoke ring at the ceiling. "Show the gentlemen in," he said.

Della Street ventured a grin. "Does that include Sergeant Holcomb?"

"Just this once, it does," Mason told her.

Della Street flung open the door. "Come in, *gentlemen*," she said.

Sergeant Holcomb pushed his way through the door. Back of him appeared several men who spread out fanwise as they entered the room, took up positions against the wall. Some of them took out notebooks. All of them had an attitude of listening intently, the attitudes of spectators at the opening round of a prize fight, who scrouge forward to the edge of their chairs lest they miss a single blow in what promises to be an encounter of whirlwind rapidity.

"Where's Douglas Keene?" Sergeant Holcomb demanded. Perry Mason inhaled a lungful of smoke, let it seep out through his nostrils in twin streams. "I'm sure I don't know, Sergeant," he said in the patient tone an elder uses in addressing an excited child.

"By God, you've *got* to know."

Mason made an unsuccessful attempt at a smoke ring. "The air's too churned up," he explained to Paul Drake in an audible aside. "It's hard to blow them when there are too many people in the room."

Sergeant Holcomb pounded his fist on Mason's desk. "By God," he said, "the day is past when you criminal attorneys can play tag with the law. You know what they're doing now to people who harbor public enemies."

"Is Douglas Keene a public enemy?" Mason asked innocently.

"He's a murderer."

"Indeed! Whom did he murder?"

"Two people. Charles Ashton and Edith DeVoe."

Perry Mason's tongue made clicking noises against the roof of his mouth. "He shouldn't have done that, Sergeant," he said.

One of the reporters snickered audibly. Holcomb's face darkened. "Go ahead and crack wise," he said, "all you want to, but I'm going to get you for aiding a fugitive from justice."

"*Is* he a fugitive from justice?"

"He most certainly is."

"He's going to surrender at five o'clock tonight," Mason said, taking another drag at his cigarette.

"We'll catch him before that."

"Where is he?" Mason asked, raising his eyebrows.

"I don't know," Sergeant Holcomb bellowed. "If I did I'd go pick him up."

Mason sighed, turned to Paul Drake and said, apologetically, "He's going to put his hands on Keene *before* five o'clock tonight, yet *he* insists he doesn't know where Keene is. I've offered to surrender him at five o'clock and yet he won't believe I *don't* know where he is. It isn't logical."

"You wouldn't promise to have that man in custody by five o'clock unless you knew where he was right now. And you're working out some scheme to beat the case while you've got him under cover," Holcomb accused.

Mason smoked in silence.

"You're a lawyer. You know what the penalty is for

131

becoming an accessory after the fact. You know what happens to people who give aid to murderers."

"But," Mason pointed out patiently, "suppose it should turn out he wasn't a murderer, Holcomb?"

"Wasn't a murderer!" Holcomb almost screamed. "Wasn't a murderer? Why, do you know what the evidence is against that boy? He went out to see Charles Ashton. He was the last man to see Ashton alive. Now get this and get it straight. Ashton had a cat. The cat slept on Ashton's bed. Douglas Keene went out to get that cat; and he got the cat. Witnesses saw him when he entered the room, and saw him leaving the place with the cat in his arms.

"Now Ashton was murdered *before* the cat left the place. The cat had jumped in through the window. There were tracks on the bed where the cat had walked up and down. There was even a cat track squarely in the middle of Ashton's forehead, proving that the murder was committed before Keene left with the cat. Ashton was killed *after* ten o'clock and *before* eleven. Keene was there in Ashton's room shortly before ten and stayed there until he left with the cat *after* eleven."

Mason, pursing his lips, said, "That would make quite a case against Douglas Keene, *if* you were certain it was Ashton's cat he carried away."

"Of course it was Ashton's cat. Witnesses saw him, I tell you. The housekeeper saw him. She wasn't sleeping well. She was looking out her window when Keene left. She saw him with the cat in his arms. James Brandon, the chauffeur, was driving a car to the garage. He turned in the driveway, and the headlights hit Douglas Keene squarely. He'll swear Keene was carrying the cat."

"You mean Clinker?"

"I mean Clinker, if that's the cat's name."

"Under those circumstances," Mason said, "the weight a jury would give the testimony of these people would depend upon their ability to convince the jury of the identity of the cat. Where's the cat now, by the way, Sergeant?"

"I don't know," Sergeant Holcomb said, then added, significantly, "Do you?"

Perry Mason said slowly, "I don't think, Sergeant, there's any law in the Penal Code against giving shelter to a cat, is there? You're not by any chance accusing the cat of the murder, are you?"

"Go ahead and crack wise," Sergeant Holcomb said. "Do you know what I'm doing here? Do you know the real purpose of my coming here?"

Mason raised his eyebrows and shook his head.

Holcomb, pounding the desk with his fist, said, "I came here to tell you that Douglas Keene was wanted for murder. I came here to tell you that we're getting a warrant out for Douglas Keene's arrest. I came here to tell you the evidence against Douglas Keene so that if you continue to conceal Douglas Keene, we can have you convicted of a crime involving moral turpitude and have you disbarred. *That's* why I'm here. I'm going to tell you all of the evidence. When I leave here you're never going to be able to tell a jury or the Grievance Committee of the Bar Association you didn't know Douglas Keene was wanted for murder and that you didn't know the evidence that was against him."

"Rather shrewd, Sergeant," Perry Mason said. "In fact, it's *very shrewd*. You're closing the door to any possible defense that I might have, is that it?"

"That's exactly it. You're either going to turn up Douglas Keene, or you're going to be arrested, prosecuted, and eventually disbarred."

"Have you," Mason asked, "entirely finished? Have you told me *all* the evidence?"

"No. I haven't even told you half of it."

"And I take it, Sergeant, that you intend to tell me all."

"You're damn right I intend to tell you all."

Mason inclined his head in the receptive attitude of one

who is about to listen intently. But Sergeant Holcomb's voice filled every corner of the office, seemed to rattle back from the windows.

"Edith DeVoe wanted to see Douglas Keene. She telephoned and left messages for him at several places. Douglas Keene went to call on her. The manager of Edith DeVoe's apartment house happened to be leaving the house just as Douglas Keene was pressing his finger against the button which rang Edith DeVoe's bell. When the manager opened the door, Keene took advantage of it by walking in. The manager naturally stopped him and asked him where he was going. Keene said he was going to see Miss DeVoe; that she had sent for him.

"Later on the district attorney went to question her. She was lying on the floor unconscious. She'd been literally clubbed to death. We went to Douglas Keene's room. We found that garments he had worn were bloodstained. There was blood on his shirt, on his collar, on his shoes, on his trousers. He had tried to wash out the bloodstains and failed. He'd tried to burn up some of his clothes and had even failed to do that. Shreds of cloth were left in the ashes, and they gave a chemical reaction which shows there was human blood on them."

"Was the cat there?" Mason asked.

Holcomb controlled himself with an effort. "No, the cat wasn't there."

"Just how would one make an absolute identification of a cat?" Perry Mason asked. "There's no way of fingerprinting a cat, is there, Sergeant?"

"Go ahead," Holcomb said grimly, "be as smart as you want to. You're a lawyer making his living defending murderers. Two months from now you'll be disbarred. You'll be walking the streets."

"So far," Mason remarked, "I haven't defended murderers. I have only defended persons *accused* of murder. You must appreciate, Sergeant, that there's quite a difference. But I'm serious about the cat. Sergeant. Suppose

134

the housekeeper and the chauffeur should both swear Keene was carrying Clinker in his arms; and suppose I should line up a couple of dozen Persian cats in front of the witnesses and ask them to pick out Clinker. Do you suppose they could do it, and in the event they pick out one cat and swear that it was Clinker, do you suppose there's any way by which we could definitely establish to the jury that they were right?"

"So *that's* your game, is it?" Holcomb asked.

Mason smiled urbanely. "Why no, Sergeant, that's not my game. I was just asking you a question; that's all."

Sergeant Holcomb leaned across the desk, holding both edges of it with a grip which drew the skin white and taut across the knuckles.

"After a while, Mason," he said, "we get so we know just about what to expect with you. The police department isn't as dumb as you may think it is. And, just to give you a little something to think over, as soon as you telephoned that you were going to represent Douglas Keene and that he'd surrender at five o'clock tonight, I sent some of the boys out to locate the cat. And it just happened that I knew where to send them. Just for your information, we've picked up Clinker, and he's in police custody. He was in the apartment of your very efficient secretary, Miss Della Street. And the cat has been identified at police headquarters by the chauffeur and the housekeeper, and a label has been tied around his neck. And any time you want to start juggling cats in front of a jury, you won't have to worry about taking fingerprints, or switching cats, or pulling any of your other tricks, because Clinker will be right there with a tag around his neck."

Sergeant Holcomb turned on his heel and strode toward the outer office.

For a moment, Perry Mason's face was grim and tense. Then he gave a slow smile in the direction of the newspaper reporters.

135

"We'd like to ask you," one of the men said, "if you agree . . ."

Mason said slowly, "Gentlemen, you have a damned good story. Go ahead and publish it as it is." And then clamped his lips shut in the obstinate silence of one who knows how to keep quiet.

13

PERRY MASON TURNED FROM THE TELEPHONE AND SAID to Della Street, "Nat Shuster and his two clients, Sam Laxter and Frank Oafley, are out there to see me. This is going to be a good show while it lasts. Go out and send them in. Turn on the loud-speaking inter-office telephone, sit out in your office and take down as much of the conversation as you can. You may have to testify later on about what was said."

"And I'm to keep a line open?" she asked. "And talk with anyone who calls for you?"

"Absolutely. See that nothing interferes with that. Douglas Keene may telephone in at any time. I don't want his call to be handled by the regular office system."

"Suppose he *doesn't* telephone in, Chief?"

"We've been over all that before."

"Suppose he's guilty? Can Sergeant Holcomb do all of those things he was threatening?"

Mason shrugged. "That," he said, "is where I have them fooled. Holcomb is trying to stick me for concealing a murderer. I've told the police Keene will surrender at five o'clock. Naturally they think I know where he is. I don't know any more about it than the man in the moon."

"Therefore, there's nothing they can do?" she asked.

"Don't worry so much; go ahead and let Shuster in here. He's probably going to deal a couple of cards from the bottom of a cold deck."

"Such as what?"

"Such as suing me for defamation of character."

"Why?"

"Because I told the district attorney what Edith DeVoe told me about that automobile exhaust business."

"But you were just passing on what she told you."

"I can't even prove that she told it to me now. She's dead and there weren't any witnesses. Go ahead and bring Shuster in, and don't forget to listen to everything that's said, and take notes so you can testify to it later on."

She nodded, slipped through the door, and, a moment later, ushered Shuster, Laxter and Oafley into the room.

Shuster twisted his lips back from protruding teeth. The perfunctory smile over, his face became a mask of reproachful gravity. "Counselor, did you inform the district attorney that my client, Samuel C. Laxter, was guilty of the murder of his grandfather, Peter Laxter?"

"Want me to answer that yes or no?" Mason inquired casually.

Shuster frowned. "Answer it," he said.

"No."

"Didn't you intimate to him that such was the case?"

"No."

"Didn't you tell him that Edith DeVoe had accused him of that crime?"

"No."

Shuster's face was a study. "Mr. Burger says you told him that."

Mason remained silent.

"Burger told Sam Laxter," Shuster went on, "that you said Edith DeVoe told you Samuel Laxter had a tube running from his exhaust to the hot air pipe that went to Peter Laxter's room."

Perry Mason's face was as grim and uncompromising as granite. "Perhaps he did, because she did, and I did."

Shuster blinked his eyes as he tried to figure out those answers, then, with a look of triumph on his face, he said, "You told Burger that she made that accusation?"

"It wasn't an accusation; she simply said she saw him seated in the automobile with the motor running and a flexible tube extending to the hot air pipe. She told me that, and I told Burger that."

"It's a lie."

"What's a lie?" Mason asked, getting to his feet ominously.

Shuster backed up nervously, holding out his hand before him. "A slander, I meant," he said, "a defamation of character."

"Has it ever occurred to you that it might be a privileged communication?" Mason inquired.

"Not if it was actuated by malice," Shuster remarked, shaking his finger at Perry Mason, but moving back of the big overstuffed leather chair so that it was between him and Mason. "And you were actuated by malice. You were trying to protect your client, Douglas Keene."

"So what?" Mason asked.

"So we want a retraction."

"Who wants a retraction?"

"Samuel Laxter does, and I do."

"Very well," Mason said, "you want a retraction—so what?"

"We want your answer."

Mason said, "I told Burger nothing but the truth, as it was told to me. I didn't vouch for the facts; I only vouched for the statement having been made for what it was worth."

"We want an apology."

"Go to hell."

Samuel Laxter stepped forward. His face was white

"Mr. Mason," he said, "I don't know you, but I do know there's something rotten in Denmark. I'd heard that a story was being circulated, linking me with the death of my grandfather. It's a damnable lie! I've also heard that you led the officers to a surreptitious and unwarranted search of my car, in my garage, after first picking the lock of the garage in order to get across to my car. Someone had planted a long tube in my automobile without my knowledge. I don't know what protection the law gives me—that's up to Mr. Shuster—but I certainly intend to see that *you're* held to strict accountability for what you've done."

Mason yawned.

Shuster laid a restraining hand on Sam Laxter's arm. "Now let me do the talking," he said, "let me do the talking. Don't get excited. Keep calm, keep calm. I can handle him. You let me make the statements."

Mason sat down once more in his big swivel chair, leaned back and took a cigarette from the cigarette case on the desk. "Anything else?" he asked, tapping the end of the cigarette on his thumb-nail.

Frank Oafley said, "Mr. Mason, I want you to understand my position. My relationship with Edith DeVoe is no longer a secret. She had done me the honor to marry me shortly before her death."

He stopped for a moment while a spasm of expression crossed his face; then he went on, "She had told me about what she had seen, but I hadn't been inclined to give it much thought until after the district attorney pointed out to me how easy it would have been for someone to have put carbon monoxide into Grandfather's room.

"Naturally, this came as a big shock to me. I know my cousin well. I can't believe that he was capable of any such thing, and then I remembered that Edith had never told me that she had positively recognized Sam as the one in that car. The man in the car had his face concealed under the broad brim of Sam's hat. That was what led Edith to believe the man in the car was Sam Laxter.

"Now, if you told the officers that Edith said Sam Laxter was seated in that car, you have made a statement which was unwarranted by anything Edith said."

Mason, studying Frank Oafley's face, said speculatively, "So that's *your* story, is it?"

"That's my story," Oafley said, blushing.

Shuster's face was cunning. "Consider, Counselor, what a position you're in," he said to Mason. "You make a charge against my client. You can't back that charge up; you have got no evidence. You can't testify what Edith DeVoe told you because that's hearsay. Dying declarations are admissible when a person making them knows he is going to die, but this wasn't a dying declaration. When she told you this, she thought she'd live to be a hundred, so you haven't got a leg to stand on. My client can take you into court. He can trim you. He can stick you; he can soak you—but he won't do it if you make a retraction."

"What Shuster means," Oafley said, "is that you emphasize that Edith didn't know who it was in the car."

Sam Laxter's face was scowling. "I want more than that," he said. "I want a retraction and an apology. I never sat in that car, and Mason knows it."

Perry Mason stretched forth his hand to a row of books which stood on his desk, supported by book ends. He pulled out a book, opened it, and said, "Speaking of law, gentlemen, *I'll* read you a little law. Section 258 of the Probate Code reads as follows: 'No person convicted of the murder of the decedent shall be entitled to succeed to any portion of the estate; but the portion thereof to which he would otherwise be entitled to succeed goes to the other persons entitled thereto under the provisions of this chapter.' There is some law for *you* to think over, Frank Oafley."

Shuster sputtered into speech with moist vehemence. "What a trick!" he exclaimed. "What a scheme! He tries to turn you one against the other, reading from his law books, making his dirty slanders. Close your ears to his words, close your hearts to his thoughts, close your . . ."

Mason interrupted, speaking directly to Frank Oafley. "You would like to protect your cousin," he said, "but you know as well as I do that Edith DeVoe wasn't the sort of girl to jump at false conclusions. Perhaps she didn't see the man's face, but she saw the man's hat, she heard his voice and she *thought* that man was Sam Laxter."

Oafley's forehead knitted thoughtfully as he said slowly, "She *did* hear his voice."

"Go ahead," Sam Laxter said bitterly, "put on an act, Frank; pretend you're being convinced, but you're not fooling me any. The minute this lawyer showed you that you could hog all of my inheritance by getting me convicted of murder, I knew what was going to happen."

"Gentlemen, gentlemen!" Shuster half screamed. "Don't do it; don't fight. It's a trap. Don't walk into it. He gets you fighting between yourselves and then his damn cat inherits the estate. What a scheme! What a scheme! Oh, what a trick!"

Mason, looking at Sam Laxter, said, "How do you account for that tube being found in your car?"

"Someone planted it," Laxter said belligerently. "You led the officers to the garage and they 'found' a tube in my car, *after you suggested they look for it.*"

Mason said, "Do you think I planted the tube in your car?"

Shuster rushed in front of Sam Laxter, grabbed him by the lapels of his coat, pushed him back and shouted, "Don't answer! don't answer! It's another trap. He gets you to charge that he planted it and then *he* sues *you* for defamation of character. You can't prove he planted it there; don't say it; don't say anything. Let me do the talking. Keep quiet, everybody; keep calm. Don't get excited. *I'll* handle it."

Oafley moved a step closer to Laxter and said, over Shuster's shoulder, "Are you insinuating that I planted it there, Sam?"

Laxter, his voice edged with bitterness, said, "Why not? You don't fool me any, Frank Oafley. You'd do a damn sight more than that for half a million dollars. I'm commencing to see this thing in a new light now."

"You forget," Oafley said, with cold dignity, "that it was Edith DeVoe who saw this. I didn't see it, and when she first told me, I didn't attach any significance to it."

"Gentlemen, gentlemen," Shuster pleaded, turning his head rapidly to look beseechingly first at Laxter, then at Oafley. "Gentlemen, calm yourselves. This isn't what we came here for. Keep cool. Remember what I told you to say. Let me do the talking. Shut up, everybody."

"Edith Oafley," Sam Laxter sneered, paying no attention to the lawyer. "If she weren't dead, I could say plenty about her."

Oafley, with an inarticulate expression of rage, pushed Shuster aside with his right hand and slapped Laxter's face with his left.

"Gentlemen, gentlemen!" Shuster screamed. "Remember . . ."

Sam Laxter's left fist, swinging in a sizzling blow aimed at Oafley's jaw, caught Shuster full in the face as the little attorney pawed at Laxter's coat. Shuster went to the floor, moaning. Laxter swung his bandaged right arm, struck Oafley a glancing blow on the cheek. Oafley stepped in, swinging his right. Laxter missed with a left. For a moment the two men stood toe to toe, slugging wildly, their blows doing but little damage.

Shuster, on the floor, tugged at their trousers legs. "Gentlemen, gentlemen," he pleaded, his voice half muffled by his cut and rapidly swelling lips.

Perry Mason elevated his feet to the desk, tilted back

in his swivel chair and puffed complacently at his cigarette, watching the melee with whimsical humor.

Abruptly, Oafley stepped back. "I'm sorry, Sam," he said. "I forgot your arm was hurt."

Shuster bobbed up between them, a palm against the vest of each, trying to push them apart. The men, breathing hard, paid no attention to his futile efforts, but stood staring at each other.

"Don't worry about my arm," Sam Laxter said bitterly, then glanced at the bandage. It showed a red stain where the wound had been reopened.

"Come away, come away," Shuster said; "he's full of tricks. He's clever. Didn't I warn you before I came in here?"

Oafley said slowly, his chest heaving, his face flushed, "Just keep your tongue off Edith, that's all."

He turned abruptly, crossed the office, jerked open the corridor door. Shuster hesitated a moment, then ran after him, shouting, "Mr. Oafley! Mr. Oafley! Come back here a moment, Mr. Oafley!"

Oafley called back over his shoulder, "You can go to hell. I'm going to get a lawyer of my own."

Shuster looked at Sam Laxter with an expression of consternation on his face, then turned to Perry Mason. "You did it!" he screamed. "You did it deliberately! You turned these men one against the other. You put suspicion in their minds. You made an issue out of Edith DeVoe. You . . ."

"Close the door," Perry Mason interrupted in a calm tone of voice, "as you leave."

Shuster put his hand through Sam Laxter's arm.

"Come," he said. "The law gives us our remedy."

Sam Laxter said bitterly. "He'll get a lawyer and try to pin Granddad's murder on me. What a sweet mess that is."

Shuster pushed him through the door.

"Don't forget to close the door," Mason called.

Shuster banged the door shut with a force which threatened to pull the wall down. The effect of the slam was still shivering the pictures on the walls when Della Street opened the door from the outer office.

"Did you do that on purpose?" she asked.

Mason, smoking calmly, said with a detached air, "There was no sense having both of them support Shuster. As a matter of fact, their interests are adverse. They should have realized it. If Shuster is representing one of them, the other will get another lawyer. That'll mean two lawyers fighting, and that'll be a break for Douglas Keene."

She sighed, as a mother sighs who is confronted by a hopelessly naughty child, then suddenly laughed. "Well," she said, "I got it all down, even including the sound of the blows. Winifred Laxter is in the outer office. She's got a cat with her."

"A cat?" Mason asked.

"Yes, a Persian cat."

Mason's eyes were twinkling as he said, "Tell her to come in."

"And that was true about the police getting the cat from my place," she said. "They told the manager they had to search my apartment. They got a pass-key from her."

"Did they have a warrant?" Mason asked.

"I don't think so."

Mason, smoking his cigarette, said thoughtfully, "It puts you in something of a hole, Della. I'm sorry I didn't think they'd look out there. Sergeant Holcomb is getting better and better—or worse and worse—whichever you want to call it."

"Why does he hate you so much?"

"Simply because he thinks I'm shielding murderers. He's all right; he's just zealous. I don't blame him. And you must admit my manner toward him is a little irritating at times."

144

"I'll say it is."

Mason looked up at her and grinned. "Purposely irritating," he said. "Send Winifred in, and wait in your office. You might listen in."

She opened the door and beckoned. Winifred Laxter entered, a big gray Persian cat on her arm. Her chin was up, her eyes defiant. There was a pugnacious set to her head.

Perry Mason looked her over with amused tolerance. "Sit down," he told her.

"I lied to you," she said, standing by the side of the desk.

"About the cat?" he asked, looking at the Persian.

She nodded. "That cat wasn't Clinker—*this* is Clinker."

"Why did you lie to me?"

"I telephoned Uncle Charles, the caretaker, you know, and told him I wanted him to get rid of Clinker, that I wanted him to let me keep Clinker. He refused. So then I suggested as a next best thing that we could fool Sam Laxter into thinking he'd parted with Clinker. I told him to keep Clinker under cover and I'd send Douglas Keene out with another cat that would look like Clinker. He could use this other cat as a double and let it be very much in evidence, then, if Sam was going to poison any cat, he'd poison the other cat. Don't you see?"

Perry Mason, watching her shrewdly, said, "Sit down and tell me about it."

Her eyes were apprehensive. "Do you believe me?"

"Let's hear the rest of it."

She sat down on the edge of the overstuffed leather chair. The cat struggled to free itself. She held it tightly, smoothing the fur of its forehead, scratching it behind the ears.

"Go on," Mason said.

When she saw that the cat was quiet once more, she said, "Douglas Keene went out there. He took the cat out with him. He waited for some little time for Ashton to show up. Then, he came back to me for instructions. He left the cat with me."

"Why did you tell me that cat was Clinker?"

"Because I was afraid other people would say Douglas had taken Clinker with him, and I wanted to see if you thought that would be too serious. In other words, I wanted to get your reactions."

Mason was laughing now. The cat squirmed restlessly.

"Oh, for goodness sake," Mason said, "let the cat down. Where did you get him?"

She stared steadily at him and then said defiantly, "I don't know what you're talking about. This cat is Clinker. He's very much attached to me."

The cat jumped to the floor.

"It would be a good story," Mason said with a voice that was almost judicial in its complete detachment. "It would help me out of a jam and it would be a swell out for Della Street. The cats sure look alike. But you couldn't get away with it. They'd find out sooner or later where you got the cat. There might be a big difference of opinion as to whether it was Clinker or wasn't Clinker. But in the long run it would put you on a spot, and you're not going to get put on a spot."

"But it *is* Clinker. I went out there and found him. He'd been frightened to death—poor cat—all the noise and excitement and finding his master dead, and everything. . . ."

"No," Mason told her, "I'm not going to let you do it, and that's final. I suppose the papers are on the street and you've read that the police found Clinker in my secretary's apartment."

"They found the cat they *thought* was Clinker."

Mason said good-naturedly, "Baloney! Take your cat and go on back to your waffle parlor. Is Douglas Keene going to get in touch with me and give himself up?"

"I don't know," she said with tears in her eyes.

The cat, arching its back, started exploring the office.

"Kitty—kitty, come, kitty," Winifred pleaded.

The cat paid no attention to her. Mason's eyes were sympathetic as he stared at the tear-stricken countenance. "If Douglas gets in touch with you," he said, "tell him how important it is that he back my play."

"I don't know that I will. You d-d-d-didn't have to go ahead and s-s-s-say that. Suppose they should convict him and hang him for m-m-m-murder?"

Mason crossed to her side, patted her on the shoulder. "Won't you have some confidence in me?" he asked. She raised her eyes.

"Don't you think you've got to take the responsibility of this thing," Mason told her soothingly. "Don't go out picking up cats and figuring how you can work out an alibi for Douglas. You just dump all of that onto my shoulders and let me carry the load. Will you promise that you'll do that?"

Her lips quivered for a moment, then straightened. She nodded her head.

Mason gave her shoulder one last pat, crossed the office to where the cat was sniffing about, picked it up, and carried it back to Winifred and put it in her arms.

"Go home," he said, "and get some sleep."

He held the corridor door open for her. When he had closed it, Della Street stood in the doorway of his private office.

Mason grinned at her. "A dead game kid," he said.

Della Street nodded her head slowly.

Mason said, "How'd you like to cut corners, Della?"

"What do you mean?"

"How'd you like to go on a honeymoon with me?"

She stared at him, eyes growing wide. "A honeymoon?" she asked.

Mason nodded.

"Why . . . oh . . ."

He grinned at her. "Okay," he said, "but first lie down

147

there on the couch and get some sleep. If Douglas Keene rings in on the telephone, tell him that he must back my play. You can put up a stronger talk than I could. I'm going down to Paul Drake's office for a little while."

14

PERRY MASON, SEATED IN PAUL DRAKE'S OFFICE, SAID, "Paul, I want you to turn your men loose on the new car agencies and find out if a new car has recently been sold to a Watson Clammert."

"Watson Clammert," Drake said. "Where the devil have I heard that name before?"

Mason grinned as he waited for Drake's recollection to function. Suddenly the detective said, "Oh, yes, I remember. He's the person who shared a lock box with Charles Ashton."

"I presume the police have gone into that lock box," Mason said.

"Yes, and found it practically empty. They only found some of the paper wrappers used by banks in bundling bills of large denomination. Evidently Ashton had pulled out the bills and left the wrappers behind."

"Ashton or Clammert?" Mason inquired.

"Ashton. The bank records show that Clammert never did go to the safety deposit box. He's nothing but a name signed upon the card, so far as the bank knows."

"How much money do the police figure was taken from the box?"

"They don't know. It may have been a lot. Ashton was seen by one of the attendants stuffing bills into a suitcase."

"Did you check into that automobile accident Laxter had?" Mason asked.

"Yes. He was crowded into a telephone pole, just as he said—some drunken driver whipped around a corner."

"Any witnesses?"

"A few people heard the crash."

"Get their names?" Mason asked.

"Yes. They saw the tracks where Laxter had put on his brakes and skidded. They say he was on his side of the road at the time. He seemed excited, but perfectly sober."

"Where had he been before that?"

Drake said slowly, "I'm checking on that, Perry. When the police first talked with him they were investigating the death of Peter Laxter, the grandfather, and later on the death of Ashton, the caretaker. Laxter had a perfectly good alibi on Ashton's death. He'd left the house about nine o'clock and hadn't returned. Ashton was murdered between ten and eleven."

Mason nodded.

"Later on, Shuster did the talking. He gives Laxter an alibi."

"He does?"

Drake nodded. "Shuster says Laxter was in his office."

"Talking about what?"

"Shuster refuses to state."

"What a sweet alibi that is," Mason said scornfully.

"Wait a minute, Perry, I think it checks."

"How?"

"Jim Brandon, the chauffeur, had been with Laxter. He drove him up to Shuster's office. Around eleven o'clock. Laxter told Brandon to take the car and go on home; that he'd come later. Brandon took the green Pontiac back to the house. That's when he saw Keene. It was shortly after eleven."

Mason started pacing the detective's office, his thumbs hooked in the armholes of his vest, his head thrust forward. At length, he said, in the mumbling monotone of one who is thinking out loud, "Laxter, then, left the house with Jim Brandon in the green Pontiac, but he returned in Ashton's Chevvy. How the hell did he get that Chevvy?"

Drake stiffened to attention. *"That's* a thought," he said.

Mason said slowly, "Paul, put out a bunch of men to cover the apartment house where Edith DeVoe lived. Talk with all the inmates. See if any of them noticed the Chevvy parked anywhere near the apartment house."

Drake pulled a pad of paper toward him and scribbled a memorandum.

"That would make a swell break," he said, "but it would take more than that to make Sam Laxter the fall guy. You see, the person who murdered Ashton must have killed him between ten and eleven. Then he must have taken Ashton's crutch with him and sawed it up into sections. Then he must have gone to Edith DeVoe's place. Now, if Sam Laxter can prove he was in Shuster's office . . ."

"If that's the sketch," Mason interrupted, "and Brandon saw Douglas Keene leaving the house carrying the cat, where was Ashton's crutch? Douglas Keene wasn't carrying it with him."

Drake nodded thoughtfully. "That's so," he admitted, "but, of course, Keene could have tossed the crutch out the window that was always left open for the cat, then driven by in his car and picked it up. I tell you, Perry, you've got a tough case here. If Keene doesn't get in touch with you, it's going to put you in a spot. If he surrenders himself, circumstantial evidence is going to hang him in spite of all you can do."

The telephone rang. Drake answered it, and said, "For you, Perry."

Della Street was on the line. Her voice was excited.

"Come on up quick, Chief," she pleaded. "I've just heard from Douglas Keene."

"Where is he?" Mason asked.

"He's at a public pay station. He's going to call back in five minutes."

"Get a line on that stuff, Paul," he said, "and get it fast. I'm going to be on the move from now on." He dashed out of the office, climbed a flight of stairs and ran down the corridor to his own office. "Is he going to give himself up?" he asked Della Street as he rushed into his private office.

"I think so. He seemed sullen, but I think he's okay."

"Did you give him a good argument?"

"I told him the truth. I told him you were doing everything on earth for him and that he simply couldn't let you down."

"What did he say?"

"He sort of grunted, the way a man does when he's going to do what a girl wants him to but doesn't want to let her think she's having her own way."

Mason groaned, and said, "My God, you women!"

The telephone rang.

"Wait a minute before you answer it," Della Street said. "Do you know who's hanging around the street by the office?"

"Who?"

"Your little playmate—Sergeant Holcomb."

Mason frowned. The telephone rang again.

"Serious?" she asked.

"Yes," he said, "they'll try to arrest him before he can surrender and claim they nabbed him as a fugitive from justice, and . . ."

He picked up the receiver and said, "Hello."

A man's voice said, "This is Douglas Keene, Mr. Mason."

Mason's eyes narrowed thoughtfully.

"Where are you now?"

"Out at Parkway and Seventh Streets."

"Have you got a wrist-watch?" Mason asked.

"Yes."

"What time does it show?"

"Thirteen minutes to eleven."

151

"Make it closer than that. How are you on seconds? Say 'thirty' when it's twelve minutes and thirty seconds to eleven."

"I've passed that," Keene said. "I'll say eleven when it's just exactly eleven minutes to eleven."

"Be sure and call it right on the dot," Mason said, "because . . ."

"Eleven!" Douglas Keene interrupted.

Perry Mason held his watch in his hand. "All right," he said, "you're about twenty-five seconds slow, as compared with my time. But don't change your watch. I'll change my watch so it'll be even with yours. Now, listen, they're going to tail me when I leave the place, hoping I'll lead them to you. You walk down toward my office and stand on the corner of Seventh—that's just west of my office building—you know where that is?"

"Yes."

"At exactly ten minutes past eleven," Mason said, "walk out to the corner and catch the first eastbound street car that comes down Seventh Street. Pay your fare, but don't go inside the car. Stand right by the conductor where you can get off the car when I give you the word. I'll get aboard that car, but won't recognize you or speak to you in any way. A girl will drive right alongside the car in a convertible coupe with the rumble seat open. She'll be going at the same rate of speed the car's going. It may be a block or it may be two blocks after I get aboard, but when I yell, 'Jump,' you make a jump for that rumble seat. Can you do it?"

"Sure I can do it."

"Okay, Douglas, can I depend on you?"

"Yes, you can," the young man said in a voice which had lost its sullen tone. "I guess I've made a damn fool of myself. I'll play ball with you."

"Okay," Mason said. "Remember, ten minutes past eleven."

He hung up the telephone, grabbed his hat and said to Della Street, "You heard what I told him. Can you do it?"

Della Street was adjusting her hat in front of the mirror. "And how!" she said. "Do I leave first?"

"No, I leave first," Mason said.

"And you don't want me to get the car out until after you've reached the corner?"

"That's right. Holcomb will tail me. If he thinks I've got a car, Holcomb will use a car. He'll have one parked somewhere near here. If he thinks I'm walking, he'll walk."

"What'll he do when you take the street car?"

"I don't know. How's your wrist-watch?"

"I was listening over the extension telephone. I synchronized it with his."

"Good girl. Let's go."

Mason ran down the corridor, caught the elevator and managed to give the appearance of strolling casually as he crossed the lobby of the building and reached the street. The thoroughfare was well crowded. Mason took the precaution of glancing hastily over his shoulder, but saw no sign of Sergeant Holcomb. He knew, however, that the Sergeant was on his trail. The officer was too old a hand at the game to crowd his quarry too closely, particularly at the start.

Mason walked half a block up the street, paused in front of a store, looked at his watch, frowned, and looked in a show window, ostensibly trying to kill time. After a minute, he looked again at his wrist-watch, then turned to look up and down the street. He walked a few aimless steps, lit a cigarette, took two puffs, threw the cigarette away and looked at his watch for the third time.

In the street, directly opposite from the place where Mason was standing, was a safety zone. Mason walked aimlessly toward the corner, as though he had a few minutes to kill.

His wrist-watch showed eleven-ten.

Mason watched the signals a block away. A street car came through the signal, rumbled slowly down the block, and came to a stop at the safety zone. The signal changed so it was against the car. Mason acted as though he intended to cross the street, and then, as though changing his mind, paused, undecided. The signal changed. The motorman clanged the bell of the car and sent it across the intersection. As the car rolled past him, Mason swung aboard the rear platform. Douglas Keene was standing by the conductor.

Mason heard the sound of running feet. Sergeant Holcomb, sprinting, just managed to catch the car as it gathered headway. Della Street, driving Mason's convertible coupe with the top down, was coming just behind the street car, holding a line of traffic behind her. As soon as Holcomb boarded the car, Della Street shot the automobile forward, so that the rumble seat was just even with the place where Keene was standing.

"Jump!" shouted Mason.

Keene made a leap for the rumble seat, landed on the cushions, clutched at the top of the car. Mason jumped to the runningboard and clung to the back of the front seat with one hand and the well of the rumble seat with the other. Sergeant Holcomb, who had dropped his fare into the box in front of the conductor, shouted, "Stop! You're under arrest!"

"Give it the gun, Della," Mason said, "and cut in front of the street car."

Della Street's shapely foot pushed the throttle against the floorboards. The car leapt forward. Mason flung one leg over the side of the car and got into the rumble seat.

"Police headquarters," he said to Della, "and give it everything it's got."

Della Street didn't even bother to nod. She cut the corner in a screaming turn. A traffic officer raised a whistle but she was halfway down the block by the time the first blast echoed through the street. Her right palm pressed down on the horn as she drove with her left hand.

Mason paid no attention whatever to the traffic, but concentrated his attention on Douglas Keene.

"Tell me about it," he said, "and don't waste words. Put your lips up close to my ear and shout, because I've got to hear every word you say. Give me just the high-lights."

"Edith DeVoe telephoned me. She'd already told me about finding Sam in the car pumping exhaust fumes into the pipe. She wanted me to come out at once and see her. She said something important had developed. I went out. I rang her doorbell, and there was no answer, but the manager of the apartment house was just coming out. I started to go in through the door as he opened it, and he stopped me and asked me who I was and whom I wanted to see. I told him I had an appointment with Edith DeVoe, and kept right on going. He hesitated for a minute and then went on out. I went down the corridor to Edith DeVoe's room. She was lying on the floor. There was a club near her, and . . ."

"Yes, yes," shouted Mason. "Never mind that. What happened next?"

"I went directly to my apartment. Someone had been there before me. A suit of mine was spattered with blood. I didn't notice it right away."

"That was after you'd taken the cat to Winifred?"

"Yes, I left Winifred and went to my apartment. That was where I got Edith DeVoe's message."

"And you went from your apartment to see Edith?"

"That's right."

"How long after you got back to your apartment did you notice your suit had blood on it?"

"Almost at once."

"Then what did you do?"

"It was a nightmare. I tried to get rid of the bloodstains and couldn't."

"Why didn't you call the officers when you saw Edith DeVoe had been murdered?"

"I just lost my head, that's all. I was afraid they'd try to pin it on me. I was shocked and frightened. I just ran away. Then when I saw my clothes all spattered with blood . . . Ugh! It was a nightmare!"

"Did you kill Ashton?"

155

"Of course not; I didn't even see him."

"Did you go to the house to get the cat?"

"Yes."

"Were you in Ashton's room?"

"Yes."

"Did you look around any?"

The man hesitated. Della Street swung the car to avoid a truck. The car swerved out of control, lurched toward a telephone pole. Della Street fought with the steering wheel. Perry Mason gave but a passing glance to the road ahead as Della struggled to get the car back under control, leaned close to Douglas Keene's ear and said, "Did you look around any while you were in the room?"

Keene hesitated.

"Go on and answer."

"Yes, I was looking for something."

"What?"

"Evidence."

"Evidence of what?"

"I don't know; I thought there was something fishy in the way Ashton had been spending money. I was just looking around. Jim Brandon hinted Ashton had the diamonds in his crutch."

"Did you wear gloves or did you leave fingerprints?"

"I must have left fingerprints."

"Now, look here, Keene, wasn't Ashton there? Wasn't he dead? Aren't you trying to cover up something?"

"No," Keene said, "he wasn't there. I'm telling you the truth."

"You left before he came in?"

"So help me, Mr. Mason, that's the truth."

Della Street had the car back under control. Street intersections whizzed by in flashes. She braked the car for a turn.

"Don't tell anyone what you've told me," Mason said. "You're going to surrender at police headquarters. Refuse to talk unless I'm with you. You've got to do that in order to protect Winifred. If you so much as open your mouth,

Winifred is going to become involved. Can you keep quiet for her sake?"

The youth nodded.

The car skidded as Della Street made the turn, slammed on the brakes and slid to a stop in front of police headquarters. Mason grabbed Keene by the arm, rushed him out of the car and up the steps. As they were about to enter, a commandeered automobile screeched to a stop at the curb and Sergeant Holcomb, with a gun in his right hand, jumped from the car and sprinted after them. Mason rushed Keene down the corridor to a door marked "Homicide Squad," kicked it open and said casually to the man at the desk, "This is Douglas Keene. He's surrendering himself into custody, in accordance with the understanding I had . . ."

The door burst open. Sergeant Holcomb tore into the room.

"I've got you this time," he said to Perry Mason.

"For what?" Mason inquired.

"Resisting arrest."

"I didn't resist arrest."

"I was trying to arrest this man and you took him away from me; I don't give a damn if you did take him to headquarters. I had him arrested before you took him here."

"You can't arrest a man," Mason said, "until you've actually taken him into custody. After you've taken him into custody, he can escape, but there can't be any arrest until the man is in custody."

"But you helped him beat it so I couldn't make the arrest. I'm going to get you for that."

Mason smiled, and said, "You overlook one thing, Sergeant. A private citizen can make an arrest when a felony has in fact been committed and he has reasonable ground to believe that the person he is arresting is the one who committed the felony. *I* put Douglas Keene under arrest."

Sergeant Holcomb pushed the gun back into his holster.

157

The officer behind the desk said, "Take it easy, Sergeant. Mason has surrendered him."

Sergeant Holcomb turned without a word and pushed out of the door. A newspaper reporter came running into the room. He grabbed Mason by the arm. "Do I get an interview with Keene?" he asked.

"Certainly," Mason told him. "I can tell you exactly what Douglas Keene will say, and all he will say. He will say that it is remarkably nice weather we are having for this time of year, and that is all, my dear boy, *ab-so-lute-ly* all."

15

PERRY MASON WAS CHUCKLING AS DELLA STREET DROVE the automobile toward his office. "Turn to the left at Fifth Street, Della," he said, "and go straight to the Union Depot."

"The Union Depot?" she asked.

He nodded. "The office is going to be too hot—you know, too many newspaper men, cops, detectives, district attorneys, and what have you. I want to use the telephone, and I'll go down to the depot while you're packing up."

She deftly avoided a jay-walking pedestrian, and gave Mason a sidelong glance. "What do you mean, while I'm packing up?"

"A couple of suitcases," he said, "a light airplane trunk if you have one."

"I have one."

"All of your party clothes. You're going to stay at an exclusive hotel, and I want you to put on a good show—act the part, you know."

"What's going to be my part?"

"A bride."

"The man in the case?" she inquired, as she slid the car to a stop when a traffic signal turned against her.

"He will only appear long enough to be very suddenly called back to town, interfering with his honeymoon most materially."

She was facing him now with calm, steady eyes, in which there was a mischievous light. "And who is the husband going to be?"

He bowed. "Unaccustomed as I am to honeymoons, I shall do my best to act the part of an awkward groom during the few minutes between the time we register and when I am called back to town upon most urgent business."

Her eyes dwelt upon his profile. Ahead of her a traffic light flashed from red to orange, through orange to green and was unheeded. Behind her a chorus of protesting horns sought to call her to her senses. Her voice was vibrant. "You always believe in acting a part perfectly," she said. "Would it be natural for a newlywed husband to interrupt his honeymoon? . . ."

The growing protest of blaring horns suddenly called her attention to the fact that the traffic on her right was streaming by, while the traffic on the left and directly behind her, being blocked by the car she drove, was expressing its sentiment with all of the impatience which a modern automobile horn is capable of registering.

"Oh, well," she said with whimsical philosophy, as she snapped her eyes back to the road and saw the green light of the traffic signal, "how are those poor fishes behind me going to know I'm a bride just starting on a honeymoon?"

She kicked the gear in, stepped on the throttle, and sent the convertible shooting across the intersection with such speed that she was half way down the block before some of the protesting drivers had fully awakened to the fact that the cause of their protests had departed, and only their own sluggish reactions were holding up the stream of traffic.

Mason lit a cigarette, offered it to her. She took it, and he lit another for himself. "I'm sorry," he said, "to wish this on you, Della, but you're the only one I know whom I can trust."

"On a honeymoon?" she asked dryly.

"On a honeymoon," he answered tonelessly.

She snapped the wheel savagely, making the tires scream as the car slid around to the left and headed toward the Union Depot.

"You don't necessarily need to collect any traffic tickets en route," he observed.

"Shut up," she told him. "I want to collect my thoughts. To hell with the traffic tickets."

She sped down the street, deftly avoiding the vehicles, slid to a stop in front of the Union Depot.

"I meet you here?" she asked.

"Yes," he told her, "with plenty of baggage."

"Okay, Chief."

He left the car, walked around the hood, took off his hat and stood for a moment by the curb. She sat very straight in the seat. Her skirts, well elevated to allow free action of her legs and feet in driving the car, showed her legs to advantage. Her chin was up, her eyes slightly defiant. She smiled into his face. "Anything else?" she asked.

"Yes," he said, "you'll have to practice your best honeymoon manners, and quit calling me Chief."

"Okay," she said ... "Darling," and, leaning forward, pressed her mouth close to his surprised lips. Then, before he could move, she had shot back the clutch, stepped on the throttle and whizzed away from the curb like a bullet, leaving Perry Mason standing on the curb blinking with surprise, lipstick showing on his lips.

Mason heard a chuckle from a newsboy. He grinned rather sheepishly, wiped the lipstick from his mouth, and strode toward the telephone booth.

He put in a call for Winifred Laxter, heard her voice on the telephone, "It's okay, Winifred," he said. "Your boy-friend came through like the trump that I knew he was."

"You mean . . . he's in touch with you?"

"He's in jail," Mason said.

She gave a gasp.

"And," Mason promised her grimly, "he won't stay there long. Don't try to get in touch with me. I won't be at my office. I'll call you as soon as there's anything new. Don't give out any statements to the press, in case any reporters should start looking for interviews. Pose for all the pictures they want, back of your waffle counter, or in front of the place. If you play it right, you should get a lot of advertisement for Winnie's Waffles."

"Advertisement!" she exclaimed contemptuously. "I want Douglas. I want to go to him. I want to see him."

"That's the one thing you can't do. If they'd let you in to see him he'd talk to you, and I don't want him to talk. They probably wouldn't let you in anyway. I don't think it's going to be long now until I have the case cleared up."

"You don't think Douglas is guilty, do you?"

Perry Mason laughed light-heartedly. "No boy that came through the way he did is guilty of anything," he said. "The kid's young, and he lost his head. You can't blame him for that. He was confronted with a frame-up that would have stampeded an older man."

"Then it was a frame-up?"

"Of course, it was a frame-up."

"May I quote you as saying that—you know, in case someone . . ."

"You may not," he told her. "For the next forty-eight hours you may concentrate your attention upon making waffles. Good-by. I'm catching a train," and he hung up before she could protest.

Mason dropped another coin and called Drake's office. Paul Drake, himself, answered the telephone.

"Got a lot for you, Perry," he said. "Do you want it over the telephone?"

"Spill it."

"It's an earful."

"What is it?"

"There was a poker game going on—in the apartment house where Edith DeVoe was murdered. The poker game was on the same floor."

"So what?" Mason inquired.

"So one of the participants in the poker game, reading about the murder, considers it his civic duty to report to the police all about the poker game and about a mysterious gentleman who broke in on the game, saying he was the occupant of an adjoining apartment. That was just about the time the police showed up, and the man had an idea the chap might have been connected with the crime. The police showed him photographs of all the principals in the crime and then, after they checked up on his descriptions, showed him a photograph of you, and he identified it instantly."

"The moral of that story," Mason said, "is: Don't play cards with strangers. What are the cops doing? Are they taking it seriously?"

"I think they are. Sergeant Holcomb is all worked up about it. You sure as hell *do* get around, don't you, Perry?"

"I can't spend *all* my time in my office," Mason grinned. "This was after office hours, wasn't it?"

"Yeah. I thought you should know about it. But here's another funny development. The bird identified one of the other pictures—that of Sam Laxter. He said that he'd seen Sam in the corridor about eleven fifteen. They confronted him with Laxter and he made a positive identification."

"What does Sam say?"

"He isn't saying anything. Shuster is doing all the talking. Shuster says the man was drunk; that the illumination in the hallway wasn't good; that Sam wasn't anywhere near the place; that the man's a publicity seeker; and that Sam Laxter and Douglas Keene look very much alike and that Keene was the one the man saw; that the man wasn't wearing glasses, and that he's a liar."

162

"That's all he's said so far?" Mason asked, grinning into the transmitter.

"Yeah, but give the boy a little time and he'll think up something else."

"I'll say he will. Have the police put Sam under arrest?"

"They're questioning him in the district attorney's office."

"And Shuster isn't present?"

"Shuster naturally isn't present, and Sam isn't talking."

"Do they know just when Edith DeVoe was killed?" Mason asked.

"No. She was dead when the ambulance arrived. Her skull was fractured. Death itself took place shortly before the ambulance got there, but when the blow was struck is another question. She may have died instantly. She may have been unconscious for an hour or two and then died. They can't fix the time of the attack. The police know about the marriage now. They've got a statement from Milton, and Oafley has told them all he knows. The marriage ceremony took place right around ten o'clock. The boys from the poker game came in and helped celebrate. They were in there fifteen or twenty minutes. Then they left. Oafley says he left about ten minutes to eleven."

"Rather strange that Oafley should leave within an hour after the ceremony was performed," Mason said slowly.

"As far as Oafley's concerned, he's in the clear," Drake said. "The officers have checked his story. He left about ten minutes to eleven. He arrived at the house about five or ten minutes after eleven. That gives him a perfect alibi on the Ashton killing. Ashton was killed right around ten thirty. Four or five people can prove that Oafley was in Edith DeVoe's apartment as late as ten twenty anyway, and one person saw him leaving the apartment house a few minutes before eleven. The housekeeper saw him come in about ten minutes after eleven."

"Could Oafley have smashed Edith DeVoe's head before he left her apartment?"

"No, she was alive at eleven o'clock. She knocked on the door where the boys were playing poker and asked to borrow some matches."

"Everyone in the case seems to have been going to Edith DeVoe's apartment last night," Mason said thoughtfully. "She must have been holding a reception."

"It's only natural," Drake told him, "when you consider that she'd been telling what she knew about Sam Laxter. These things get around, you know.

"Frankly, Perry, you've got a swell break. Things look pretty black for Sam Laxter right now. The only alibi he has to tie to is that he was in Shuster's office while Ashton was being murdered. It's now come out that Shuster had been tipped off when Burger made arrangements to exhume Peter Laxter's body, so Shuster telephoned Sam and Sam came to his office."

"Find out anything about that Chevrolet?" Mason asked.

"I can't prove it's the same Chevrolet," Drake said, "but a couple of people noticed an old Chevvy with a crumpled fender parked in front of the apartment house where Edith De Voe lived, about eleven o'clock. One witness remembered it because he said there was a new Buick parked right behind it and he noticed the contrast in the two cars."

Mason said slowly, "Could you see that the police were tipped off to ask Sam Laxter how it happened he left his house in the green Pontiac and came back in the caretaker's Chevrolet?"

"I could tip them off to ask, but it wouldn't do any good. Laxter is keeping quiet. He's making a lot of mysterious references to the old stand-by—the married woman with whom he spent an hour after leaving Shuster's office. He won't jeopardize her good name."

Mason laughed heartily. "My God," he said, "hasn't

Shuster worn out that alibi yet? Every one of his clients has used it for the past ten years."

"It sometimes gets by with a jury," Drake pointed out. "But, anyway, it gives your man, Keene, a swell break if you play it right."

"I'm going to play it right," Mason promised him grimly. "How about the Clammert automobile, did you find out anything?"

"Some," Drake said. "I find that Watson Clammert purchased a Buick sedan and had a state license issued to him. The number is 3D44-16. I haven't been able to get the engine number or the body number, but we'll get them. He took a full coverage policy with the International Automotive Indemnity Exchange."

"Did you get a description of him?" Mason asked.

"No. But I'm working on it."

"Quit working on it, then. Drop Watson Clammert like a hot potato. Call in your men. Tell them not to ask any more questions. You've done a swell job, Paul. And now you can go get some sleep."

"You mean you don't want anything more?"

"Not another thing. So far as you're concerned, the case is closed. Further inquiries are just going to make trouble."

Drake said slowly, "Well, you know your business, Perry. . . . Here's a tip for you. I got it from headquarters. The police are planning to rush through a preliminary hearing for Douglas Keene and call Sam Laxter as a witness. Then they'll ask him where he was at the time the murder was committed. Laxter will be given his choice of naming the woman or going to jail for contempt."

"Under the circumstances, he'll probably go to jail for contempt and get a lot of newspaper sympathy," Mason said. "Anything else?"

"Ashton is mixed up in things pretty deep," Drake said. "The detectives are beginning to think he copped off most of Laxter's coin. Does that mean anything special to you?"

"Sure, it does. It's the whole case. The whole business hinges on Ashton," Mason replied.

As Paul Drake asked an excited question, the lawyer pretended not to hear and said, "Well, I'm taking a train, Paul. Good-by."

He hung up the receiver, looked at his wrist-watch, crossed to a haberdashery store which made a specialty of supplying the needs of travelers, purchased several handbags, a few articles of clothing, and then returned to the depot. He went to the telegraph office and sent a telegram addressed to Watson Clammert, care of the Hotel Biltmore, Santa Barbara. The telegram read:

LONG DISTANCE TELEPHONE CONVERSATION WITH YOUR NEW YORK ASSOCIATES ADVISES INDUSTRY THREATENED WITH NEW CODE CONTAINING REGULATION AFFECTING YOUR PROPOSED CONSOLIDATION DISASTROUSLY STOP ABSOLUTELY IMPERATIVE YOU BE ON GROUND AT EARLIEST POSSIBLE MOMENT STOP PLEASE CHARTER AIRPLANE FROM SANTA BARBARA FLY TO LOS ANGELES AND CATCH FIRST TRANSCONTINENTAL PLANE EAST STOP ADVISABLE KEEP THIS MOVE CONCEALED FROM OPPOSITION THEREFORE HAVE PURCHASED TICKET FOR YOU UNDER ASSUMED NAME AND WILL HOLD HERE AWAITING YOUR ARRIVAL

Mason unhesitatingly signed the partnership name of the leading law firm in the city, a law firm of financial and political prestige, which specialized only in the most remunerative of corporate and probate business.

He paid for the telegram and saw that it was dispatched.

He consulted his wrist-watch, stretched, yawned, and then, with a chuckle, proceeded to the telephone booth. He looked up the number of Hamilton Burger's residential telephone, together with the address, then called the

166

telephone company and said, "I want to send a telegram, please."

After a moment, a young woman's voice said, "To whom is your message going?"

"Thelma Pixley, 3824 East Washington Street."

"And what is the message?" the feminine voice asked.

"Greatly impressed by your personality appearance and ability," Mason dictated slowly. *"In view of what has recently happened you will probably be out of a job. I would like very much to have you work for me. I am a bachelor and will pay you good wages. I will treat you with every consideration. Please come to my office at your earliest convenience bringing this telegram with you and we can discuss wages."*

"By whom is the telegram to be signed?" asked the business-like feminine voice.

"Hamilton Burger."

"It's to be charged to your telephone, Mr. Burger?"

"Yes."

"What's the number, please?"

"Exposition 96949."

"And the address?"

"3297 West Lakeside."

"Thank you, Mr. Burger," the voice said.

Mason hung up, left the telephone booth, and stood by the main entrance to the depot smoking cigarettes until Della Street swung his car in close to the curb, then Mason nodded to the red-cap porter. The porter piled Mason's baggage into the rumble seat, having some difficulty to find room for it.

"Now then," Mason said, "I want to buy a new Buick sedan, but I want to stop at one of the outlying agencies. First we'd better stop by the bank and pick up some money."

Della Street was all crisp business efficiency. There was no reference, by word or look, to the manner in which she had played the part of a bride when she had first driven away from the station.

"Okay Chief," she said.

Mason smiled slightly, but said nothing.

She ran the car through the snarl of traffic, stopped at the bank. Mason, consulting his watch to see that he had time before the bank closed, said, "Park in front of the fire plug, Della; I'll only be gone long enough to cash a check."

He entered the bank, secured three thousand dollars in cash, thrust it into his pocket, returned to the car and said, "We want a Buick agency away from the business district. I have a list of them. Let's see, here's one in Franklin that should be just about what we want."

Mason sat back and smoked. Della Street drove the car with silent skill. "This the place?" she asked.

"Yes."

"Do I come in?"

"No. You stay out here with this car. I'll drive the other one away."

Mason entered the car agency. A suave salesman came toward him smiling. "Interested in the new models?" he asked.

"I wish to buy a new sedan. What's the price, fully equipped?"

The salesman took a notebook from his pocket, mentioned the amount. "Now if you'd like a demonstration,' he said, "we can arrange to . . ."

He broke off in gasping surprise as Mason pulled a wallet from his pocket and started counting out bills.

"I'd prefer to purchase a demonstrator, if you have one in that model," Mason said.

The salesman gasped, then adjusted himself to the situation.

"Ah, yes, I'll fix up the papers at once. What's the name please?"

"Clammert, C-l-a-m-m-e-r-t, Watson Clammert," Maso

said. "I'm in a hurry. I want to get a certificate of ownership, or whatever it is I need."

Fifteen minutes later, Mason, impatient at the delay, drove a spotless demonstrator from the side door of the agency. He gave an almost imperceptible gesture to Della Street and she followed him around the corner. A block away, Mason stopped and transferred the baggage from the convertible coupe to the sedan. "Now," he told her, "we stop at the first storage garage we come to and store the convertible. You drive the Buick. I'll drive the coupe. I'll take the lead. When I turn in to a garage, you stop out in front."

"When does the honeymoon start?" she asked.

"Just as soon as I emerge from the garage," Mason told her, grinning.

"And you want to make a real honeymoon of it?"

He looked at her sharply.

"I mean," she said, with wide-eyed innocence, "do you want it to *look* like a real honeymoon?"

"Of course."

She nodded and chuckled.

Mason drove down the street some half-dozen blocks, then turned into a storage garage. A few minutes later he came out sliding the storage check into his pocket.

"The next move in our honeymoon," he said, "is the Biltmore in Santa Barbara. You are now Mrs. Watson Clammert. I'll give you more detailed instructions on the way up. And, incidentally, this car is supposed to have plenty of speed under the hood. Have you ever been pinched for speeding?"

"Not this year."

"It might, then, be advisable to take a chance."

He settled back against the cushions.

"Yes, dear," Della Street said demurely and slammed her neatly shod foot against the accelerator with such violence that the resulting forward leap of the automobile all but jerked Mason's head off.

16

Swift-moving bellboys deftly removed the baggage from the new Buick. The western sun, slanting into the Pacific Ocean, silhouetted the fronds of the palm trees, etching them blackly brilliant against the gold of the ocean and the deep blue of the sky. The luxurious hotel, with its exotic setting, seemed to radiate the calm tranquility of the days of the Spaniards.

"An ideal place for a honeymoon," Mason said, escorting Della Street through the door.

Mason approached the desk. The clerk handed him a registration card and a fountain pen.

Mason wrote the name, "Watson Clammert," and then heard a startled feminine exclamation from behind him, followed by a titter.

He turned. Della Street, shaking out her coat, had cascaded a shower of rice to the floor. The clerk smiled. Mason looked completely nonplused, then sighed as he caught the roguish twinkle in Della Street's eyes.

"I'm sorry, dear," she said.

Mason turned to the smiling clerk.

The clerk turned the card to look at the name, then reached into a compartment below the desk. "A telegram for you, Mr. Clammert," he said.

Mason frowned, opened the telegram, and spread it on the counter. Della Street came near, sliding her hand around his neck as she pressed her cheek up against his shoulder.

She gave a startled gasp as she read the telegram. Mason's exclamation was one of annoyance.

"But you're not going, dear!" Della Street protested.

Mason turned away from the counter, leaving the telegram unheeded. "Of course not," he said. "I wouldn't think of going . . . and yet . . ."

"Business has always interfered," she said, her voice seemingly perilously near to tears.

The clerk and bellboys watched the tableau.

"At any rate," Mason remarked, somewhat stiffly, to the clerk, "we'll go to our room."

He strode toward the elevator.

"But you didn't tell me what you wanted," the clerk said. "We have . . ."

"The best in the house," Mason snapped, "and make it snappy."

"Yes, Mr. Clammert," the clerk said, handing the key to one of the bellboys.

They stood waiting for the elevator. Della Street started to cry. "I know you're going," she sobbed into her handkerchief.

Mason stood very erect, frowning. His eyes dropped to his handbag. And old shoe dangled from the handle. "How the devil," he asked, "did . . ."

Della Street continued to sob into her handkerchief.

The elevator slid to a stop. The door opened. Mason and Della Street entered, followed by the bellboy. Five minutes later they were ensconced in a corner suite which looked over the calm blue waters.

"You little devil," Mason said as the door closed. "What was the idea of all the rice business and the old shoe?"

Her eyes were too innocent. "I thought you wanted to make it seem convincing," she said, "and I had to do something. After all, you weren't very much like a bridegroom. To my mind, you seemed to fall down on your acting. You seemed to play more the part of a business man or a busy lawyer than a bridegroom. You didn't show any affection whatever."

171

"Grooms don't kiss their brides in the hotel lobbies," he said. . . . "Say, were you really crying? You sounded like it."

Della Street ignored his question. "You see I haven't been married before. All I know is what my friends have told me and what I've read. What are we supposed to do next? Do we stroll out hand in hand to watch the sunset?"

Mason grabbed her shoulders and shook her. "Snap out of it, you little devil, and quit your kidding. Do you remember the part you're to play?"

"Of course, I do."

Mason opened his suitcase, took out an onion. Gravely he cut it in two and handed it to her. "Smell," he said.

She made a grimace of distaste, held the onion under her eyes, moved it back and forth. Mason, standing by the telephone, watched the result of the onion application with a nod of approval. Della Street dropped the onion and reached for her handkerchief. Mason took down the receiver and said to the operator, "Get me the room clerk."

Della Street came and leaned against his shoulder. Her sobs were plainly audible.

When Mason heard the voice of the room clerk, he said, "This is Watson Clammert. I want to charter a plane at once. Will you make the necessary arrangements and get me transportation to the airport? I'm leaving my wife here and she'll keep my car. She isn't going with me to the airport."

"Very well," the clerk said. "Incidentally, Mr. Clammert, you left your telegram here on the counter. I'm having a bellboy bring it up."

"Okay," Mason said. "The boy can take my baggage down with him. I want to leave within ten minutes. Can you arrange it?"

"I can try," the clerk promised.

Della Street rubbed her tear-reddened eyes.

"The honeymoon is over," she sobbed. "I knew you'd

go busting away on business. You d-d-d-don't l-l-l-love me."

Mason grinned at her. "Save it for the lobby," he said.

"How do you know I'm not s-s-s-sincere?" she sobbed.

A puzzled look came over his face. He strode to her, stood for a moment staring down at the slender sobbing figure.

"The devil," he said, and pulled her hand from her face.

She looked up at him with a grin, but there were tears on her cheeks.

Mason's state showed puzzled perplexity.

"Onion tears," she said, grinning.

There was a knock on the door. Mason crossed to the door and opened it. A bellboy handed him the folded telegram and said, "You had some baggage?"

Mason indicated his bags. The boy picked them up. Mason and Della Street followed him to the lobby. Della Street managed to convey the impression of a young woman who has been crying, who is very much hurt, somewhat angry, and defies the public to do its damnedest in the line of speculating.

She glanced with haughty defiance at the clerk. The clerk averted his gaze from her tear-reddened eyes. She turned to a bellboy, and the boy's incipient smile faded into expressionless servility.

"Remember, dear," Perry Mason said, "about that automobile. Now you're inclined to drive too fast. That's a new automobile and it isn't broken in yet. Don't drive it too fast, and change the oil just as the instruction book says."

"Yes, dear," Della Street said.

"And remember, if anyone should ring up, don't tell them I'm not here. Tell them that I can't come to the telephone, tell them that I'm down with influenza; tell them I'm out playing polo; tell them anything, but don't let on that I'm not here."

"Yes, dear."

"And I'll come back just as soon as I can make the round trip. I won't need to be in New York more than two hours."

Della Street turned away and said nothing.

A taxi driver entered the hotel. The clerk nodded to Perry Mason. "Your arrangements are all made, Mr. Clammert."

"That," Mason grunted, "is what I call service."

He nodded to the bellboy, started for the door, then stopped, turned awkwardly to Della Street.

"Good-by, darling," he said.

She flashed across the distance between them, a bundle of flying clothes and outflung arms. She clasped her arms around his neck, drew his head down to her savagely, clung against him while her lips sought his, found them, and held them in a long, close embrace.

There was something of startled surprise in Perry Mason's face as she released him. He took a quick step toward her. "Della," he said, "you . . ."

She pushed him away.

"Hurry, Watson Clammert," she said, "and get that airplane. You know how vitally important it is for you to get to New York."

For a moment Mason stood uncertainly, then turned and strode from the hotel lobby.

Della Street placed her handkerchief to her eyes, walked unsteadily toward the elevator.

The hotel clerk shrugged his shoulders and turned away. After all, it was none of his business. He was there to give service. A guest had demanded an airplane at ten minutes' notice, and the clerk had seen that he was accommodated.

17

DELLA STREET CAME RUNNING INTO THE LOBBY OF THE hotel. "Oh!" she screamed. "Oh."

The clerk gave one glance at her face, then moved swiftly from behind the counter, and came to her solicitously. "What is it, Mrs. Clammert? . . . Not the plane? It couldn't be the plane!"

She held her knuckles to her lips, shook her head at him, her eyes wide and startled. Twice she tried to talk, and both times managed only to give a little gasp.

The clerk was solicitous, as became his position. Nor was he unaware of the beauty of this fragile and disappointed bride, whose husband had been called away from her side at the very inception of the honeymoon. His hand patted her shoulder comfortingly. "My dear young woman," he said, "what is it?"

"The car!" she gasped.

"The car?"

"Yes. Watson's new Buick. Oh, he thinks the world of it."

"I've seen it," the clerk said; "it's a beauty. What's happened to it?"

"It's been stolen."

"Stolen? From the grounds here? Impossible!"

"Not from the grounds," she said, shaking her head. "I drove up the road for a ways, parked the car, and went down to sit on the beach. I guess I was careless and left my ignition keys in it. I came back and it was gone."

"Well, we can get it," the clerk said grimly. "It doesn't stand much chance of getting out of the county without being caught. What's the license number?"

Della Street shook her head helplessly. Then seized with a sudden inspiration, said, "Oh, I know. Call up the International Automotive Indemnity Exchange. Call them at my expense. We had the car insured a few days ago. They can look up the insurance records. My husband has the policy and I don't know where it is. But you can explain to them the car has been stolen, and they'll give you the license number and the engine number and all of that data you require."

The clerk was already in motion. He said to the telephone operator, "Get me the International Automotive Indemnity Exchange on long distance, and get me the sheriff's office at the court house. Better get the insurance company first."

Her fingers flew over the switchboard with swift skill.

"I'm afraid I'm making a lot of trouble," Della Street said.

"Not at all, Mrs. Clammert. I'm only sorry something like this should happen to mar the pleasure of your stay."

Then the clerk, suddenly realizing that the pleasure of her stay had been marred by much more than the loss of an automobile, became silent and embarrassed.

The girl at the switchboard said, "Do you want your call in a booth, Mr. Maxwell?"

"Perhaps I'd better."

"Booth one," she said.

The clerk stepped into the booth, and a few moments later emerged holding a slip of paper upon which he had penciled numbers.

"Now then," he said to the operator, "the sheriff's office."

"They're already waiting on the line," she told him.

The clerk stepped into the booth once more, then came out, smiling.

"You may rest assured that the car will be recovered, Mrs. Clammert. The sheriff's office is notifying the state motorcycle officers and the sheriff's office in Ventura, in

Los Angeles, in San Luis Obispo, Bakersfield, and Salinas. They'll have the roads completely sewed up. What's more, they'll have a radio broadcast giving the numbers, and wires are going out to the Division of Motor Vehicles and to the border patrol stations on the highways into Arizona, Mexico and Oregon."

"Thank you so much," she said. "Oh, I'm so completely desolated. I think I'll pack up and go to Los Angeles, and then return after my husband comes back. I don't want to stay here without him."

"We should be very sorry to lose you," the clerk said, "but I understand how you feel, Mrs. Clammert."

Della Street nodded her head with quick determination.

"Yes," she said, "I'm going to Los Angeles."

"Where can I notify you about the automobile?"

She frowned for a moment, and then said, "Oh, just notify the insurance company and my husband's lawyers will keep in touch with them. After all, I guess it's not so serious. It's up to them to supply us with a new car, isn't it?"

"Oh, you'll get your car back, Mrs. Clammert. Probably some hitch-hiker took it to get over a few miles of road. He'll abandon it by the side of the road somewhere when he runs out of gas, or, if he doesn't, he'll be picked up by some of the officers who'll be patrolling the highway."

"Well," Della Street said, "I guess the insurance company will take care of it. You've been very, very nice here, and I'm sorry I couldn't stay longer, but you understand how it is."

The clerk assured her that he understood, prepared her bill and saw that her baggage was safely started for the depot.

Perry Mason was seated in his office, reading mail, when the door opened and Della Street appeared in the doorway, carrying a hatbox.

"Well," he said, "how's the disappointed bride?"

She was all crisp efficiency. "Everything went off okay, Chief. They're notifying the motor patrols, and the border stations."

"Yes," Mason said, "I heard the reports on the police calls."

"The clerk was most solicitous," she said. "He remembered the new Buick and thought it was such a beauty and hoped I wouldn't be deprived of it more than a day or two. . . . Tell me first: Why did you go to all this trouble simply to get the police to report a car as stolen? Couldn't you have simply used a telephone and . . ."

He interrupted her with a smiling shake of the head. "You wouldn't deprive me of my honeymoon, Della!"

"You deprived yourself of it," she retorted, "and you still haven't answered my question."

"I wanted Watson Clammert arrested," he said slowly. "I wanted him arrested under such circumstances that he would appear to be a professional car thief. I couldn't have brought about that result by any ordinary means, since I didn't dare to make a formal charge in my own name and didn't dare to sign a complaint in any name. My theory may be wrong, in which event I can't afford to leave any back trail the police or Clammert could follow. We needed someone who would enlist the sympathy and active coöperation of the police without signing a complaint and without leaving a back trail. The Biltmore Hotel is a big factor in Santa Barbara and the sheriff of Santa Barbara County is sufficiently important to get all sorts of political cooperation. But the Biltmore Hotel most certainly wouldn't have acted as a cat's paw to pull our chestnuts out of the fire unless we had established ourselves so firmly with them that it would never have occurred to them to question your identity.

"It took human interest to do that, and the best way to get human interest was to give the clerk an orchestra seat and let him become a sympathetic spectator of your blasted romance."

"And would you tell me just what chestnuts you expect to have pulled from the fire?" she inquired.

Mason shook his head. "Not now," he said. . . . "Did you come down on the train?"

"No, I had the hotel take my stuff to the depot and then I chartered a car to drive me down."

"Leave any back trail?"

"No."

"Good girl. They're rushing things with Douglas Keene. They start the hearing at two o'clock this afternoon."

She stared at him with startled eyes. "You mean they're going to start the preliminary at two o'clock this afternoon? Why, it's twenty minutes to two now."

He nodded. "I was just getting my things together ready to go down there. Want to go?"

"Of course, I want to go."

"Drop your hatbox then, and come on. I'll talk things over in the taxi."

"But why let them rush things? Couldn't you have held them off?"

"I think," he told her with a grin, "things are coming along in good shape. I want to have them rushed."

"Why?"

"Partially to get the suspense of those two kids over with, and partially to get even with Sergeant Holcomb."

"How do you mean?"

"If Sergeant Holcomb solves the mystery," Perry Mason said with a grin, "*he* gets the credit. If I solve the mystery *I* get the credit."

"You think Sergeant Holcomb could clear it up?"

"I think it will be cleared up for him. That is, I think the machinery has been set in motion. It won't be long before the situation clarifies itself, and I want to beat everyone to it. You know me. I'm a great grandstander."

Her eyes were more expressive than her voice, and her voice held that peculiar, low, vibrant note which characterized her when emotions mastered her. "You're the squarest-shooting man in the world," she said. And then, as he looked up, she added with a grin, "And one of the most unsatisfactory bridegrooms. You've no idea how sympathetic that hotel clerk felt toward me."

18

SPECTATORS PUSHED AND JOSTLED, FILLING JUDGE Pennymaker's courtroom to capacity.

Dick Truslow, one of Hamilton Burger's most trusted trial deputies, grinned across the counsel table at Perry Mason.

Truslow had that attribute of a dangerous fighter—an ability fully to appreciate the strong points of an antagonist—a personal liking which could instantly be laid aside to give place to official combativeness.

"Is Shuster going to be associated with you in this case?" Truslow asked.

"He'll probably try to expectorate his way into it before we get done," Mason remarked. "The other day saw him talking in the bright sunlight and there was a rainbow in front of his lips."

Truslow laughed, then lowered his voice confidentially. "You should see Hamilton Burger," he said. "He's having a fit."

"What's the matter?"

"Of course," Truslow said, closing one eye, "I wouldn'

want to be quoted, but the Chief has been shooting off his face that it's all bosh and poppycock, this contention of yours that anyone could send a telegram in another person's name if he had a reasonable amount of assurance and a knowledge of the address and telephone number of the person he was impersonating."

Mason managed to look innocent.

"So *someone*," Truslow said, chuckling, "sent the widowed housekeeper out at Laxter's place a telegram, and signed the Chief's name to it."

"What was in it?" Mason asked, with a perfectly straight face.

Truslow said, "Don't look around—she's looking this way—wait a minute. . . . There, now take a look—over your left shoulder. See her standing there with the telegram? Look at the simpering look on her face. She thinks it's nothing less than a proposal of marriage."

"What does the district attorney think?" Mason inquired.

"I can't tell you," Truslow said, "not unless you put cotton in your ears."

Mason smiled. "Has it changed your contention in regard to the source of that Winifred Laxter telegram?"

"Well, my instructions were not to bear down too hard on it . . . but I'm afraid I've got you this time, Perry. We've got a pretty damn good case of circumstantial evidence. You're not going to resist having the defendant bound over, are you?"

"Oh, I think so," Mason said.

"Ten to one you can't get anywhere. You might kid a jury into giving you a break, but you're never going to be able to get past the preliminary."

Mason lit a cigarette, then almost immediately dropped it into a cuspidor, as Judge Pennymaker pushed open the door of his Chambers and took his place on the Bench. The court was formally called to order. Dick Truslow rose to address the Bench. "Your Honor, the preliminary hearing in this case is for the purpose of determining whether there are reasonable grounds to hold over Douglas Keene on a charge of first degree murder—to wit, the murder of one Edith DeVoe, but, in order to show the motive for that murder, it will be necessary for us to introduce evidence relating to the murder of one Charles Ashton. However, may it be understood that any evidence looking to the death of Ashton is limited solely for the purpose of fixing a motive so far as the murder of Edith DeVoe is concerned, and we will not introduce that evidence or seek to have it considered for any other purpose."

"Any objection on the part of the Defense?" Judge Pennymaker asked.

"We'll make our objections at the proper time," Mason said, "as the questions themselves come up."

"I'm not trying to limit Counsel," Truslow said, "I merely wanted to explain our position to the Court. I thought perhaps I might eliminate some objections by the Defense in stating my position."

"Proceed with the case," Pennymaker said. "The defendant is in court?"

"He is coming in now, your Honor," Truslow said.

A deputy led Douglas Keene into the courtroom. He looked somewhat pale, but his head was back and his chin held high. Mason crossed to him, squeezed his arm reassuringly. "Sit down, lad," he said, "and keep your head. It won't be long now until the whole thing is cleared up."

"The first witness on behalf of the prosecution," Truslow said, "is Tom Glassman."

Glassman came forward, was sworn, testified that he was an attaché of the district attorney's office; that on the evening of the twenty-third instant he had gone to the apartment of Edith DeVoe; that in the apartment a woman lay sprawled on the floor, there were wounds on er head, and nearby lay a club; that the club was smeared with blood.

"I show you a photograph," Truslow said, "merely for the purpose of identification, and ask you if that is a photograph showing the features of the young woman you saw lying on the floor at that time."

"It is."

"We'll connect up the photograph and introduce it later," Truslow said. "We would now like to have it marked for identification."

He asked several more perfunctory questions and said to Perry Mason, "You may cross-examine."

"On that bit of club which you found by the body of the unconscious woman," Mason said, "there was a fingerprint, was there not?"

"There was."

"You photographed that fingerprint?"

"I did."

"Was that a fingerprint made by the defendant?"

"It was not."

"Was it a fingerprint of Sam Laxter, Frank Oafley, or any of the servants in the Laxter household?"

"It was not."

"Naturally, you made an attempt to identify that fingerprint?"

"Naturally."

"You were unable to do so?"

"That's right."

"You had been to the Laxter residence earlier in the evening, had you not?"

"I had."

"And you there found the body of Charles Ashton, the caretaker?"

"I did."

"That body was lying on the bed of Ashton's room?"

"It was."

"Ashton was dead, was he not? And death was due to

strangulation inflicted by a cord which had been throw around his neck and drawn taut?"

"That is correct."

"And there were cat tracks up and down the bed?"

"Yes, sir."

"Did you make any attempt to ascertain whether tho cat tracks had been made before or after the death Charles Ashton?"

"I did."

"When were they made—before or afterwards?"

Truslow's face showed surprise at this line of interrogation.

"Afterwards."

"I thought," Truslow said, with a slightly nervous laug "that we were going to have quite a fight to get this ev dence in, but I see you are bringing it out. While it pro ably isn't proper cross-examination, strictly speaking, certainly am making no objection."

"I want to get all the facts in," Perry Mason said. An turning to the witness, went on, "When you arrived the Laxter house, Samuel Laxter was not there?"

"He was not."

"He showed up later on?"

"That is right."

"His automobile was damaged and his right arm w injured?"

"That is correct."

"But Frank Oafley was there?"

"Yes, sir."

"Where was he when you drove up?"

"I don't know where he was when we drove up, b cause we stopped in the garage to make a search of t automobiles, but when we reached the main terrace which the house is situated, we noticed a man digging the ground near a corner of the house. We turned o flashlights on him, and it was Mr. Oafley."

"That's all the cross-examination I have," Mason sa

Truslow, looking rather puzzled, remarked, "I think we'll get the *corpus delicti* definitely established, your Honor."

Mason slumped back into his chair with the manner of a man who has no further interest in the proceedings. Nor did he ask so much as a question while Truslow called the autopsy surgeon, then put on witnesses who identified the dead woman; who identified the club as having been sawed from a crutch; witnesses who testified to the type of crutch used by Charles Ashton and who stated that, to the best of their belief, the blood-stained club which was offered in evidence by Truslow, was part of Ashton's crutch, or, at least, a crutch similar in appearance.

Truslow brought Babson the cabinetmaker to the stand, who positively identified the section of the crutch, due to certain scratches which appeared on it, and testified how Ashton had employed him to hollow a receptacle into the crutch, and line that receptacle with chamois skin. Then, by other witnesses, Truslow brought out the value of the Koltsdorf diamonds, the fact that Peter Laxter was very much attached to them and never let them out of his possession.

"Call Samuel Laxter," Truslow announced at length.

Samuel Laxter took the witness stand.

"Your name is Samuel Laxter; you reside in the Laxter household?"

"That is correct."

"You are a grandson of Peter Laxter, deceased? You resided in what was known as the country house for several months prior to the time it burned, and then you took up your residence in what is known as the town house?"

"Correct."

"You were acquainted with Edith DeVoe?"

"Yes, sir."

"You saw her body in the morgue?"

185

"Yes, sir."

"She was dead?"

"That is right."

"And the body you saw was the same as that picture in the photograph, People's Exhibit No. 1?"

"That is correct."

"And that was Edith De Voe?"

"That is right."

"Where were you on the evening of the twenty-thir between the hours of nine o'clock in the evening and ap proximately eleven-thirty at night?"

"I refuse to answer."

Truslow smiled. "You can't refuse to answer," he sai "without being guilty of contempt of court. That sto about protecting some mysterious woman won't go her Laxter. You're in a court of justice—you've got answer."

Nat Shuster came bustling forward.

"If the court please," he said, "it now appears that attempt is being made to malign the character of th witness by extraneous questions. He is not accused of t murder and if he was not accused of the murder, it mak no difference where he was unless he was present at t place where the murder was being committed."

"You're appearing for Mr. Laxter?" Judge Penn maker asked.

"Yes, your Honor."

"I," Mason observed, "am making no objection to t question."

"I am going to order the witness to answer the qu tion," Judge Pennymaker stated.

"I refuse to answer."

Judge Pennymaker's face clouded.

Shuster leaned across the counsel table. "Go on," said; "say the rest of it."

"Upon the ground that the answer might tend to

186

criminate me," Laxter said, after the manner of one who has learned his speech by heart.

Shuster smiled, and turned toward the Court.

"I want the Court to understand," he said, "that the answer would not tend to incriminate him, so far as any crime under discussion is concerned, but I believe there is a city ordinance which might have been violated by this witness, and, inasmuch as we are technically able to back up our position on such grounds, I have instructed my client to protect the good name of the young woman involved in the case."

"Bosh and nonsense and grandstand!" Mason said.

Judge Pennymaker pounded with his gavel.

"That will do, Counselor. You have no right to make any such statement."

Perry Mason nodded. "That is right, your Honor, but on the other hand, Counsel for Mr. Laxter has no right to make any such statement—a statement which is intended only to appeal to the newspapers."

Shuster waved his arms excitedly. "Your Honor, I resent that accusation."

Truslow's voice boomed out over the hysterical comments of the excited lawyer, "I agree with Counselor Mason, your Honor. However, it is all immaterial. I now offer this witness immunity from prosecution for any crime other than that of murder and again repeat my question."

"Again I refuse," Laxter said doggedly, "on the ground that the answer would incriminate me."

"You were not at the Laxter residence at the time Ashton was murdered?" Truslow asked.

"I was not."

"Where were you?"

"I was in Nathaniel Shuster's office. I was there from before ten o'clock until after eleven."

"Was anyone there with you?"

"Nathaniel Shuster."

"Anyone else?"

"James Brandon."

"Who is James Brandon?"

"He's employed as chauffeur and butler."

"Was he present in the discussion which took place between you and Nathaniel Shuster?"

"No, sir, he sat in the outer office."

"When did he leave?"

"About ten minutes before eleven o'clock I told him that he might go home. There was no need for him to wait any longer."

"Then what did you do?"

"I stayed on in Nathaniel Shuster's office for a few minutes."

"Then where did you go?"

"I refuse to answer, upon the same ground—the answer would tend to incriminate me."

"Incriminate you in what way and for what crime?"

"I refuse to answer."

Truslow said disgustedly, "I think that's all. I'm going to ask the Grand Jury to investigate this matter."

Laxter started to leave the witness stand. Nat Shuster's teeth were quite evident as he smiled triumphantly.

"Just one moment," Perry Mason said. "I believe I have the right to cross-examine this witness."

"But he hasn't testified to anything," Shuster objected.

"Sit down, Counselor Shuster," Judge Pennymaker ordered. "Counselor Mason has the right to cross-examine upon any of the testimony given by this witness."

Mason faced Sam Laxter.

"You drove to Shuster's office with Jim Brandon?"

"That's right, yes, sir."

"And you drove in the green Pontiac?"

"That's right."

"You know where Douglas Keene's apartment is?"

"Yes."

"Did you on the night of the twenty-third?"

"I can't remember. . . . I think perhaps I did."

"Hadn't you called on him there some time prior to the twenty-third?"

"I think perhaps I had been there, yes."

"After you left Shuster's office, didn't you go to Edith DeVoe's apartment?"

"I refuse to answer."

"And at that time wasn't the Chevolet automobile customarily driven by Charles Ashton, the caretaker, parked in front of Edith DeVoe's apartment house?"

Shuster fidgeted uneasily, leaned forward as though about to burst into speech.

Laxter said in an even monotone, "I refuse to answer."

"Now, then," Mason said, "didn't you enter Edith DeVoe's apartment? Did you find her lying on the floor, unconscious? Didn't you realize that she had previously made accusations which virtually amounted to charging you with the murder of your grandfather? Didn't you thereupon rush from the apartment where she was lying, enter the Chevolet automobile, drive it to Keene's apartment, cut your arm with a knife, razor blade, or other deep instrument, leave blood stains on Keene's garments, telephone Nathaniel Shuster, explain to him what had happened; that you were afraid that you might face a murder charge, and, in order to make the injury to your arm appear to have been accidentally sustained, didn't you deliberately drive the Chevolet automobile into a lamp-post on the road home?"

Shuster jumped to his feet. His hands pawed the air.

"A lie, your Honor!" he shouted. "A series of lies! An attack on the character of my client."

Mason continued to stare steadily at the white face of the witness.

"If the answer to *that* question will incriminate you, you may say so."

The courtroom was tense with silence. Even Shuster forgot his excited expostulation in order to stare as though

189

fascinated at the face of Samuel Laxter. Perspiration beaded Laxter's forehead. He cleared his throat twice and then mumbled, "I refuse to answer."

Mason motioned with his hand urbanely. "That," he said, "is all."

Truslow leaned forward and whispered, "For Heaven sakes, Mason, is there any chance this chap did what you intimated, or are you merely trying to prejudice the Court in favor of your client?"

Mason smiled and said, "Go on with the case, Truslow. I think we'll reach a solution directly."

"Call Frank Oafley," Truslow said.

Oafley took the witness stand, testified briefly as to his name, place of residence and relationship to the deceased Peter Laxter.

"On the night of the twenty-third instant," Truslow said, "you were engaged in digging in the yard of the Laxter residence?"

"I was."

"For what purpose?"

"Objected to," Shuster shouted.

Perry Mason smiled affably and said, "Your Honor, I represent the defendant in this case. Counselor Shuster is without any standing in court. If I don't object to a question and the Prosecution, by asking the question, requests an answer, the witness is forced to answer the question."

"That is right," Judge Pennymaker ruled. "Answer the question."

"I was searching for a large amount of money which had been missing ever since my grandfather died, and I was searching for certain other property."

"Why were you searching?"

"Because I had received a telegram."

"We're going to attempt to offer that telegram in evidence," Truslow said, looking at Perry Mason, his tone indicating plainly that he expected Mason to object and expected the Court to sustain the objection.

190

"No objections," Perry Mason said. "Introduce it in evidence."

Truslow took a telegram, introduced it in evidence and read it into the record:

THE KOLTSDORF DIAMONDS ARE HIDDEN IN ASHTONS CRUTCH STOP MORE THAN HALF OF YOUR GRANDFATHERS MONEY IS BURIED JUST UNDER THE LIBRARY WINDOW WHERE THE CLIMBING ROSEBUSH STARTS UP THE TRELLIS WORK STOP THE SPOT IS MARKED BY A LITTLE STICK STUCK IN THE GROUND STOP IT ISNT BURIED DEEP STOP NOT OVER A FEW INCHES

"We expect to prove," Truslow said, "for what it may be worth, that this telegram was telephoned in to the telegraph company; that it was telephoned from the telephone of Winifred Laxter, the fiancée of the defendant in this case."

Mason remained silent.

"You dug in that locality?" Truslow asked.

"I did."

"You were acquainted with Edith DeVoe?"

"I was."

"Was she any relation to you at the time of her death?"

The witness gulped. "She was my wife," he said.

Mason said to Truslow, "Go ahead and ask him about what Edith DeVoe told him concerning his grandfather's death."

Truslow showed some surprise, but immediately turned to the witness and inquired, "Did Edith DeVoe tell you anything concerning the death of your grandfather or certain suspicious circumstances she had observed on the evening of the fire?"

Nat Shuster jumped to his feet. "Your Honor! Your Honor! Your Honor!" he shouted. "This is objected to. This is absolutely hearsay evidence. This has no bearing . . ."

Judge Pennymaker banged his gavel. "Sit down, Counselor," he ordered. "You are out of order; you have no standing in this case whatever, save as you appear as the counsel of Samuel Laxter."

"But on behalf of Samuel Laxter I object to it."

"Samuel Laxter is not a party to the case. Counselor Mason is the only one who has the right to object. I have advised you of that before."

"But this is an outrage! This is convicting my client of murder without giving him a chance to defend himself. It's a great game these two lawyers are playing! They start prosecuting some other man for murder, and then they convict my client of it and I can't do anything because they don't object."

Despite himself, Judge Pennymaker smiled. "It *is* rather an ironical situation, Counselor," he said, "but there can be no question concerning its legality. You will sit down and refrain from interrupting the proceedings."

"But he shouldn't answer. He'll get himself into trouble I advise him not to . . ."

This time there was no smile on the Judge's face.

"You'll sit down and keep quiet," he said, "or you'll be ejected from the courtroom and fined for contempt Now, which will it be?"

Slowly, Nat Shuster sat down.

"And you'll remain seated and remain quiet," Judge Pennymaker ordered, then turned to the witness. "Answer the question," he said. "That is, unless there's an objection by Counsel for the defendant. If there is such an objection, I will sustain it as the question calls for hearsay evidence too remote to be a part of the *res gestae.*"

"No objection in the world," Mason remarked urbanely

Shuster half-arose from the chair, then sat back with a pathetic air of dejection.

Frank Oafley said slowly, "My wife told me that on the night of the fire she was walking past the garage. She saw Samuel Laxter sitting in an automobile, with a hose running from the exhaust to the hot air pipe which furnished heat to my grandfather's room."

"Was the motor running?" Truslow asked.

"She said the motor was running."

"Were there any indications that the motor had been running for some time?"

"Yes, there were no lights on in the garage until she switched them on, yet the hour was long after dark."

"Did she," asked Truslow, "tell you to whom else she had told this story?"

"Yes, she did."

"To whom?"

"To Perry Mason, the attorney, and to Douglas Keene, the defendant."

"That's all," Truslow said. "You may cross-examine, Counselor."

Perry Mason remarked, almost conversationally, "I believe you'd been with her until just before she discovered Samuel Laxter in the automobile on the night of the fire?"

"That's right. She and I had been walking and . . . making plans for the future." The witness broke off abruptly, averted his eyes. A spasm of expression crossed his face. He seemed fighting to control himself, then he looked back to confront Perry Mason and said, in a voice which was harsh with emotion, "I was afraid my grandfather wouldn't approve of the match. Our meetings were surreptitious, but we had planned to be married just as soon as we could."

"Now, was she absolutely certain that the person seated in the automobile was Samuel Laxter?" Mason inquired.

"Yes, I think she was," Oafley said, "although she did say that she didn't see his face clearly. Sam Laxter wears a rather distinctive type of hat, and she saw that very plainly."

"Did he speak to her?"

"Yes, he spoke to her, and she thought the voice was

that of Sam Laxter, although, when I asked her about it, she remembered that the voice had been rather muffled because the man had been slumped over the steering wheel, apparently in an intoxicated condition."

"Do you know of any motive that Sam Laxter might have had for murdering his grandfather?"

"Why, yes, of course. There was the will."

"Do you know of any motive he might have had for murdering Charles Ashton?"

Over at the counsel table, Nat Shuster went through an elaborate pantomime of registering extreme protest, but remembering the judicial admonition, he remained seated and kept silent.

"No, I don't," Oafley said.

"Do you know where Sam Laxter was when Ashton was murdered?"

"No, I don't."

"Where were you at the time?"

"You mean at the time Ashton was murdered?"

"Yes."

"I was with Edith DeVoe."

"Getting married?" Mason inquired.

The witness showed that the subject was very painful to him.

"I think the time of the murder has been established as just after the ceremony," he said.

"I'm sorry to have opened up the wound," Perry Mason told him kindly. "I think that's all."

"That's all," Truslow said.

Shuster looked hopefully at the Court, but Judge Penny-maker avoided his gaze. "That's all," he said.

Truslow turned to give Perry Mason a fraternal wink. "Call Thelma Pixley," he said.

Thelma Pixley came forward and was sworn.

"Do you know the defendant in this case?"

"Very well."

"Did you see him on the twenty-third—the night Charles Ashton was murdered?"

"I did."

"What did he do? . . . I will state to the Court and Counsel that this is merely for the purpose of fixing a motive for the subsequent murder of Edith DeVoe. I think the fact that the caretaker's crutch was found in the apartment of Edith DeVoe indicates . . ."

"No objection whatever," Perry Mason interrupted. "The witness may answer the question."

"Answer the question," Judge Pennymaker instructed.

"I saw the defendant's automobile come up the driveway. He circled the house then went back below the garage and parked the car. I expected he would ring the bell and I waited to let him in, but he had a key to the back door. I saw him go in. I wondered what he was doing, so I went to my door and listened. He walked down the stairs, and I heard him open the door of Charles Ashton's room."

"Do you know how long he stayed there?"

"I saw him leave."

"What time was it when he arrived?"

"Just before ten."

"When did he leave?"

"It was just a few minutes after eleven."

"As much as five minutes after eleven?"

"I don't think so. The clock had struck eleven just before—I don't think more than a minute or two before I saw him leaving."

"Was he carrying anything with him?"

"A cat."

"Could you see the cat clearly?"

"It was Clinker."

"That's the caretaker's cat?"

"Yes."

"Would you know that cat if you saw it again?"

"Certainly."

Truslow motioned to a bailiff who had evidently been

195

waiting for the signal. The bailiff stepped through the door to an ante-room and shortly emerged, carrying a big Persian cat, about the neck of which was affixed a tag.

"Is this the cat?"

"That's Clinker, yes."

"Your Honor," Truslow said, smiling at Perry Mason, "let it appear that the witness identifies the Persian cat, about the neck of which is affixed a tag bearing the words 'Clinker' and the initials 'H.B.,' in the handwriting of Hamilton Burger, the district attorney."

Judge Pennymaker nodded.

Truslow turned to Perry Mason and said, "Cross-examine."

"Could you see the cat clearly enough to identify it?" Mason inquired.

"Yes," the witness snapped belligerently. "I'd know Clinker anywhere—even if they *had* let you substitute cats, I could have picked Clinker out. . . ."

Judge Pennymaker pounded with his gavel. The courtroom broke into laughter.

"That last remark may be stricken from the records," Judge Pennymaker suggested to Perry Mason.

Mason nodded. He seemed to have lost interest in the proceedings.

"No further questions," he said.

"Call James Brandon," Truslow instructed the bailiff

James Brandon, his face seeming to leer sardonically because of the distinctive scar, came forward and was sworn.

"You're employed by Mr. Samuel Laxter?" Truslow asked.

"And by Mr. Oafley," Brandon said. "I'm employed a chauffeur and butler."

"And were so employed on the night of the twenty third?"

"Yes."

196

"Did you have occasion to see the defendant on that night?"

"I did."

"Where?"

"Just below the garage of the Laxter house."

"Did you see his car parked near there?"

"His car was parked about twenty yards farther down the road."

"What was he doing when you saw him?"

"He was coming from the direction of the Laxter house with a cat in his arms."

"Did you recognize the cat?"

"I did. It was Clinker."

"The cat which has been tagged with the name 'Clinker,' and which is now here in court?"

"That's the cat."

"What time was this?"

"Right around eleven o'clock, perhaps two or three minutes after eleven."

"You were driving an automobile?"

"Yes."

"Where had you been prior to the time you saw the defendant?"

"I'd been in Mr. Shuster's office. Mr. Sam Laxter asked me to take him to Mr. Shuster's office. I arrived at Shuster's office shortly before ten o'clock and remained there until a little before eleven, when Mr. Laxter told me I could take the car and go home. I then drove back to the Laxter house, put up the car, entered the house and remained there during the evening."

"Was Mr. Oafley there when you arrived?"

"No, sir; he came in some ten or fifteen minutes later."

"You may inquire," Truslow said.

"Was the defendant carrying a crutch when you saw him?"

"No, sir."

"You're certain it was Clinker that he was carrying?"

"Yes, sir; I saw him very clearly in the lights of the automobile."

"Did he subsequently return to the house?"

"I don't know. I think he did."

"What makes you say that?" Mason inquired.

"I heard a car drive around the driveway and stop at a point opposite the window to Ashton's bedroom. I thought it was the defendant's car, but I didn't look. That is, I thought the motor sounded like the motor on his car."

"How long was the car there?"

The witness leered at Perry Mason. "Two or three minutes," he said. "Plenty long enough for the defendant to pick up a crutch and put it in the car."

The courtroom tittered.

"Exactly," Mason said. "Now *if* he had driven back to pick up the crutch, why didn't he pick up the cat at the same time? What was the object in carrying the cat in his arms if he was going to return later on with the automobile?"

"I don't know," the witness said after a moment.

"I'm quite certain you don't," Mason observed, getting to his feet. "Now, you'd been taking quite an interest in Charles Ashton, hadn't you?"

"Me, sir?"

"Yes, you."

"Why, I don't think so."

Mason stared steadily at the witness, and Brandon, squirming uncomfortably in the chair, avoided his eyes.

"Do you know when Ashton came to consult me about his cat?"

"I can't say," the witness said.

Mason, staring at him coldly, said. "You're under oath, remember that. When Ashton came to my office, you followed him, didn't you?"

"No, sir."

"You had the green Pontiac," Mason said slowly. "You parked it in front of my office. You waited until Ashton

198

came out and then you followed him, driving slowly in the car, didn't you?"

The witness wet his lips, remained silent. Judge Pennymaker leaned forward, his face showing interest. Truslow looked puzzled.

"Go on," Mason said; "answer the question."

"Yes, sir," the witness said finally; "I did."

"And you went to Babson, the crutch maker, and asked him about Ashton's crutch, didn't you?"

Once more, there was a perceptible period of hesitation, then Brandon said slowly, "Yes, sir; I did."

"And found out that Babson had hollowed out a receptacle in Ashton's crutch."

"Yes, sir."

"Why did you do that?"

"I was instructed to."

"Who instructed you?"

"Frank Oafley."

"Did he say why he wanted you to do that?"

"No, sir. He told me to shadow Ashton every time Ashton left the premises. He asked me to find out where Ashton went, report on everyone Ashton saw, and find out how much money Ashton spent. He was particularly anxious about the money."

"When did he tell you that?"

"On the twentieth."

"And when did he tell you you didn't need to shadow Ashton any more?"

"On the evening of the twenty-third."

"At what time?"

"At dinner time."

Perry Mason returned to the counsel table, sat down in his chair and smiled over at Truslow.

"That," he said, "is all."

Truslow hesitated, then slowly said, "I think that's all. Dr. Robert Jason will please take the stand."

Dr. Robert Jason took the stand, testified to the fact

that the body of Peter Laxter had been exhumed; that he had made a careful post mortem examination for the purpose of determining whether the burns had been inflicted before death or afterwards.

"What did you determine?" Truslow asked.

"The body was almost incinerated, but there were several places where the clothing had protected the flesh. It is an established fact that, where death results from burning, at points where the clothing is tight around the body, there is less damage to the flesh. On these areas I was able to make an examination from which I reached my conclusion."

"What was that conclusion?"

"That the deceased met his death prior to the fire."

"Cross-examine," Truslow announced.

"Did you determine whether the cause of death had been burning or carbon monoxide poisoning?" Mason asked.

Dr. Jason shook his head. "In all cases of burning there is usually present carbon monoxide residue in the tissues."

"So it would be virtually impossible to tell whether a person had met death from carbon monoxide poisoning, which was administered through fumes liberated from the exhaust of a motor vehicle, or by being asphyxiated and burnt in a burning house. Is that right?"

"That is approximately correct; yes sir."

"Therefore, acting on the assumption that the body would show evidences of carbon monoxide poisoning in either event, you failed to make any test for it in this post mortem examination?"

"That's right."

"Did you make any x-rays of the bones?"

"No. Why?"

"I was wondering if the body showed that the right leg had recently been broken."

Dr. Jason frowned.

"What would that have to do with it?" Truslow inquired.

"I would just like to have such a test made," Mason remarked, "and, if we are going to have this evidence introduced at all, I feel that I am entitled to know whether there was evidence of carbon monoxide poisoning."

"But," Judge Pennymaker pointed out, "the witness has just stated that such evidence would be present, regardless of how the man met his death."

"Oh, no, he didn't," Mason said. "He simply testified that such evidence would be present whether death had been from burning or from carbon monoxide. I would like to have this witness · instructed to ascertain immediately those two things and return to court."

"I can telephone to my office and have one of my assistants make the test immediately," the witness said.

"That will be quite agreeable," Perry Mason observed.

"That would be irregular," Judge Pennymaker pointed out.

"I know, your Honor, but the hour is getting late and would like to have the matter completed today. After all, this isn't a case in a superior court before a jury. The function of this hearing is only to determine whether a crime has been committed and whether there is reasonable ground to suppose the defendant is guilty."

"Very well," Judge Pennymaker said; "you may do that, Dr. Jason."

Dr. Jason left the witness stand.

Della Street came pushing forward toward the rail which separated the place reserved for court officials from the balance of the courtroom. She caught Perry Mason's eye.

"Just a moment, if the Court will indulge me," Perry Mason said, and went to the rail.

Della Street whispered to him, "I've been calling the insurance company and asking for information. They've just advised me that the police in Santa Fé, New Mexico, have recovered my car. A man was driving it who claims he is Watson Clammert, but can offer no proof of his identity other than some receipts which the police think are forged, because the receipts show that he purchased and paid for the car, as Watson Clammert. But the peculiar thing is that they think he's a bank robber, as well, because in a suitcase in the car there was over a million dollars in currency."

Mason sighed with satisfaction.

"Now," he said, "we're getting somewhere."

"We'll call Winifred Laxter to the stand," Truslow said, "as our next witness."

He lowered his voice slightly and said to Judge Pennymaker, "The Court will undoubtedly bear with us that this is a hostile witness, and permit the use of leading questions."

"You may examine the witness," Judge Pennymaker said, "and rulings will be made when the necessity for leading questions becomes apparent."

"Very well. Take the stand, Miss Laxter."

Winifred Laxter walked forward, as a princess might approach the sword of a headsman.

She held up her right hand, took the oath and then walked to the witness chair and sat down.

"Your name is Winifred Laxter and you are engaged to the defendant?"

"I am."

"You were acquainted with Charles Ashton?"

"I was."

"You are familiar with the cat now in court, with a tag around its neck upon which the word 'Clinker' appears?"

Winifred Laxter bit her lip and said, "I knew the caretaker's cat."

"Is this the caretaker's cat that you have mentioned?

Winifred Laxter looked pleadingly at Perry Mason, but Perry Mason remained silent. She took a deep breath hesitated, seemed about to shake her head, but the cat, with a throaty "meow," jumped from the table, crossed the courtroom, leapt into her lap and curled up contentedly. Some of the spectators tittered. The Judge pounded with his gavel. The girl glanced once more at Perry Mason.

"Answer the question, Winifred," Perry Mason said, "and tell the truth."

"Yes," she said, "this is Clinker."

"Did you have Clinker in your possession on the night the night the caretaker was murdered?"

"Answer the question," Mason told her, as she looked helplessly at him.

"I'm not going to answer."

"Answer the question, Winifred," Mason repeated.

She stared steadily at him, then said slowly, "Yes, I did."

"Who gave you the cat?"

Her manner was vengeful now. "A friend of mine gave me the cat and I gave it to Perry Mason—that is, Perry Mason took it with him. He said that the police mustn't find it in my apartment."

Spectators stirred restlessly.

"Was this friend Douglas Keene?" Truslow asked.

"I refuse to answer."

"Go on and answer," Mason ordered.

Judge Pennymaker cleared his throat. In a voice which obviously contained sympathy for the young woman, he said, "Of course, gentlemen, it is only fair to advise this witness that the answer might incriminate her, in that it would make her an accessory . . ."

"There is no necessity," Perry Mason said. "I am representing the interest of this witness. Go ahead and answer the question, Winifred."

"Yes," she said.

"You may cross-examine," Truslow announced.

"No cross-examination," Mason said.

Truslow got to his feet. His manner was cold and pur-poseful.

"Your Honor," he said, "I regret being forced to do this, but it appears that the murder of Charles Ashton is inseparably connected with the murder of Edith DeVoe. The murderer must have taken the crutch from Ashton's room to the place where Edith was murdered. The mur-derer must have sawed up the crutch, taken out the diamonds and used a part of the crutch as a club with which to injure fatally Edith DeVoe. Therefore, the mur-derer of Charles Ashton must be the murderer of Edith DeVoe. It therefore becomes necessary to prove that Ashton was murdered before the cat was taken from the Laxter house and that the cat did not return to the Laxter house at any time after the murder. It is, as I see it, incumbent upon the Prosecution to account for the time of the caretaker's cat from the moment it was taken into the custody of the defendant in this action until the police recovered it. Therefore, I am going to ask that Della Street take the stand."

Della Street gasped with surprise.

"Take the stand, Della," Perry said.

Della Street stepped forward and was sworn.

"Your name is Della Street and you are the secretary of Perry Mason, who is appearing as an attorney in this case. On the night of the twenty-third, did Perry Mason appear at your apartment carrying the cat known as Clinker and which is now in Court?"

"Answer the question," Perry Mason told her.

"I don't know," she said defiantly.

"Don't know?" Truslow asked.

"No," she said.

"What do you mean by that answer?"

"I mean that I don't know."

"Why don't you know?"

"Because I don't know whether this cat is the cat which belonged to the caretaker."

"But Winifred Laxter says it is."

"I am not responsible for what Winifred Laxter testified to; *I* am testifying under oath."

"But the cat shows that it knows Winifred Laxter."

"I am not responsible," she told Truslow icily, "for the cat's circle of acquaintances."

There was a laugh from the spectators. Judge Pennymaker smiled, even as he called the courtroom to order.

"But you admit that Perry Mason brought a *cat* to your apartment."

"I admit nothing of the sort. The question is not pertinent unless it has to do with the murder, and it can have nothing to do with the murder unless the cat which you claim was brought to my apartment was the caretaker's cat, and I have no knowledge whatever on that. I think you will have to ask these questions of Mr. Mason."

Truslow smiled ruefully and said to the court, "Perhaps the legal knowledge this young woman has acquired is responsible for some of Counselor Mason's success."

"She seems to have a very excellent grasp of the legal points involved," Judge Pennymaker observed.

Mason smiled.

"I am going to call Perry Mason to the stand," Truslow said. "I am aware that the procedure is unusual, but I am also aware that it is unusual for Counsel to take so active a part in the cases involving his clients as Perry Mason apparently takes. I am not asking for any confidential communication which came to him from one of his clients; I am going to ask him only what he did in connection with sheltering a criminal."

"Very well," Judge Pennymaker ordered; "Perry Mason will take the stand."

Mason stepped to the witness stand, took the oath and sat down. Judge Pennymaker looked at him with some sympathy, then said to Truslow, "After all, Counselor, while your comment as to Counselor Mason's methods of representing a client may have some justification, the fact remains that Counselor Mason is an attorney at law. He is not restricted to the representation of any one client. If it should appear, as I think it will appear, that he also represented Winifred Laxter, the Court will hold as a privileged communication anything which Winifred Laxter may have said to him. As you have so aptly pointed out, Counselor Mason's methods are perhaps somewhat unusual, but you must admit that his history shows a long line of successes which have been achieved, not through a defense of the guilty, but through strikingly original methods of demonstrating the innocence of his clients."

"I'm not talking about the past," Truslow said grimly; "I'm talking about the present."

"I thank your Honor for holding out a lifeline to me," Mason said smilingly, "but I hardly think it will be necessary."

Truslow said, "Your name is Perry Mason? You are an attorney at law?"

"That is right."

"You are the attorney representing Douglas Keene?"

"I am."

"Did you go to the waffle place operated by Winifred Laxter on the night of the twenty-third?"

"I did."

"Did you take into your possession a cat at that place?"

"I did."

"What did you do with that cat?"

Perry Mason smiled. "I'll even go farther than your question, Mr. Truslow, the cat was given to me with the statement that it was Clinker, the caretaker's cat, and Winifred Laxter stated that the cat had been in her possession ever since shortly after eleven o'clock when it had been delivered to her by Douglas Keene, the defendant in this case.

"I told Miss Laxter that it was important the police

did not find the cat there, and I took the cat and personally delivered it to my secretary with instructions to keep it in her possession."

"And just why did you do that?" Truslow asked.

"I did it," Perry Mason said, "so that there would be no chance for the cat to escape and return to the Laxter residence."

It took a moment for the meaning of Mason's words to penetrate to Truslow's consciousness. He frowned and said, "What?"

"I did it so the cat couldn't get back to the Laxter residence."

"I don't understand," Truslow stated.

"In other words," Mason remarked calmly, "I wanted to establish that if the cat tracks on the counterpane of the bed in which Charles Ashton was found dead were those of Clinker they must have been made prior to the time Douglas Keene left the house."

Truslow frowned. For a moment he forgot his role of questioner as he sought to follow Mason's reasoning. "That," he said, "doesn't benefit your client any."

"It does to this extent," Mason answered. "It clarified the situation so that the real murderer could be found."

Truslow asked no question, but stood in puzzled contemplation, waiting for Mason to go on, while Judge Pennymaker leaned forward in order to miss no word.

"I acted on the assumption," Mason said, "that Keene was innocent. I couldn't definitely prove his innocence except by proving someone else was guilty. The police officers jumped to the conclusion that Keene was lying. On the face of it, Keene must have been lying. Ashton was undoubtedly killed at ten thirty. Keene was undoubtedly in Ashton's room, where the body was subsequently found, at ten thirty. There were cat tracks on the counterpane. The police jumped to the conclusion those tracks were made by Clinker. But Keene said he had left the house shortly after eleven, taken Clinker with him, and, at the time he left, Ashton's body was most certainly not in the room.

"In place of following the reasoning of the police and acting on the assumption Keene was lying, I decided to act upon the assumption Keene might be telling the truth. In that event, the cat tracks could not have been those of Clinker; in that event Ashton could not have been at the place where his body was found at ten thirty. Yet, since he was undoubtedly killed at ten thirty, it becomes very apparent that he must have been killed at some place other than that in which his body was found. In that event, the cat tracks must have been made by some cat other than Clinker.

"When I had reasoned this far I suddenly realized the importance of proving just that point and of accounting for every minute of Clinker's time, from the moment Keene took him from the house. I could think of no better manner than to take him into my personal custody and keep him where the murderer couldn't find him."

"Why," Truslow demanded, "did you want to establish the fact that this cat, Clinker, was taken from the house by your client?"

"Because," Mason said, "Clinker was the only cat who had access to the residence. Moreover, Clinker kept other cats chased out of the neighborhood. Therefore, if Keene was telling the truth, Ashton's body must have been brought to the house after Ashton was murdered, and the murderer, in order to make it seem that Ashton had been murdered in bed, and to direct suspicion toward Douglas Keene, must have gone out into the night in search of a cat and brought it forcibly to the house, taken it to the bed where Ashton's body lay—a bed, by the way, on which the sensitive nostrils of a cat could have detected the odor of Clinker—and forced that cat to make tracks on the counterpane.

"If that is what happened, one who is at all familiar with the nature of cats would realize that the cat would

208

be very apt to resent such treatment and that his resentment would take the form of deep scratches on the murderer's hands. I therefore looked over the possible suspects to find someone with scratched hands. When I found that person, I found he had sought to conceal the scratches on his hands by making additional scratches under circumstances which would seem to offer an explanation for scratched hands—to-wit—digging around a rose bush, apparently in an attempt to discover treasure, but the digging was certainly not the type of digging one would indulge in if trying to unearth a million dollar treasure. Therefore, I came to the conclusion that the digging was for the sole purpose of furnishing him an excuse by which he could account for scratches on his hands, claiming that they had been inflicted by the rose thorns."

Truslow's eyes were opened so wide that they seemed to bulge.

"You mean Frank Oafley? Why, Frank Oafley was with Edith DeVoe at the time Ashton was murdered."

"Yes," Mason said, "I let this entire trial proceed merely because I wanted to get that admission from his own lips, because Ashton *was not murdered in his bed, but was murdered in the apartment of Edith DeVoe.* He *must* have been murdered there. It is the only explanation which satisfies all of the physical facts in the case. Remember that Ashton was a frail, wizened individual, and that a driveway went directly past the window over his bed. A strong man could have slid Ashton's body through that window with the greatest ease."

"Just a minute," Truslow objected, suddenly aware of what was happening. "You're on the witness stand as a witness, yet you're making an argument in the case."

"Called to the witness stand," Perry Mason remarked urbanely, "as a witness on behalf of the prosecution, and I am testifying in response to a question from you asking that I explain my motive in taking the cat from Winifred

Laxter and concealing it where none of the parties to the action could find it until after the police had taken it into their custody for safekeeping. And to issue the fact that the police *would* keep it safe, I led the police to believe that by holding the cat they could implicate my client and perhaps cause me some embarrassment as an attorney."

Judge Pennymaker smiled and said, "I think Counselor Mason is probably making rather an argumentative answer; but the Court is certainly going to hear it. Go on with your explanation, Mr. Mason."

"I felt certain," Perry Mason said, turning to the Court, "that Peter Laxter was not dead."

Judge Pennymaker shook his head, as though trying to clear his senses. "Felt certain that *what?*" he asked.

"That Peter Laxter was not dead. Everything pointed to the fact that Edith DeVoe and Frank Oafley had plotted against his life; that they had decided to introduce carbon monoxide gas into his bedroom. The evidence in this case shows that Charles Ashton, the caretaker, and who was a devoted servant, apparently received from Peter Laxter a large sum of money, and the famous Koltsdorf diamonds; that this property was delivered to him for safekeeping, the reason being that Peter Laxter must have known in advance that his country house was going to be destroyed by fire.

"In other words, either Peter Laxter or Charles Ashton knew that an insidious attempt at murder was going to be made by someone. Edith DeVoe told me it was made by Sam Laxter, but I am inclined to think she said that as part of a prearranged scheme by which she and Frank Oafley had conspired to murder Laxter, and then, by accusing Sam Laxter of the murder, eliminate him from sharing in the estate, leaving Frank Oafley as the sole heir.

"Peter Laxter decided to let the conspirators go ahead with the murder plot. For reasons of his own, he wanted to disappear. One of those reasons was probably that he wanted to bring Winifred Laxter to her senses by letting her see how the two men who professed to love her would behave if she apparently were disinherited. So Ashton, the caretaker, who was in Peter Laxter's complete confidence, went to the charitable ward of the hospital. He found there a man—a Watson Clammert—who was dying; who had no relatives and no property. Ashton gave this man the best medical attendance and nursing, knowing in advance that it was a hopeless case. He built up, by this means, a fictitious relationship, so that no question was raised when Ashton took the body after the man had died.

"Undoubtedly, the conspirators had been watching for just the right opportunity to perpetrate their crime, and undoubtedly Peter Laxter had shrewdly deprived them of this opportunity until he had completed his preparations, which included getting a body and reducing all of his negotiable property to cash so that his ostensible heirs could not loot his estate.

"Watson Clammert, however, had a driving license and certain papers of identification, so it was easier for Peter Laxter to assume the name of Watson Clammert than it was to adopt an entirely new name. When the stage had been set, he let the conspirators burn up his country house, after going to the elaborate trouble of introducing carbon monoxide gas into his bedroom. They then went ahead and probated his will while Peter Laxter sat on the sidelines and laughed at them.

"You understand, your Honor, I am now stating the reasons which lay behind my actions. Much of this is, of necessity, assumption, but I think the assumption is well taken.

"Everyone has acted upon the assumption that because Dafley was not present *where Ashton's body was found* at the time Ashton was murdered, he has a good alibi. As a matter of fact, there is nothing which actually indicates that Ashton was murdered at the place where his body was found. I believe that he was murdered in Edith DeVoe's apartment. I believe that he went there, or was lured there by the conspirators when they found out that Ashton knew of their conspiracy. I think that they both believed Peter Laxter was dead. I think that they killed Ashton, cut up the crutch, took out the diamonds, and, knowing that they had to dispose of Ashton's body, slipped it out of the window into Oafley's waiting automobile. Then Frank Oafley drove his machine to the Laxter residence sometime after the defendant had left the premises with the cat, and slid the body through the window which was customarily left open to enable the cat to go in and out.

"The murderer knew that Clinker customarily slept on the bed. He wanted to show that everything was as it should be. So he looked around to find Clinker and found that Clinker had been taken a few minutes earlier by Douglas Keene, so he immediately realized what damaging evidence he could pile up against Keene if there were cat tracks on the bed. So he went out, found a cat and forced the cat to make tracks on the bed. In doing this his hands were scratched.

"Oafley wanted to have some logical explanation by which he could account for his scratched hands. So he arranged to have a telegram sent to him, and, in order to make that telegram appear natural, he arranged that a check-up would apparently show it had been sent by Winifred Laxter. This telegram gave Oafley an opportunity to dig in the rosebush, so that he could have a logical explanation for his scratched hands.

"Now then, your Honor, we enter upon the phase of the case which so far can only be a matter of speculation. As soon as I realized that it was contemplated a Watson Clammert might be given access to the safety deposit boxes Ashton had rented, I realized that Peter Laxte

212

had, for the sake of convenience, taken the name of Watson Clammert, probably in order to use Clammert's driving license, rather than apply for another. I don't *know* what happened in Edith DeVoe's apartment shortly after eleven o'clock, but I can surmise what happened. Oafley assisted her in killing the caretaker. Then he took the caretaker's body, leaving the crutch in Edith DeVoe's apartment. They sawed up the crutch and intended to burn it up, after having removed the diamonds. Sam Laxter went to his lawyer's office in the green Pontiac. He returned home in the caretaker's Chevrolet. Therefore, he must have found the Chevrolet parked at some place which he visited after leaving Shuster's office.

"He wouldn't have taken this car unless he had thought Ashton was dead, or unless he was in a hurry caused by panic.

"I feel certain that he and Shuster discussed the fact that Edith DeVoe was making charges against him. I think Shuster found out what was happening from remarks dropped by Oafley. I think Sam Laxter went to see Edith DeVoe, either with or without Nat Shuster's knowledge. Sam Laxter went to the apartment and found her dying. He left in a panic, and it is reasonable to surmise that he called his attorney, Nat Shuster. I will not speculate as to what he said to Shuster or what Shuster said to him, but the fact remains that a very shrewd attempt was made to fasten the crime on Douglas Keene. In view of the statements Edith DeVoe had been making charging Sam Laxter with murder, Sam Laxter realized at once that if it could be shown he was at Edith DeVoe's apartment at about the time the murder was committed, he would stand but little chance of being acquitted.

"Now then, the question arises: Who did murder Edith DeVoe? I don't know; but I do know that Peter Laxter, masquerading as Watson Clammert, purchased a new

Buick sedan. I do know that a new Buick sedan was seen by witnesses parked immediately behind the caretaker's Chevrolet in front of Edith DeVoe's apartment house. The probabilities are that Peter Laxter went there to wait for Ashton to come out. After a period of waiting, Peter Laxter went to Edith DeVoe's apartment. This was probably at about eleven o'clock or a little later. He found Edith DeVoe under most incriminating circumstances. The caretaker's crutch had been sawed up and was being burned in the grate. The Koltsdorf diamonds were probably in plain sight on a table. I don't think Laxter lost his temper and struck Edith DeVoe purposely with a club. But we must remember that Laxter was an elderly man; that Edith DeVoe was vigorous and well-formed, strong and feline. She probably was the one who attacked Laxter. Laxter took the first weapon which came to his hand, pulling out a piece of the sawed-up crutch from the fireplace. We can surmise that the crutch had just started to burn, because a few minutes before Edith DeVoe had gone into the next room to borrow a match. We know that wood had recently been burned in the grate. We know that there were some evidences of heat having been applied to one end of the section of crutch which was used as a club. And I think the police will find the fingerprint on that club was left by Peter Laxter—alias Watson Clammert."

Perry Mason ceased talking, smiled at the startled prosecutor.

Dr. Jason pushed his way into the courtroom. His manner was excited. "The man didn't meet his death by burning," he said, "or from carbon monoxide poisoning, either. He apparently died from natural causes, and there isn't any break in the right leg, so the body wasn't that of Peter Laxter."

Hamilton Burger burst into the courtroom through another door. "Your Honor," he said, "halt this trial immediately. The district attorney's office demands an indefinite continuance. A man arrested as a car thief in New Mexico as Watson Clammert has telegraphed a confession, stating that he is really Peter Laxter; that he knows Edith DeVoe and Frank Oafley killed Charles Ashton and that Peter Laxter, invading Edith DeVoe's apartment to get evidence of that murder, struck the blow which killed Edith DeVoe. Panic-stricken, he wanted to escape. It's all here in this telegram. He's now willing to come back and face the music."

Pandemonium broke loose in the courtroom.

Winifred Laxter, with a glad cry, ran toward Douglas Keene, whose open arms were waiting for her.

Perry Mason uncrossed his legs, smiled at the startled face of Judge Pennymaker, reached out and snapped his fingers at the cat.

"Hi, Clinker," he said.

19

PERRY MASON SAT IN HIS OFFICE. DELLA STREET LOOKED across the desk at him with starry eyes.

"Are you going to defend Peter Laxter?" she asked.

"If they prosecute him I am."

"I don't see how you knew what had happened."

"I didn't," he said, "at first. But I had a shrewd suspicion later on. There were two or three things which gave me a pretty good idea. Notice the manner in which Frank Oafley married Edith DeVoe. During the time he was living with Peter Laxter he said his courting was of necessity surreptitious because of Peter Laxter's objections. But *he* thought Peter Laxter was dead after the house had burned up. There was no necessity for having a secret marriage ceremony and no necessity for not going on a honeymoon, but returning to the Laxter home. I am forced to conclude, therefore, that the reason both parties were so anxious to have the marriage ceremony performed was due to the fact that they realized a wife could not be examined against her husband without the consent of her husband, nor a husband be compelled to give testimony against his wife. This was because they knew the conspiracy was likely to be discovered, and that means that, in some manner, they had found out Ashton had knowledge of the conspiracy. They thought Peter Laxter was dead. Therefore, Ashton was the only one who could have known it.

"But the really significant clue is the one of the crutch. The theory of the prosecution was that the person who murdered Ashton had taken the crutch to Edith DeVoe's apartment and then murdered Edith DeVoe. That manifestly would have been impossible unless Edith DeVoe had been a party to the Ashton murder, because the crutch wasn't sawed up when taken there. It was sawed up in the apartment, and pieces of it had been burned in the grate. That would indicate that Ashton had been in the apartment; that his murderers had cut up the crutch after they'd killed him."

"Where would you have been if the police hadn't apprehended the grandfather?" Della Street asked.

"I don't know," Mason said. "I might have been able to make it stick, and I might not, but I think I could have pieced the facts together."

"Why didn't you accuse Oafley earlier?" she asked.

"Because," said Mason slowly, "of various factors involved. In the first place, I wanted Douglas Keene to come through, and, in the second place," and he chuckled, "I wanted to grandstand. If I had tipped off the police, they'd have taken all the credit, and they might have bungled the case so that Keene would never hav been really vindicated. They might even have framed him. And I wanted Oafley to admit under oath being with Edith DeVoe at the exact time Ashton was murdered."

"And," she said, "last but not least, you so love to skate on thin ice that you like to play people one against the other while you take all kinds of chances."

"Perhaps," he grinned. "As I've told you before, I like to play a no-limit game."

"But why didn't you get Drake to find Watson Clammert?"

"He probably couldn't have done it in time. He'd have been handicapped. The best organized law enforcement agency in the country today is the one perfected by insurance companies to apprehend automobile thieves. They've worked out a perfect system of coördination. Ordinarily police don't coördinate. They do in automobile cases. So I fixed things so Watson Clammert would be apprehended as a car thief. That got me quicker results, enabled us to have him arrested, and brought about his confession. After all, it was really very simple. By going to the Biltmore Hotel, establishing our identities as honeymooners, letting the clerk see our new car, and get interested in you, then having you conceal the car and report it as stolen, we started in motion the machinery which was bound to put a finger on Clammert. He was entirely unsuspecting. He was driving the car he had purchased under his assumed name. It was only a matter of hours until he'd be arrested."

"Well," Della Street said, "the Lord knows your methods are unconventional, but I *will* say this for them, they're effective."

He grinned at her.

"And," she said, "now that we've finished up this case, we have an extra Buick sedan on our hands. What are we going to do with it; sell it, or sell the convertible?"

"No," Mason said slowly, "we'd better keep them both."

She raised her eyebrows.

"You see," he said, "it's a handy car to have around—in case I should ever want to go on a honeymoon."